To Betty,

Thank you for being a legend and for never
learning to bite your tongue

Prologue

I can't breathe.

The water is burning at my chest and creeping down into my throat, little by little. Suddenly my mouth opens involuntarily, trying desperately to swallow the water pressing through. There's too much, it's starting to go into my windpipe.

I can't move.

I feel helpless but as my body's natural survival instinct kicks in, my mind overrules it and I open my mouth further to let more of the water rush in. It tastes disgusting, I'm gagging and choking as the moss-green liquid and, no doubt, duck shit continues to flood into my mouth.

I can't see.

I squeeze my eyes tight so I can no longer be tempted by the dull light of the sun above the water. It's taking too long to sink to the bottom. I didn't think it would take this long.

I can't feel.

The initial burn of the icy water on my skin no longer bothers me; everywhere is numb. It's finally matching how I feel on the inside. It won't be much longer, then oblivion. I tell myself all the pain will stop soon.

I feel his arms first. They pull at my top desperately, but the algae soaking into my clothes make me a slippery prize. The pulling becomes more violent, urgent even. The reeds, from the bank, scratch at my skin while the sunlight still tries to tempt my eyelids to open once more. I refuse.

I smell the dog before I feel the warm tongue on my face. I start to cough and can't stop.

You can't even drown right.

"Love? Love, what's your name?" my rescuer asks.

I can't answer for coughing.

He tries again, "Can you hear me, love? Can you open your eyes? Just tell me your name; can you do that for me?"

Blinking into the sun I try to speak: "It's…it's…"

Chapter 1

"MUMMY!"

I woke with a start and a heartbeat that felt out of rhythm.

"MUMMY!" the intruder repeated, louder than before. I sat up on my elbows and looked towards the door. I tried to get my heart back into a normal beat before my youngest son bursts into the room.

A dream, it was just a dream. Breathe, you stupid woman.

I looked in the mirror, facing the bed, and realised I should have gone to sleep an hour earlier, judging by the dark circles under my eyes. My youngest son was soon to be staggering into my bedroom and I would have to answer 437 questions within the first hour of him opening his mouth.

I was not ready for that level of conversation.

My eldest will soon follow, looking angst-ridden. I will then have to coax out of him what horrible dream he's had this time.

All this wouldn't be *too* bad had I been able to leave the house without them and go to work; leaving my husband with the shit-storm that is the morning routine. However, I couldn't anymore. I was stuck here, like a prisoner of war who was trying to decide whether or not they should dislodge the fake tooth at the back of their mouth and swallow the cyanide pill.

That wasn't quite true, I wasn't there yet.

I was simply a moron who thought she could be a stay-at-home mum and keep her sanity – unfortunately for all involved, this moron had not.

Before I left my job, I had daydreams about a wonderful homeschool scenario, where I'd bake bread in between lessons for the kids; all the while keeping my home looking immaculate and awaiting my husband to return from his day spent being a successful hunter-gatherer.

These antiquated roles, I'd decided, were exactly what the family needed in these formative years for my children.

What an idiot.

To say my expectations had disappeared up shit creek, along with my waistline, was a slight understatement. I felt certain that villagers at the top of the creak had erected a monument in my honour reading: 'This statue is to commemorate the monumental fuck-up that ruined her children's future and her marriage in less than six months of staying at home'.

I hope they didn't have to pay for that thing by the letter.

As I lay in bed and contemplated the pointlessness of my contribution to the universe, I heard the pudgy footsteps of my youngest child, Arthur.

He is a three-year-old butterball of mischief and undoubtedly my favourite human on the planet. He preferred his father.

"MUMMY! Why are you not answering me?" he called.

"Sorry, Artie, I'm awake now, what's wrong?" I answered, in my best *Maria-from-the-Sound-of-Music* voice.

This voice never lasted the day. By the time I wrestled the children into the car for the school run, it was replaced by something that sounded similar to a demonic possession.

"I need the toilet."

Christ.

"Ask your dad," I muttered, as I pulled the duvet back over my head.

"I want *you*."

As I heard those words, I forgot that I was exhausted. I threw my legs out of the bed, my heart swelled with love because my baby wanted me and not 'fun' dad.

I always thought it was unfair that he got the 'fun' label.

I could have been the fun one if I didn't have to spend all my time separating the kids from killing each other. All he had to do was walk in the door and play for a half hour before ushering them up to bed.

It's not my fault I couldn't do the funny voices when I read the stories, or make the robot tigers (a fearsome creature of my son's imagination).

None of that mattered though because I was the favourite, this morning, and I got the honour of wiping my son's arse.

I think I need to reevaluate the meaning of 'favourite' in my vocabulary

"How did you sleep, Artie?"

"Good," he answered, as he swung his legs, whilst he sat on the toilet.

"And you wanted mummy this morning, that's nice."

"Not really, but daddy was sleeping."

This was just one example of a metaphorical kick in the gut I regularly received from my children, but I wasn't ridiculous enough to cry about it. Instead, I ate chocolate biscuits and buried my hurt feelings down into my cold dead soul, like all functioning adults did.

"Have you finished?" I asked, a little more sharply than I intended.

"Not yet. What's that?" he asked, innocently, as he pointed to my hair removal cream.

I foolishly decided to try it last night and the bathroom still stank from it.

"It's mummy's cream."

"What's it for?"

I knew the ambiguous answer of 'mummy's cream' was never going to be enough information for this one.

Well, mummy and daddy haven't seen each other naked in months and mummy decided that she should probably sort out the yeti-like winter fuzz she's got going on if she stands a chance at peaking her mate's interest ever again.

I decided against landing that particular information at my son's door and instead opted for:

"It's to make me smell nice."

"Ok. Is that because you smell like poo?"

"No, Artie."

"Poo!"

The fit of laughter that followed was so energetic that I decided to look past the fact he'd said I smell like shit and he *does* actually prefer his father.

All this and it's not even 8 am.

I dutifully wiped his tiny bum and let him loose back into the world just in his tiny superhero pants.

Throughout the day I lose count of the number of times I ask Artie where his trousers are.

I didn't mind too much in the morning time. I was happy to let him strut around upstairs in his underwear because his dad did the same and 'that's what boys do' apparently (well, according to his father).

I think they're even wearing the same underwear.

Collapsing back into bed - with an extra pair of elbows to contend with - I didn't have long to wait before my eldest, Adam, joined us.

Not before his usual routine, of course.

My five-year-old likes to knock our bedroom door before coming in and announcing himself. This isn't as a result of him being emotionally scarred by walking in on his parents doing something lurid, he's just a formal kid.

Every morning, I wait for the knock followed by:

"Mummy?"

"Yes, sweety?"

"It's me, your son - Adam."

For the love of -

"Yes, sweety. I know."

"Can I come in?"

"Yes, sweety."

He was leaner than Arthur but just as awkward to lie in bed with. His blonde hair was a surprise to everyone. I spent the first six months of his life holding him up to the light at the window in the hope of seeing a fleck of ginger (so I could say for definite he was part me) but alas it wasn't to be. Not even a hint of a curl, straight as an arrow and his father's brilliantly blue eyes.

They both looked like their father. Had I not seen them come out of me I would have questioned if we were related at all.

Finally, the breadwinner awoke and welcomed the intruders into the bed.

Although the longer we left it to have sex I had begun to feel like the intruder here. It was much easier to ignore the chasm between us when the children were in the bed too.

"My boys!" he exclaimed.

"The heir and the spare, welcome to the kingdom of Bedfordshire."

Affection and fun came easily to Ben. He had a hard time at the start of our relationship trying to get me used to hugs and general tenderness.

As a rule, displays of physical affection make me feel uneasy and awkward. I'm one of those people who stiffly stand there when being hugged. Sometimes – usually when alcohol has been consumed – I offered a limp pat on the back to signal that I wanted this torture to end. According to Ben, it was endearing and just a 'quirk' of mine. Now, it was considered more of a sign of depression.

I decided it was probably best not to pull at that thread, early on a Tuesday morning.

"How did you sleep, Adam?" Ben asked.

"In my bed, Benjamin."

"Don't call me that, call me 'daddy'."

"But it's your name? You don't call me 'son'"

Ben's eyes pleaded with me to *do* something about this conversation. Naturally, I pretended not to see him and turned my attention to my phone.

My phone was the reason for my being a half-assed parent.

It called to me like an old friend when my kids have demanded my attention. It told me to give them biscuits and look up organic oatmeal cookies that I will definitely make tomorrow. It reassured me that by tomorrow I would be a much better parent so I wouldn't have to feel bad about reading internet articles like: 'Help! My daughter wants to marry the microwave.'

A lot of my ambition and drive to be a better parent and housewife waited for me in that magical place called 'tomorrow'.

It's great; I never had to feel guilty about my online habits because 'tomorrow' I would definitely rectify all my failings.

I was stuck in a hole of looking up other people's wonderful gardens. I hated my garden, I wanted the lot of it concreted over and turned into some beautiful Italian-looking courtyard, so I can sit in my fairy-light covered haven and sip wine.

There were many problems with this scenario: I had no money to do any work in the garden and, more importantly, I lived in Ireland. This meant it was only summer for 24 hours and the rest of the time it's freezing.

These pretty convincing problems weren't enough to stop my garden-porn binge. I salivated at the prospect of a fire pit and then had a stroke of inspiration:

I remembered that there were always 'DIY garden transformation' videos online and I convinced myself that they couldn't be that hard to follow.

I decided I was a genius and felt confident that I was one step closer to realising my Italian courtyard dream. It was because of this I decided to zone back into my family and find out if they were still in the room.

"I don't know why goats are called goats, Artie," said Ben, "Maybe Mummy knows."

I've come back too soon.

"Who wants breakfast?" I offered, in an attempt to escape more questions.

If you ever wanted to find out how little you know about the world around you, you just needed to have a conversation with my children. They specialised in asking the most obscure questions. At first, they don't seem that difficult, but when I had to give them some sort of answer I found myself staring at them, blankly, at a complete loss as to what to tell them.

Breakfast had to be served in a particular order and if it wasn't done in that particular order then there would be a fit of epic proportions. I don't mind admitting that I had no control in my house at mealtimes. I'd like to say it was because I saved my authority for the bigger things, but I was just trying to get through the day, one hideous hour at a time.

Cereal had to be put in certain bowls, (red for Adam, blue for Arthur) yoghurts were served next, (strawberry for Adam, apricot for Arthur) then toast (cut in triangles, not squares).

If any of these steps were put in the wrong order - or presented on the wrong plates - it resulted in tears and the refusal to eat anything. The stars aligned most mornings and I could get through the first meal of the day relatively painlessly, however, dinner was a whole other story. It was a battle of wills just to get Arthur to eat something that wasn't beige and covered in breadcrumbs.

I read all those 'no-fail' tips that the internet provided about dealing with fussy eaters but I was convinced the authors behind them were all sadists and talked out of their arse.

I told myself it was a phase that he would eventually grow out of, but that was one of many lies I told myself on a daily basis. I knew he'd end up as one of these complete weirdoes in a tabloid feature entitled: *I eat 150 chicken nuggets a day and it's all my mum's fault.*

I was always envious of my husband's ability to get ready within 15 minutes of waking. It was not like it took me much longer since I had dispensed with such frivolities like brushing my hair or showering in general but, still, he looked put together and ready for the outside world in the same time it took me to convince Artie to sit at the table for breakfast and keep his underwear on for this one particular meal.

Ben kissed us all good-bye and I couldn't help but think he was hiding a smug smile because he got to escape from us for nine hours a day. He never suffered the guilt I did when I left the boys for work. That was a catalyst in my decision to stay at home, but the nail on the head was 'the incident'.

My mother came up with that name, I'd rather call a spade a spade; or a failed suicide attempt a failed suicide attempt, but, perhaps, 'the incident' rolls off the tongue a bit better.

It's definitely too early in the morning to think about that.

"Will you be late?" I asked, in the hope that he was going to say he was only working a half-day and had forgotten to tell me.

"I don't think so."

Liar

"One of these days I'm going to find out that you've been secretly finishing at 5 pm on the dot and you're out having a life before coming home to us lot."

"A life? What's that? Between you three, the office, my hot mistress and golf on the weekends I really don't have time for anything else."

I threw a tea towel at him, which he caught effortlessly and threw back at me.

"I count down the hours until I'm reunited with my family, you know that."

"Liar."

"I am not!" he countered, incredulously.

"Did I say that out loud?"

He shot me a sulky look and called to the kids:

"I love you, boys. I'll be home on time."

I spent the next hour pleading for Adam to get ready, at a speed faster than a drunk snail but - as usual - it ended with me screaming at him to 'get a move on' because - as usual - we would be late. The school run was stressful enough, without the added pressure of battling traffic in less time.

Parents were feral at this time of the morning. I knew I wasn't alone in this stress because everyone seemed to have the same look of grim determination on their face as they tried to park illegally or battle the jam at the drop-off point at the front of the school.

When I was lucky enough to get there on time, and parents worked as a collective being with seamless drop-offs, it was usually when Adam told me he'd lost a shoe or had forgotten to put his socks on.

If I didn't get him out of the car in less than ten seconds I was going to be lynched by a stressed-out office worker, in the car behind me, who needed to leave their own kids down immediately so they could get a large, bizarrely named coffee and into their work on time before that bitch, Sandra, from the office tapped her watch and tutted at them for being late again – or so I imagine...

In order to prevent this anxiety-filled moment I usually opted to park on the road outside. It was a free-for-all too but at least if I managed to find an illegal parking spot I'd be able to let Adam put his shoe back on before I dragged him up the drive to the school.

Today, we were stuck in the traffic and we were late. I noticed that the woman in the car behind us was using her time in the traffic jam to apply her make-up.

I didn't remember the last time I wore make-up. I caught a glimpse of my very pale, tired-looking face and decided to never look in the mirror again. I used to wear make-up every day but sheer laziness and a talent of avoiding mirrors at all costs meant I was now free of that responsibility.

Perhaps that's why we haven't had sex in a while.

The mistress crack was one of his stupid attempts at a joke but it hit a nerve.

Maybe it wasn't a joke at all.

My destructive train of thought was interrupted by the make-up applicator, who beeped at me for not driving forward the five foot the traffic had moved. She'd obviously finished her eyeliner and was, once again, conscious of the time. I waved my hand as a fake apology in the rearview mirror and continued on the slog that was the school run.

In a miracle of miracles, there was a space and it was big enough that I didn't have to embarrass myself by attempting to parallel-park under pressure.

"Before we get out, do you have everything?" I asked, nervously.

"Yes, mummy."

"Shoes on both feet?"

"Yes, mummy."

"Great, we're just about going to be on time! Good work, team!"

"Mummy, I forgot my school bag."

"Fuck."

"FUCK!" echoed Arthur, with glee.

"Don't say bold talk, mummy!" cried a stressed-out Adam.

"Do you really need it?"

"Of course, mummy," his eyes were filled with tears.

"Ok, sweety. We'll go back and get the bag."

With a heavy heart, I left behind my beautiful, big parking spot and trekked back to the house. The school bag sat in the driveway.

At least it hadn't been taken away by the neighbour's dog – who had a penchant for stealing towels from my washing line.

It was already after 9 am by the time we made it back to the school, so I had no choice but to face the drop-off line at the door. If Adam's shoes hadn't survived the second trip to the school he was going in with whatever was left on his feet.

"Now, do you have everything?"

"Yes, mummy."

"Shoes on both feet?"

"Yes, mummy."

"Great, just jump out and tell the teacher you're sorry for being late. I love you, have a great day."

I got no reply and he didn't even look behind to wave us off, as he ran into the school.

Ungrateful wretch.

I comforted myself in knowing that his teacher (and not me) was going to have to sit through a blow-by-blow account of the forgotten schoolbag incident.

"Ok, Artie. The world is our oyster, where shall we go?"

"To get chocolate from the shop," he demanded.

"No, Artie."

"How about some crackers?"

"Ok, we're going home then."

"Yay!"

While Arthur was happy to look out the window and say 'crackers' over and over, I took the opportunity to revisit my bad mood about my philandering husband.

Could he really be having an affair? Was it the lack of sex? The lack of make-up?

I stopped myself in my tracks for even thinking that this alleged affair was because of something I had done.

As far as I was concerned I deserved sainthood for giving up my career to raise his children. Instead, I was being repaid by him screwing the 'other woman'.

That utter bastard. I'm not going to stand for this.

I pulled the car over to a screeching halt and dug around in the handbag for my phone.

It was time for Benjamin Cole to get a piece of my mind.

Chapter 2

"Hello?"

The fool answered.

"What do you mean you have a mistress?" I raged.

"What?"

"This morning, you said you had a mistress?"

"Amy, I'm in the middle of the office can I phone you back?"

"No, you bloody well can't. Do you think I'm going to give you time to get your story straight? You're going to tell me what you meant by that."

"It was a JOKE."

"Oh yeah, likely story. I bet it was one of those jokes that are actually true, but you're trying to put me off the scent by admitting to it. I'm wise to you, gobshite."

"What?" he sounded genuinely confused.

"It makes sense, think about it." I offered, with a little less fire in my belly than before.

"No, I won't think about it nor am I entertaining this bizarre argument after I told a joke."

"So you're not going to admit it?"

"Admit what? That you've lost your sense of humour?"

After we remained silent on either end of the phone for almost thirty seconds I said: "There's no mistress is there?"

"No, Amy."

Fuck.

"Right, bye then."

I clicked the phone off and wondered how I could spin this round so that I could also claim that I was joking.

I worked in PR for years, spin was my skill; but even this may be a tough one to get around.

Was I hungry? I tend to get cranky when I'm hungry. Damn it anyway, what was I even thinking?

Ben had never given me a moment's worry when it came to fidelity.

In all the years we'd been together I couldn't remember a time he had given another woman a second glance, let alone wanted to strike up a conversation with them. I was going to have to pin this on school run stress and hope he had a terrible day at work so this paled in significance.

Best keep my phone off for a while just in case.

By the time we were home, I was lost in thoughts of the early days of our courtship.

We met through mutual friends and it wasn't an instantaneous spark of everlasting love, it was just: easy.

Everything with him was so simple. We had our first date and I was off the market ever since. There was no big dramatic declaration of love or stormy years of fights that eventually turned into a settled existence together, it was all like falling into the easiest transition of my life.

After years of horrible boys, I was wary of how easy the relationship was but it didn't stop me. I think that's always been a problem with me, I didn't seem to learn as I bumped from one turd to the next. I didn't protect my heart as I should have, even after the umpteenth heartbreak, but I was glad I didn't. If I had been a hardened cynical wretch I might have lost Ben before it had even begun.

For the first few months, I waited for the other shoe to drop so I could discover the 'real' him that he was obviously hiding – the horrible version. It never came. Instead, I fell deeper in love with a kind and thoughtful man.

Getting married was the logical next step. Next came buying the house and having children; it was all textbook.

Up until that December.

"Right, Artie. Crackers?" I asked.

A pointless question, this child had never said 'no' to a cracker in his life.

"How about chocolate?"

"Nice try, kid."

I handed over the crackers and hummus and asked for 15 minutes so I could check my work.

"You don't work, mummy. I'm your job." He said, sweetly.

"This is just the other little job I have."

"Oh, your secret job that we don't tell daddy about?"

"Yes, that one."

"Ok, can I have cartoons on then and I won't tell daddy?"

I was quite obviously being played by an extortionate three-year-old. I shouldn't have let him get away with it but I really wanted those 15 minutes.

"Ok, love."

The television clicked on and so did my laptop.

It wasn't exactly a secret job, it was still my old job. I just liked to check in from time-to-time and offer any little ideas or advice.

I didn't feel like telling Ben that I hadn't completely cut the cord on my old career. By trying to keep an 'in' with the company I had a backup plan just in case I needed it.

It seemed logical to me that perhaps I would have needed to return to work if I had accidentally lost both the kids in a supermarket and realised I was completely unqualified to be a parent.

I told myself it was easier to keep this little part of my day a secret - for now.

I wouldn't have long as I had promised that I would make a bigger effort to get involved with other parents in my position – those who were staying at home, not those who were losing their grip on reality – and Ben had 'helpfully' found a local parent and toddler group that was on this morning.

I really hated those things, mostly because I generally didn't want to spend time with people other than those I'm related to; but a promise was a promise.

There was nothing of great consequence in my inbox so I decided to send one of those easy-breezy emails just to see what everyone was up to.

I preferred to communicate via text or email, that way I could think about what I needed to say instead of letting nonsense pour out of my mouth.

I found it hard to remember how to have a proper conversation with adults, other than Ben. I spent the majority of my day with Arthur and, as talkative as he was, the topics were limited to cartoons and what junk food he could extort out of me.

An email was safer; I could form actual sentences without stuttering or tumbling over my words.

I opted to reach out to my old partner in crime, Rita. She would know what was going on in my accounts.

I wished I had bothered to change my old university email address - it wasn't exactly professional. I was left using it because the one for work was decommissioned when I left.

To: rita@RSNCommunications.com
From: RaveyAmy1985@gmail.com
Subject: What's up??
Hi there,
Just having a look at the usual suspects and I haven't had an update on the plan for the week ahead. I usually get something, at the latest, by lunchtime on Mondays. I hope you lot aren't slacking off without me already??

I decided to add a few smiley emojis with my signature just in case she thought I was being a complete bitch, but I'd worked really hard to get some of those clients and I wasn't about to be shut out, just because I'd left.

I was aware of how ridiculous my thinking on this was, but I didn't care. Thankfully it didn't take long for her to get back to me.

Good old Rita; I knew I could depend on her.

From: *rita@RSNCommunications.com*
To: *RaveyAmy1985@gmail.com*
Subject: Re: What's up??
Hi Amy,
We had a little meeting yesterday and we thought with you gone for so long now, all campaign business should be sent directly to the account directors. You've been such a great crutch during this transition but I think we can take it from here. All the best and keep up the Facebook pictures of the boys, they are just THE cutest.
Coffee soon?
Xxx
Rita

I read and reread the email then slammed the laptop closed. I resisted the urge to write back "fuck you, Rita" and locked myself in the bathroom to cry.

That's it, I'm officially unemployed. Fucking, Rita.

Rita had always been my competition but we seemed to bounce off each other, spur each other on, and get the results. I considered her a friend; although she had cancelled plans to meet up for lunch four times over the last six months, and now this.

The more I thought about, the more I knew it was ridiculous to think of our relationship as a friendship.

She was five years younger, single and determined to make her name in the business. After two maternity leaves and that 'inconvenient' bout of insanity, I had been treading water - at best – near the end of my time there. However, the rejection still stung.

Fucking, Rita.

I took a big breath and decided to leave the bathroom and face Arthur.

"You look funny, mummy."

Thanks, kid.

Taking a look in the mirror, I saw my eyes were red and puffy from the tears. My cheeks were blotchy and I really did look rather rubbish. I decided if I was going to have to face the outside world then I would have to put on some sort of make-up.

In deciding this I was presented with another problem: how much effort does one put into these things?

Should I look up a video tutorial and get some smoky eyes going on or do I just do the basic cover up the bags under my eyes?

The answer to this was easy because my make-up collection consisted of a very questionable looking sponge, foundation that was at least three shades too dark for my un-tanned body and dry looking mascara.

"Right, au naturale it is," I said, to no-one.

I decided the make-up fiasco was also Rita's fault.

I justified the lack of effort I was making for my appearance at this group was because I didn't want to give these people unrealistic expectations on how I look; this way they would get to know the real me.

The real me was a puffy-eyed mess and if they didn't like it, they could lump it.

I was always much braver in the safety of my own home; in reality, I knew I would be a self-conscious mess from start to finish.

"Television is going off now, Arthur," I called into him, as I tried to locate my keys.

"But WHY?" he whined.

I resisted the urge to shout back: "Because I'm a bastard" and decided it was more constructive to not feed the tantrum.

"We're going to a new playgroup and you're going to make lots of friends and have fun," I said, trying to fake some enthusiasm.

He eyed me suspiciously and stayed rooted to the spot.

"Afterwards we can go get sausages somewhere?" I added, to sweeten the bargain.

Sausages or chicken nuggets were the way to get Arthur to do most things. The way to this boy's heart was definitely through his stomach - as long as what you were trying to give him wasn't, in any way, construed as healthy.

A quick check over my clothes revealed that this particular top had several yogurt-y handprints splattered on it from when both boys pretended to give me hugs after breakfast – clearly, they had been really using me as a giant tissue.

Turds.

After a quick change of t-shirt, we were out the door before I could go back on my word and lock us in the house for the rest of the morning.

I decided to face the music and turn on my phone to see if there was a message from Ben.

There were three texts and four missed calls.

Shite.

Ben: Amy, pick up the phone

Meh, that wasn't so bad maybe he wasn't too mad about my slight overreaction.

Ben: Amy, you can't avoid me for the whole day. I think we need to talk about therapy again.

Ok, well that escalated fast.

Ben: AMY, PICK UP THE DAMN PHONE!

Contrary to popular opinion I actually love reading messages done in capitals. People think they're shouting at me when really they're just making it easier for me to read the text without my glasses.

"Jokes on you, angry texter! I'd better reply all the same," I say to an oblivious Arthur.

Amy: Sorry, sweety! Phone died, all charged up now though. Hope you're having a good morning after that crazy person took my phone and pretended to be me. What a bitch, eh?!

I figured that I might as well curve into the insanity. He must have been waiting for my message because I received his reply within seconds.

Ben: THAT'S what you're going with?

It wasn't a great response, but at least most of the angry capitals were gone.

Amy: Yes, yes it is. Can't really talk now, going to bring Artie to a playgroup and get out into the big bad world again. Love you xx

As soon as I hit 'send' I turned the phone off once more.

I completely disagree that modern technology makes you completely reachable all the time – you just need to turn the damn thing off.

My problem had been, albeit momentarily, solved.

However, it meant I would have to pay attention to my surroundings during the time at playgroup. I had been hoping to get back to my garden porn binge.

It was pleasant out so I thought I could pretend to be someone who enjoyed being active and walk to the playgroup.

It could be my first lie to the group, should I get up the courage to actually talk to anyone.

I hadn't always been like this.

In pre-incident times I liked people, or at least tolerated social situations a hell of a lot better than I did now.

It was months since 'it' happened and I still couldn't stomach the thought of actually letting my brain open up long enough for me to process it.

I knew that this level of avoidance was unhealthy, I knew it was the real reason I talked Ben into agreeing with my plan to become a stay-at-home parent.

I had told him it was so I could be with the kids more, instead of running off to work every day. The reality was that I just couldn't face being part of the outside world anymore. I felt better in my bubble at home. I could keep the four of us safer there.

Even thinking about 'it' in this peripheral capacity caused a feeling of uneasiness within me. The anxiety in my chest rose, when this happened it was like an elephant standing on my lungs. That's when the panic set in.

Stop, Amy. Stop.

I literally stopped in my tracks. Arthur tugged at my hand to get me to start walking again, but I couldn't move. I was rooted to the spot on the footpath and all I wanted to do was run back to the house, lock the door and wait there until I could remember how to breathe again.

I hadn't had a panic attack in months, and never once in public. I'd been careful never to put myself in a situation where it might happen. I couldn't bear the thought of anyone knowing my mental health was as bad as it was – or that my grip on sanity was so tenuous.

Ben was worried enough as it was.

That wasn't my only motivation, of course. Mostly, I didn't want anyone to judge me or think I was so weak.

I knew how bad the stigma surrounding mental health could be. I knew the looks people gave, the snap judgments, and the poorly formed views – mostly because I had them before any of this happened to me. To my shame, I used to look down on anyone who dared say they were 'depressed' within my earshot. I thought it was a buzz word people used when they were having a bad week.

I remembered when an old university friend was in the throes of a depressive episode and I told her to "shake it off."

I cringed when I thought of that.

To her credit, she didn't hit me the slap I deserved. She just pulled the duvet over her head and asked me to leave her room. We didn't stay in touch after university, and to be honest, I didn't blame her.

I realised I wouldn't be able to make it back to the house in the shape I was in, so I opted for the nearest coffee shop I could find. There was an unfamiliar one ten feet away and I managed to tumble through the door, dragging a reluctant Arthur behind me.

The café was new to the area and was definitely trying too hard. There were garden gnomes everywhere and fake grass for wallpaper. Both of these décor choices were not helping my panicked state but it was starting to rain and Arthur was getting fussy so this was going to be my hideout for the foreseeable.

The interior design gave me a headache but Arthur found blocks and I knew there would be no hope of getting him to leave.

I accepted defeat and settled down on one of the battered sofas. I ordered a coffee for me, chocolate pancakes for Arthur and waited for my panic to subside.

As we were the only people in the shop our order was quickly presented and the sullen looking gentleman, who I presumed was the owner, went back to reading his paper behind the counter.

Despite the lack of customers, the coffee tasted great. I tried to enjoy the quiet of my surroundings but I ended up turning inwards and having a conversation with myself - something that never ended well.

What are you doing here, Amy? Are you seriously avoiding a parent and toddler group? Are you really that insecure? You do remember you're not in school anymore and you're an actual adult.

I was very preachy when I was right.

I decided that talking to myself was a terrible idea and opted to concentrate on my surroundings instead.

Just be present and mindful and all that other bollox.

The longer I sat in this tacky little place the more I liked it. The gnomes looked less terrifying the more I looked at them and Arthur was entertained.

By the time I spotted the sign saying 'free wi-fi' I made the decision that this was going to be my new favourite place.

I wondered how long it had been open and if it was always this quiet. I didn't have to wonder too long before the lanky man from behind the counter came walking over and sat on the sofa opposite me.

"Hi," he said, "Do you like your coffee?"

"Erm, yes?"

"Are you not sure?"

"No, I mean yes I'm sure, I like it."

"Good, good. It's good coffee, nice food too if you're staying a while longer. My son-in-law will be in to start the lunch specials."

I couldn't place his accent but his swarthy skin suggested Middle Eastern descent. To be honest I was rubbish at deciphering anyone's ethnicity he could have been from Cork.

"You are welcome to stay as long as you like, I'd be glad of the company. Business is… slow."

He gestured to the empty café as he spoke and I stared at my cup hoping he would take my complete lack of eye contact as an indication that I wanted to be left alone.

He didn't.

"What is your name? I am Joseph, it is good to be meeting you."

I smiled at the odd phrasing and I looked up at him, noting his deep brown eyes. He was in his late fifties, I guessed, but he looked tired beyond his years.

"My name is Amy and that small child who is trying to pull down your gnome display is my son, Arthur."

"Well then, Amy, tell me your story."

"My story?"

"Yes, your story. Everyone has a story and I would like to hear yours."

Chapter 3

It's true, everyone had a story; but I wasn't sure I was ready to share mine out loud and definitely not with a complete stranger in a tacky little coffee shop.

I don't know if it was the soothing feeling of the coffee or the strange little gnomes prying into my soul, but I decided to stop avoiding my memories. I sat on the worn-out sofa and let the events of the last year wash over me.

I couldn't stop it if I tried.

I woke up bleeding on 10th December. I threw myself out of the bed and ran into the bathroom. Even before I saw the blood I knew what was happening.

What is it about being pregnant that makes you think that love and sheer stubborn will can protect your child?

I gripped onto my stomach, feeling the start of the piercing pain ripping in my womb. I sat on the floor with hundreds of thoughts going through my mind.

Some relevant, others not.

Ben was in England on business and the boys were still asleep. My eyes were burning and I ached to cry but I couldn't give into tears, not just yet. I decided that I could save this baby. I knew if I just got to a doctor then I could save my little girl.

I packed up my children, who were still fast asleep, and left them with the child-minder. To this day I don't know how I kept it together that entire day. All I knew was that if I let one tear fall, it was as good as admitting defeat and I didn't know how to do that. My daughter needed me.

After a very terse conversation with a GP receptionist, I was told to go to the hospital.

By the time I got to the emergency department's reception I was shaking so badly I thought I was going to faint then and there.

They must have noticed the panic on my face as I was seen by a doctor quite quickly. I answered the obligatory questions and blood was taken for testing. I was asked to sit back in reception and I would be called soon.

The wait was agony and every time I went to the bathroom to clean more blood away I was getting more and more agitated. I didn't understand why no one was grasping how urgent this was.

I spent the next eight hours sitting on an uncomfortable plastic chair waiting for someone to give me words of comfort and tell me that the bleeding was normal.

I watched countless people come in and out. I imagined their stories and gave them names and tragic backstories - that way I could comfort myself knowing that by the time I was seen by a doctor and told everything was fine, I would go home feeling lucky. I was certain that the doctor would give me some sort of tablet or injection to stop the bleeding and I would go home to take it easy.

I decided that I would take months off work and sit on my ever-expanding arse until my daughter was ready to make her appearance.

I knew it was a girl. A mother knows these things –
one of the many bullshit things I convinced myself of
during those eight hours of waiting.

Eventually, I was told they had lost the blood samples
but they had finally located them around 9pm.

After the briefest of examinations, I was informed that
my baby was gone. They told me to go home and let
"nature do its work".

I was offered no words of comfort or an explanation,
something I so desperately needed.

Still, I did not cry.

I picked up the kids, on autopilot, and returned home
to a quiet house. They had fallen asleep in the back of
the car and I was tempted to wake them up just to have
some distraction or company. My phone had died hours
ago and, no doubt, Ben would be anxious to hear from
me, but I couldn't find the words to say it out loud.

As far as I was concerned, I had failed. I had lost our
baby.

I hated that phrase.

I hadn't 'lost' anything. My body had let me down.

The body that I had finally grown to love after years
of shallow self-loathing had become my enemy once
again.

It had killed my daughter.

The numbness carried on for weeks. My family
thought I was just being stoic and getting on with things
– while those around me offered gems like:

"Sure, it was early days anyway so it wasn't *that* bad."

This was a direct quote from an ill-informed, but
well-meaning aunt.

I had an easy to remember go-to response for when I was asked how I was feeling; I simply shrugged and said:

"These things happen."

People seemed satisfied with this, but to be honest I had no idea what that even meant in a situation like this. I knew they were all waiting for me to cry, but still, no tears came.

I tried a few times but it was as if every attempt to find my heart again was futile. I was a high functioning zombie.

Six weeks later I started to hear her; the hideous version of myself that rejoiced in my failure. I hated her, but unfortunately, by this stage, I was in no shape to defend myself against her onslaught of visceral abuse. It didn't take her long to gain more and more ground and soon I was lying awake night after night, listening to a new list of insults.

It was around 3am on a Wednesday that she first planted the seed.

If you go to the lake, all this will stop. I promise. Your family will be so much happier without you. Deep down, you know that's the truth.

After weeks of feeling shame and continuous mental and physical pain, I felt like I had an answer on how to make it all go away.

I wasn't scared or feeling guilty about who I was leaving behind. I believed her when she told me they were better off without me. It seemed like such an obvious solution.

The night before I planned to kill myself, I sat down to dinner with Ben, and my beautiful boys, to take it all in for the last time.

I memorised the crease in Arthur's chubby little arm as he hit away the food Ben was desperately trying to feed him.

I cherished the way my gorgeous husband's eyes crinkled at the sides when he smiled.

The only time I doubted my plan was when I looked at Adam. I worried about how he would take me going, but even that wasn't enough to make me change my mind.

Despite the slight waver in my determination to go through with it, I still didn't feel guilty.

I steadied my nerve and went back to feeling numb. I knew I could make it to the lake if I just stayed numb.

I casually mentioned I had a meeting in the morning and would be leaving earlier than normal. I could easily get to my destination without arousing any suspicion about why I was going nowhere near the office.

I thought about writing a note but 'she' easily talked me out of it. Besides, there was nothing I could say that would bring them comfort. I just had to get on with things.

At times I was grateful for that horrible voice. She was harsh but she handled the day-to-day functioning while I sat locked away in my own head lying in the fetal position. No one had noticed the exchange of personas, or if they did they were too afraid to mention it in case I broke down. I had checked out of reality weeks ago so really I felt like a spectator to what happened that day at the lake.

At least that's what I told myself (and others).

Afterwards, when people asked me why I did it, I told them: "It wasn't me, it was 'her'. I didn't have a choice."

But that was a lie.

I had a choice and I chose the easy way out. I wanted to die and leave everyone else to pick up the pieces. At my core, I was a coward.

I don't remember if I slept the night before, all I know is that I took my time getting ready. I tamed my hair and put on more makeup than I ever normally would.

I wasn't playing for time - I thought as it was my last day on the planet then I should, perhaps, make an effort.

I struggled to kiss my family 'goodbye' but as I'd spent the last few weeks shunning all affection it wasn't something they were too unfamiliar with.

I got into my car and drove, in silence, the 23 miles to a little model village off the motorway. I had found the lake years earlier when I got lost on a walk with friends. I remember the first time I walked out of the trees and came across it. It was truly breathtaking.

I had purposely never told my family about it, I kept it as somewhere secret just for me. On that day, I was glad that I had.

I walked over the first bridge and sat with the swans for a while until even depression couldn't hide the fact that I still hated birds of all kinds.

Majestic, my arse.

I was alone on my walk, apart for a smattering of dog walkers who paid little or no attention to the smartly dressed woman giving swans dirty looks.

I decided being pecked to death wasn't an advisable way to go so I took to my poorly thought out heels and headed deeper into the forest and further from the lake.

For the first time, in a long time, I was present in that forest. I could smell the trees and it started to rain. The drops on my skin were like ice and it was the first pleasant sensation I had felt in months. The experience wasn't earth-shattering, it didn't make me recognise that life is fleeting and precious or make me turn around and drive home to my family. It was simply a raindrop.

I trudged on, cursing my choice in footwear. I thought of my sons who were happy and alive and yet I longed to be with a daughter that I never knew.

I can't explain the extent of that longing. It's something I still feel all too acutely, even now.

Before I knew it, the path had returned to the lake and I found a beautiful spot where I could sit and contemplate the last few minutes of my life.

I'm an atheist, so the fact that I hoped to be reunited with my daughter in the afterlife made little or no sense, but I clung to the chance nonetheless.

I didn't spend those last few minutes talking to a God or praying for guidance or peace. I simply sat staring at the water and feeling the rain dance off the top of my head. The trees made a poor canopy but it seemed like a frivolous complaint, all things considered.

I threw the heels to one side and crept down to the waterfront. All hopes of a graceful entrance to my watery grave were well and truly scuppered when I lost my footing in some mud.

"Fucking typical," I muttered.

I started to panic and was adamant that those couldn't be my final words on this earth. I stopped wading into the water and thought about all the profound quotes that I'd read over the years. Social media was awash with them; generally shared by unsuccessful people so they feel less shitty about their Monday.

None came to mind, so I stood there freezing, waist-deep in the water until finally, my feet started to ache with the cold.

"Fuck it," I conceded, and started back to my journey to the middle of the lake.

I had to fight my natural urge to tread water and instead I dove under. It was disgusting. In all the visions I had of this moment I pictured an elegant descent into cool blue water, finally being at peace and discovering the true meaning of the cosmos.

To say it wasn't quite like that was an understatement.

The water was freezing and the smell was vile. I couldn't see centimetres in front of me never mind receive the hidden answers to the universe.

Even then I didn't start to panic, I just thought this was pretty standard for my luck up to this point. I started to feel light-headed so I closed my eyes and waited for the last of the oxygen to slip from my lungs. I would like to say my thoughts were something poignant - like my final family dinner, my wedding day or my children's births - but there was nothing.

If anything it just seemed like the most pointless end to a life, that up until a few months ago, I loved.

This also wasn't a big revelation, nor did it make me push myself above the surface, I just accepted that this was a stupid way to die but I'd got this far so it seemed like too much effort to turn back. Even in suicide, I was ridiculously lazy.

It was then I felt the pull towards the other side – not to heaven, to the other side of the lake. I was unceremoniously dragged through the water and on to surprisingly sharp reeds that surrounded the water.

I could hear him talking, asking questions but all I could do was cough. The taste of pond water was horrific.

Sometimes, even now, I can still taste it.

"Love? Love what's your name?" my rescuer asked.

I couldn't answer for coughing so he tried again:

"Can you hear me, love? Can you open your eyes? Just tell me your name; can you do that for me?"

Blinking into the sun I tried to speak: "It's…it's…"

I stopped speaking and just lay my head back on the grass to stare at the clouds. He didn't press me further for my name, just waited patiently for me to start talking again.

It took a few seconds to focus my eyes on my saviour. He was a middle-aged dog walker, who I later found out was called Malcolm.

"Are you ok? Jesus, here take my jacket. Down Jess! Get back," he shouted.

A very enthusiastic cocker spaniel licked my face and made me feel more awake by the second. I pushed myself onto my elbows and looked down to find my clothes covered in green sludge from the pond. Apparently, Jess found this delicious. I knew Malcolm was asking me questions but I couldn't understand them. He asked where I went in, so he could find my belongings, and I limply pointed across the water.

He gave Jess a command which meant she sat down right beside me while he took off in a sprint.

I remember thinking the dog was nice company. We both sat at the side of the water staring into the disgusting depths while I listened to her breathe steadily beside me. It was the first time I felt comforted by a living thing in a long time.

I don't know how long it took for Malcolm to return with my muddy shoes and handbag. He kept asking my name but he could have been speaking Norwegian for all

I could process. I may have been awake but even simple sentences were hard for me to understand.

"You're in shock, love. We need to phone someone to come here. I've already got someone to call an ambulance, they'll be here soon. Now, you have a wedding ring, can you tell me what your partner's name is? I'm going to look in your mobile if that's ok, can I phone them?"

"Ben." It was the only information I offered.

"Great, now we're getting somewhere. This is Jess, I'm Malcolm and we're not going to leave you until you're looked after. Ok, love?"

I didn't respond. I just looked back to the water again and gave up on holding my own body weight. I lay on the uncomfortable reeds and let the universe go on around me.

I felt at peace lying there.

They don't tell you about the peace you feel when you properly give up on everything. Letting go of my meaningless existence, in the grand scheme of things, was marvellously freeing.

It could have been hours before the ambulance arrived, I had no real awareness of time, but I liked watching Jess.

She had it right, just be happy. I worried about what people were going to say when they found out. I would have to put up with people saying things like:

"Have you tried not being a miserable cow?" or "Just get on with things, you have children to think of."

The kids

Adam, who we'd tried for three years to conceive and Arthur, my wild child.

I was actually going to leave them behind

It was the first time I really thought about what me ending my life would mean. I would have left Ben behind to raise our children alone. Would they have grown up hating the mother that abandoned them? Hate all women because they all represented the first one in their life to leave them?

That hurt – even more than the poisonous words I'd been listening to, on repeat, for the last few months. I allowed myself to finally think about the damage I could have caused to those I left behind and it really stung.

I don't know how long Malcolm had been silently sat beside me but when I lifted my head to look at him he smiled back, kindly.

"Are you ready to tell me your name?" he asked.

"It's Amy."

"That's a pretty name, Amy. Now, why would you want to go swimming on a day like this?"

"I wasn't going for a swim, I was trying…trying…trying to kill myself."

The tears burned in my eyes and a lump the size of a brick was lodged in my throat. When I looked back to him he had a knowing look on his face and sympathy in his eyes.

"I know, love. I just want to get you talking is all. I'm not going to ask you why, I think that's a silly question, but I will ask you about these two."

He held my phone up and there was a picture of my two beaming boys as my screensaver.

I started to cry again.

"Now, now, no need for that. Is that why you're here? Did something happen your babies?"

"No," I sobbed, "Another. My baby girl."

My shoulders shuddered with every word. It was the first time I'd ever admitted that I was still grieving for a child, despite everyone around me thinking I should have been over it by now.

To do it, finally, was such a relief. It felt like the dam wall had fallen. This kind stranger and his dog sat with me and listened to my sorry tale in between sobs.

In my mind I thought he would be less sympathetic when he found out that I was crying over a child I didn't even meet, but instead, he put his arm around my shoulder and let me cry even harder than before.

When the tears subsided enough for me to hear him, he told me about his wife: Aurelia.

"We wanted a big family," he began, "but that wasn't meant to be. We tried and tried but God decided we weren't to be blessed. Then one day she came back all excited with this test in her hand and tears in her eyes. I've never seen any person in the world look as happy as she did that day.

I was terrified from the start but she just kept calm. She took to it like a duck to water and I couldn't have been more proud to hold back a woman's hair when she got sick every morning.

"The bigger that bump got the happier she became but when she was five months pregnant she got too sick to move from bed and then we realised that something wasn't quite right."

His face darkened with every sentence and his knuckles whitened as he gripped Jess' lead.

"Cancer," he said flatly, "she needed an aggressive therapy and needed it right away. She wouldn't hear of it of course - wouldn't risk the baby.

"I tried to convince her otherwise but my Aurelia was a stubborn one. I didn't love the baby. God, forgive me, but I didn't. It was just this *thing* that wasn't even here yet and it was helping that sickness kill my wife. I remember one day I punched a wall in frustration and my dear old mum put ice on it for me, when she finished she said: 'A man becomes a father when he sees the baby, a woman becomes a mother when she finds out she's pregnant.' I never forgot those words and I stopped trying to convince her of the therapy after that."

We lapsed into silence and I waited for him to continue.

"Neither of them made it," he finished.

"I got to hold my little son but he was just too young, his wee lungs couldn't take it but I tell you what, my mum was right. I loved him as soon as I laid eyes on him. Had his whole life planned out and all. Begged him to stay with us, his mum was a fighter and he would be too. God took him three days later and took my Aurelia a week after him. They started the treatment but her wee heart wasn't in it. It wasn't cancer that took her, she just knew our boy needed her up there with him. I like to think that's where they are, happy together, you know?

"So I got to meet my wee lad but I know had he not made it that far my wife would feel just like you right now. Just because you didn't get to hold your little one in your arms doesn't mean you didn't have her whole life planned ahead of her."

It was comforting that someone understood and validated my grief. I didn't offer any words of comfort – something I regret even now. We just went back to sitting in silence, side by side, waiting for the ambulance. By the time the paramedics gave me the once over, he was gone. I didn't know his surname or how to reach him after that day.

I used to imagine inviting him over for dinner when all this was just another painful memory I wanted to hide from. We would talk like two normal people who met under extraordinary circumstances, and forge some kind of everlasting friendship. It was a nice thought but it was never meant to be - like my daughter and his family.

I was taken to the local hospital as a precaution and sat, wrapped in a blanket, in the corridor of the accident and emergency department waiting for my husband. He arrived, ashen-faced and dropped to his knees in front of me. His head collapsed into my lap like a petulant child hoping for forgiveness. I could feel him crying but I couldn't join him. The wall was back up but I already felt like a weight was gone.

"I want to go home," I pleaded.

"Not until I talk to a doctor," he said, in between sobs.

As we sat together in the hallway, I knew he wanted an explanation but I was in no fit state to tell him what had led me to this point. I knew I would have a lot of talking, explaining and apologising to do but for the first time in months, I could see the great expanse of our lives ahead of us. There was no need to rush into talking.

I don't know if it was the hyperthermia setting in, the ingestion of duck faeces or the time spent with Malcolm that set the change of mind in motion, but I knew that I had enough strength to get through the rest of the day without trying to hurt myself.

Of course 'she' wasn't happy about it but I was hoping that there was some sort of magic pill they could give me that would shut her up. There wasn't. Instead, I was given a medley of medication that would at least help to subdue her.

I was discharged after I convinced the on-call psychologist that I wasn't going to commit suicide and Ben promised to not let me out of his sight for the next 48 hours while they set up a mental health home treatment team to come and visit. The hardest thing to hear was that social services would need to be contacted and would likely want to visit our home to make sure our children weren't in any danger.

"Is this a joke? I was killing myself to protect them from my depression and now you'd think I'd harm them?" I fumed.

"It's just standard procedure," Dr whats-her-face, explained.

I resented her and her judgemental questions like: "What's your date of birth?"

Honestly, I don't remember why I didn't like her. I suspect I would have considered a mop my mortal enemy had it 'looked' at me in the wrong way at that moment.

The drive home was in silence. I stared out the window, wrapped in an overgrown jumper and leggings that were two sizes too big. In his rush to get to the hospital, Ben hadn't stopped for clothes and this was all they could find in the emergency department's lost and found box. I didn't mind, they were dry and didn't smell of algae.

As we sped silently down the motorway I decided to switch on the radio. Just as I did, the song from the first dance at our wedding came on. It was the final straw for Ben. He violently hit the brakes and stopped at the side of the road. Undoing his seatbelt in a hurry meant it sprung out and hit him in the face. I pursed my lips together to stifle the laughter reflex and he glared, daring me to giggle. He got out of the car, slamming it behind him. I waited for a few seconds before undoing my belt. I took a deep breath and got out of the car to face the man I loved and try to explain why I was planning on leaving him a widower with two young children.

"Ben," I began.

"Don't, Amy. Just… don't." He said, with his hands in the air in exasperation.

"Don't make a joke about this or try and play this down. You were going to kill yourself today. If this had gone the way you wanted it to I would be picking up your corpse. Your fucking corpse! How? How did we get to a point where I'm this oblivious asshole who didn't know this was coming?"

"Are you really making this about you? How YOU didn't know? I'm the one this is happening to."

"No, Amy, it's not. It's happening to all of us: You, me, Adam and Arthur - we are a team, remember? The days they were born we sat staring at those little balls of fat with complete love. We vowed there and then we would do everything within our power to make sure they didn't have a day of unhappiness if we could help it. So what do you think would have happened with you gone? We'd just move on and get over you? YOU ARE EVERYTHING TO ME. EVERYTHING."

I didn't have the strength to fight with him so instead, I sat on the barrier waiting for him to finish.

"Please, Amy. Please promise me you won't try this again. If you can't keep yourself safe for me or you then do it for the boys. Yes, I'm using all the emotional blackmail in my arsenal. I will fight dirty and for as long as there's a breath in my body to keep you with me. Do you understand that? I don't work without you. I just don't."

His words didn't touch my heart at the time but I would call on them in my darkest times in the weeks to follow.

I knew I would keep myself safe for them.

I tried to speak but nothing came out so I stood up and hugged him at the side of the road. Commuters drove past on their way home from work and stared at this odd couple. They probably thought we were just some ordinary people who were fighting over a flat tyre or whose fault it was they were lost. Little did they know we were trying to put a broken woman back together.

We made another vow at that roadside, one that was more sacred than the ones we nervously swapped in a church years previously. We vowed that it was him and I against the world and I believed him.

After we returned to the car the rest of the journey was, once again, done in silence - but not like before. Instead, I was mentally picking up tiny fragments of my soul and tentatively fixed them back together.

When we got home, I picked my son up for the first time in months and kissed him on his beautiful, tiny lips. That was a fragment put back in place. Later, that night, I lay my head on my husband's chest and listened to his heart like I used to. Another one connected.

That's the way it was, that's how I found my way back to a new normal. It wasn't some shocking realisation or epiphany as I washed the dishes. It was the simple, somewhat boring, yet beautiful routine of my daily life that brought me back to life.

I was shopping one day when I saw one of those god-awful shabby chic plaques that are in every bargain home store in the world, and it said: 'Remember the little things, because one day you'll look back and realise they were the big ones'; or something equally as trite, but that's the only way I could describe my journey home.

I had no grave to go to and grieve for my daughter, but I gave her a life, if only in my head. I named her Lily and she had the most beautiful red curly hair and green eyes, like me. Her smile was like Ben's and she would wrap him around her little finger. Even now, when nosy people ask when I'm going to 'try for a girl' after my two sons I swallow down the lump and refuse the urge to tell them that I had a daughter. Even if I never got to hold her, she was mine and she was as real to me, in those short weeks, as both my sons are now.

That was the hardest part of coming back into the world: people. Well-meaning as they were, they were all dumbfounded at how badly I'd taken it all.

Apparently, there's a socially acceptable amount of grief a woman is allowed to express after a miscarriage (an early one at that) and I'd far exceeded my quota.

I gladly accepted the medication they gave me. There was one that levelled out the sadness, one to help me sleep, one that helped the anxiety. They had covered all their bases, but it didn't stop there.

I was sent to therapy.

I spoke about my childhood, the relationship with my parents and a whole host of other things that I thought they wanted to hear. If I had enough of a 'dodgy' background then maybe my little swim in the lake would make sense.

It was all lies, of course. I had a wonderful childhood. The truth of the matter was: my baby died and I was suffocating with grief. I didn't even last a full session before I left. I refused to go back since.

As the months rolled on, I successfully managed to completely alienate myself from all of my friends. It didn't help that while I was trying to collect my sanity, my whole persona changed. The natural air of confidence, the surety in my voice and my abilities as a writer had all but gone.

All this meant I was floundering at work so I decided to make the leap out of the viper's nest and retreat back home where I felt safer – citing rising childcare costs as the reason.

Looking back, I know I wasn't pushed out per-se but the way I was treated in the office had certainly changed. I couldn't figure out if they were deliberately hiding scissors and other sharp stationery or if I was being paranoid, but I thought it was for the best if I just got out of there.

Sometimes I missed the adult conversation but mostly I managed to convince myself that I hated people. Small talk, although tedious, became something I grew to almost fear. I stopped short of becoming agoraphobic but I was frightened that's where I was headed.

The panic attacks and the social anxiety as a whole were getting out of hand and it was building. Now, I was avoiding a parent and toddler group.

I weighed up how much of my story I was willing to reveal to this stranger but I decided to open up as best I could.

What have you got to lose? It's not like you'll ever be back here again and this is a kind of therapy.

I couldn't bring myself to tell him what had led me to this point in my life (or into his café) so I spoke to him about other things. I told him about my old job, my new job and the fact that I was still adjusting to life at home - nothing of real consequence.

I avoided mentioning my daily dance with sanity. I did, however, confess that I was using his establishment to avoid meeting new people at a playgroup that I had felt pressured into joining so I could keep my husband off my back.

He didn't laugh at my childishness or tell me to be honest with Ben, he simply absorbed the information and shrugged. I didn't need an opinion on my behaviour, it was just nice to have someone to talk to and I knew my inner voice wasn't great at the sympathy. We only stopped talking when his son-in-law, Michael, came in to start cooking.

Only then our bubble of intimacy was truly burst.

Chapter 4

"I enjoyed that Amy," he said.

"So did I, Joseph."

For the first time, in a long time, I meant it. As a rule, if it involved small talk I would run a mile, but his strange mannerisms and his voice that sounded like honey made me relax and talk about the little things in my life. I almost felt a bit more like myself. I refused the offer of lunch and promised that I would be back the same time next week.

"This can be your haven, Amy. Perhaps we can help each other in some way?" he asked.

That piqued my curiosity, "How's that?"

"You said you did PR, yes?"

"Well, yes in a previous life, but I can refer you to someone in my old work who can give you advice for this place?"

"No, I like you Amy and I think you and I will do great things together."

He said it so confidently that I almost believed him.

"You come again and we'll make a plan together, I will pay you and we will make my café work."

"You can pay me in coffee and tray bakes," I said with a greedy smile, "I'll be back next week and we can plan our world domination."

"Good, good. I'll see you then."

His back was already turned before I got to the door. The fact there was no lingering 'goodbye' made me like him even more.

The encounter with Joseph was enough to bolster my spirits and make me brave enough to face the playgroup, or it could have been the caffeine boost. Either way, I was marching towards it with purpose while Arthur's little legs could barely keep up.

When I walked into the freezing cold community hall I saw all the little cliques forming already.

Wasn't this the first day? How am I already on the back foot of this?

I tried not to let the paralysing fear of forming new friendships stop me so I let go of a restless Arthur's hand, who sprinted towards the blocks knocking a smaller child out of his way.

Please don't cry, please don't cry, please don't cry.

She cried - loudly.

The mother appeared from behind me and swooped up the little crying girl, soothing her as only a parent can do, whilst simultaneously throwing me a look of disgust.

"Well this couldn't have gone better," I muttered.

I vowed to give it 15 minutes then I could sneak out the back while they were all drinking watery tea and, no doubt, judging mothers who chose to formula feed their children.

Bunch of bitches

Of course I'd no idea if that's what they were talking about; but it was easier to decide that they were the problem, rather than me. I felt completely awkward in my own skin at the best of times, so I knew this wasn't going to be easy. I had to remind myself that they were just normal people. Since Lily, the 'new' me was cautious of everything. Afraid of expressing an opinion in case I offended someone, afraid of offering words of advice to anyone that needed it in case I was wrong and I ruined their life, afraid of raising my voice in case someone actually heard me.

Arthur was happy and had managed to find a little group of like-minded hooligans, who also liked piling blocks on top of each other and kicking them over. I wouldn't go as far as saying they were playing 'together', more like tolerating each other's presence.

The fifteen minutes were up and as I gathered up our coats and manoeuvred my way over to the blocks I felt a tap on my shoulder.

"Not leaving are we?" she said.

I just stood, dumbfounded, not thinking of an excuse to leave quick enough. As the silence extended she introduced herself and I realised soon enough I wasn't going anywhere.

"My name is Margaret Clunting and I'm the Chairwoman of S.M.U.G"

"Smug?" I asked, slightly concerned that she was having a laugh at my expense.

"No, dear: S.M.U.G. It stands for: 'Special Mums United in Growth'. It's my brainchild and we run several of these little groups across the town to reach out to struggling mothers so they can get out and feel like they're part of a wider community. It can be very isolating as a mother, you know?"

I stared at her blankly and before I had a chance to offer my name or any type of verbalisation she had already left to introduce herself to another woman who just walked through the door. I hoped she would be as clueless as me but she knew all about S.M.U.G and was "delighted" that there was one on her doorstep. My eavesdropping gleaned that she was already attending two others in different parts of the town.

This recognition earned her an automatic 'in' with the other women who were stood in the corner scrutinising those who they did not recognise, namely: me.

I put down the coats and settled back down on to my hard plastic chair knowing I wasn't going to get out of there anytime soon.

Time stood still in Smug Club and I vowed never to darken its doors again. I was bored out of my mind and I didn't want to run the risk of taking out my phone to play around with a new game I'd downloaded. It had the world's catchiest little theme tune. Judging by Mrs Clunting and her gaggle of Cluntettes, I had a feeling that anything but utter adoration and all-consuming supervision of one's child during Smug Club would be frowned upon.

I called Arthur over to see if I could somehow convince him to leave, but he decided he'd prefer to stay with his new 'friends'.

"Traitor," I mumbled under my breath.

The door opened once again and that's when I spotted her. A vision of colour, warmth, and light who exuded unadulterated confidence and had the air of some sort of bohemian goddess. I'd never been more jealous of a person. She had tattoos down both arms, a nose ring and her hair fell loosely at her shoulders. She lit up the room and I wanted to be her friend.

Unfortunately, Mrs Clunting had spotted her too and was quick as a flash to head over and introduce herself.

"Well, that's that then."

I resigned myself to solitude and got back to hoping time would move faster.

Within seconds I heard a howl of laughter reverberating throughout the room.

"You're fucking kidding me, right? Your actual name is 'MRS CUNTING'? Fuck me, that husband of yours must have the tongue of a rock star in order to convince you to take that shite name."

I can't be sure, but in my recollection, everything went instantly silent around the room. Cups shattered on the floor as the Cluntettes gasped and someone fainted at the vulgarity of this vile woman's language. The fainting was an exaggeration but you get a general idea.

"I would ask you to refrain from using that type of language in any situation where there are young people around. It's highly offensive and isn't very big or clever. My name, madam, is Mrs *Clunting* and I am the founding member and present Chairwoman of S.M.U.G. You are very welcome to join our gathering here today with your children but I suggest you revise your use of the English language or you will be asked to leave."

I was waiting for her to sheepishly apologise for the outburst but she smiled a sickly sweet smile and said in a very posh revision of her normal voice: "But of course, Mrs *Clunting*, I will take my needlework to the corner and continue to mend my husband's socks, while my darling children increase their intelligence by playing with that decapitated doll. I shan't be any more trouble."

The sarcasm was lost on Mrs Clunting, she returned the smile before tottering back to her gaggle of followers in the corner.

To my happiness the bohemian was coming my way, dragging a reluctant looking pair of twin girls behind her.

"Right then you heard the woman; go play and don't make any trouble or there will be no iPad until you're 13."

The threat was believed and the two children skulked off to find the aforementioned decapitated doll.

My new best friend (and hero) sat two chairs away and took out her phone. Within seconds I could hear world's catchiest theme tune.

I groaned inwardly at her devil-may-care attitude and went back to staring at Arthur. He was now trying to hit everyone else's towers with a wooden hammer.

"I am Thor!" He roared as he bashed the last one out of existence, leaving a total of three children in tears.

I ran over and picked him up from the carnage, offering a weak smile to the mothers who were trying their best to comfort their devastated children. I believe this counted as our second strike. If I was lucky he'd pee on the slide and we'd be asked to leave.

I took my wriggling miscreant over to the seats and explained that he wasn't allowed to play 'Thor' with his hammer like he does at home because it would scare the other children. I knew this was not sinking in – nor did he care about the emotional well-being of other children. Instead, he just rubbed my cheek with his chubby hand before running off again.

"He's a great character," the woman said.

The softness in her voice caught me off guard and I blushed because someone was actually speaking to directly to me.

"He's the devil," I replied.

"Nah, he's spirited. I like that with kids. I want to keep as much mischief in mine before ones like Cunting, over there, try and beat it out of them. What kinda name is Cunting anyway?"

"It's *Clunting*," I corrected.

"Yeah, sure it is," she said with a roll of her eyes, "My name is Elle, by the way. Have you been to one of these things before?"

Without thinking I said: "I'm Amy. Do you mean like a parent and baby group or a Smug Club one?"

Her laughter echoed through the hall again.

"Smug Club? Fuck me, yeah. That sounds about right. I pity the next father that tries to come into the room. They might just crucify him for trying to parent equally. I mean, really? What makes them 'special'? We're all special. My husband is a bit of a plonker but I wouldn't make him feel like that, you know? I sound just like them, don't I? Spouting these judgements before I even know the facts.

She paused for a second and I thought she was going to change her mind about her evaluation on them. After a heartbeat, she said: "Nah, I'm going to stick with it. Screw 'em."

Her South African accent made the constant cursing sound like something more beautiful. I'm not even denying it, I had a huge crush. I was desperate for a friend and this magical cursing unicorn ticked all the boxes.

The conversation was easy. She had moved to Ireland when she was 12 with her mother after her parents' divorce. She admitted that she worked hard on keeping the accent because the alternative would be "hideous".

I tried to decide if I should be offended by this or not but I decided she could probably punch my child in the face and I'd blame him for getting in the way of her fist. I told you: I was desperate.

I had no idea what she was talking about when she eventually stopped speaking. She'd obviously asked a question but I had no idea what it was.

Keep it light, keep it light, keep it light, keep it light.

"Sorry?" I asked in a panic.

"What do you do when you're not sat with outcasts like me?" she repeated.

"Oh, well I used to work in a PR firm before I lost my baby and my mind."

Fuck.

"Cool," was the only answer she offered in response to my miserable attempt at light-hearted conversation.

Well done, Amy.

We went back to looking at our children.

I was mortified but when I looked at her I noticed she wasn't remotely bothered about my social faux-pas. After an eternity of awkward silence (in reality less than five minutes) I worked up the courage to finally say something.

"I'm sorry, I'm really sorry," I said.

"For what?" She sounded confused as to why I was apologising.

"I didn't mean to overshare; I'm really bad at this," I continued.

"No, I think you're great," she offered, "If your goal is to make people feel really uncomfortable."

Her voice was kind and she was smiling as she spoke.

"How about some tea," she asked.

I nodded in agreement and watched as she headed up to the counter. It didn't take long before I heard the raised voices.

"For fuck sake, all I said was 'shift your arse'. I meant it in a nice way," said Elle.

"I think you should leave," said Mrs Clunting, "I don't think S.M.U.G is the place for you or your parenting...style."

"Are you kicking me out of Smug Club? Oh, no! How will I survive?" she said in mock terror.

Her theatrical gasp was paired with the flailing of arms that nearly knocked a tray of tea out of the grip of a passing woman.

"Does this mean I don't fall under the 'special' category?" she continued, "You know what? You judging bastards are the reason why mums don't think they're good enough. I bet you spend your free time on those websites making others feel like shite for formula feeding, or using jars or going to work. Like anyone needs the advice of you lot on what makes a good mum.

"We're all trying our best and as long as the kid is happy and healthy then who the hell cares if I curse or let them pick out their own clothes or stay up when they like?"

"I care," said Mrs Clunting, stepping in front of the line of fire once again, "We all care here and that's what makes us 'special.'"

Her use of air quotes made me want to gag.

"Now, I don't know what type of hippy commune you were raised on but we don't need the aggravation of a *free spirit* or whatever you think you are," she continued.

"You're no better than us. Don't dare look down on those who make the effort to go organic or care that our children aren't dressed like they've been dragged through a ditch. I know there's a rise in the 'anti-mum' club online but I refuse to expose my child to this type of behaviour, so just leave."

For a second Elle looked taken back, unsure of herself even. I doubt many people had stood up to her quite so vocally, or publicly, before. The blush in her cheeks was rising but she refused to take her gaze from Mrs Clunting.

The room had been in silence from the start of the altercation. I hadn't taken a breath since it began, and I had started to get dizzy. I'm not sure if my light head was caused by a lack of oxygen or if it was down to my complete discomfort at any type of confrontation.

"Kids," she called in the direction of her stunned daughters, "it's time to leave this poorly disguised cult for brain-dead conformists and get back to the real world."

The venom in her voice was dripping with every word uttered and her gaze didn't leave Mrs Clunting for a second. The kids must have recognised the tone as serious and dutifully joined their mother. Only when she could feel the children beside her did the staring match end. She went to pick up her belongings that were still on the chair beside me. I knew I should have picked up her jacket or at least given one of my ever-so-useless sympathetic smiles. I was embarrassingly bad at empathy but it was the only way people who knew about the breakdown looked towards me now, so I had managed to practise mirroring it back to them. I just sat there in shock waiting for my brain to kick in again but nothing happened.

"You coming?" asked Elle.

Is she serious? Of course, I'm not going; what would all the other people think if I left? They'd think I was some sort of rebel mum who was in cahoots with this woman.

"No, I think Arthur is happy where he is for now," I replied, meekly.

"Suit yourself, but if you think you're going to get a sympathetic ear or genuine advice from this bunch of wankers then you're sorely mistaken."

I could feel the other women look at our exchange trying to gauge if I was going to leave too. To my shame, I kept my head down and pretended that Arthur needed me.

As she left, I heard one of her children say: "Scew 'em, mum. You're the best."

I didn't look back or watch as she left. I kept my gaze transfixed on the blocks that Arthur was building. I assumed she had gone when the noise level began to increase again.

I didn't leave the floor for the remainder of the group. I must have seemed like a dedicated builder, but the reality was: I was ashamed of myself.

Why do I care what this bunch of strangers thought of me?

I instantly regretted not taking Elle up on her offer. Sure, she had the mouth of a sailor, and she scared and fascinated me in equal measure, but at least she was real.

When they gathered the children round for a group sing-song I took the opportunity to get our stuff together so we could make a swift exit after the nineteenth verse of 'The wheels on the bus'.

I hoped that Arthur wouldn't make a scene before we left – something that was never guaranteed.

The last strains of the song were in the background when I felt a hand on my shoulder, it was Mrs Clunting.

"Amy is it?" she asked.

"Yes," I replied, curtly. I wasn't being rude because of her talk-down to Elle, I was just trying to keep the conversation as short as possible so she would lose interest and leave me alone again.

"Well Amy, on behalf of the S.M.U.G I would like to apologise for that outburst earlier," she said with a voice that sounded almost earnest – almost.

"That's an unfortunate part of being a community group. Any old person can walk through the door and there's very little we can do to stop it – well other than asking them politely to rethink their attendance," she said with a smile.

"Hmmm yes, it was uncomfortable."

"Well, anyway I shan't keep you I'm sure you've a busy day ahead with your little one. I'll look forward to seeing you next week, same time?"

"Sure thing," I replied. I hoped the fake enthusiasm in my last statement was disguised better than it sounded in my head.

It was in that moment that I vowed never to return to Smug Club.

Chapter 5

I packed Arthur up with only three tantrums – all caused by my refusal to steal the toys he was playing with and bring them home. If I managed to leave situations like this with under five meltdowns it was considered a success.

We toddled home for lunch and to my surprise - and horror - Ben was home and met us at the door.

He couldn't still be mad at the mistress gaff? I felt my text message explained it, didn't it?

There was something odd about his demeanour but I was too hungry to challenge him on it, in the hallway.

He fussed around Arthur while I prepared something to eat for the three of us. He was acting happy but there was an artificial air about it all.

"What's going on?" I asked.

"Nothing, I just fancied lunch with my favourite people." He tried to present this in a nonchalant tone but it just came out high pitched.

"Is this about the phone call this morning? It really was just a crazy person momentarily taking control of my phone. I don't think you're having an affair."

"What? That? No, no, it's nothing. I just wanted to see you both." His voice was soothing and when he crossed the room to kiss me on the forehead I almost believed him.

"You know I love your cooking so I'm thinking I should make this a regular thing."

One lie too far, Benjamin.

I banged the knife down on the counter making him and Arthur jump.

"Now I know you're lying," I said, "You refer to my cooking as your 'daily punishment' for something terrible you did in a previous life, so tell me why you're here. Have you been fired from your own business?"

"No of course not, I was just... concerned."

"Concerned?"

"No, not concerned really. Worried is maybe better."

"Of what *now*?" I was really getting tired of this conversation, "I'm being the perfect little depressed zombie. All tablets and doctor appointments are taken and attended without a fight. I get out of the house at least once a day and don't shut myself away from anyone, so what do you want now? CCTV feed to your mobile? Half-hourly check-ups?"

I didn't realise I was shouting, or that I'd picked up the knife and was gripping it so hard my knuckles were turning white, until Ben put his hands in the air in a sign of peace and asked me to put the knife down.

I shook myself out of whatever type of rage trance I was stuck in and stepped away from the counter leaving the knife behind me. I put my hands up to my eyes to shield me from the sympathetic smile that was, no doubt, plastered on Ben's face.

"I'm sorry," he said, "I tried phoning your mobile but it's been off most of the morning and when I realised there were no appointments or anything in the calendar I got worried. I drove straight here and that's when I saw you both walking home. I didn't want you to think I was checking up on you but I was just worried when I couldn't reach you."

"I'm trying, Ben," I replied, failing in my attempt to not sound fed up with his constant state of worry, but I couldn't hide it from my voice.

"I just went to a parent and toddler group for an hour just to see what it was like. I did text you about it."

The look of relief on his face was instantaneous.

"That's brilliant news," he said, "I thought you were taking the piss with the message. I'm so proud that you were out of your comfort zone and went to that. You've no idea how worried I've been, but hearing that you're seeking out other like-minded people to spend time with is a huge relief. How often is it?"

"Like-minded people? So, just because we've pushed a bowling ball out our vagina means I'm going to be instant friends with these people? I can assure you that's about the only thing we have in common at this stage."

"No, Amy you know what I mean. It's just great that there's something a bit sociable for you to do. This is great. Is it a daily thing?"

"No, once a week but I think maybe-"

"Weekly? Well, that's a start but we should sit down tonight and look at other's in the area and really fill out that calendar of yours."

"We should?" The sheer joy in his eyes was uncomfortable to look at it. He'd obviously been put through hell and back with me and I never really put my head above the water long enough to check how he'd been coping.

Not well, judging by this farcical display

"One step at a time," I replied, "I just want to give this a proper go first and then we can look and see how we get on with fleshing out the rest of the week. Don't want to do too much, the therapist told me to set realistic goals for my week."

"You mean the therapist you're refusing to go back to because you don't like the temperature of her office?

"Look, it's fine I'm just so excited that you tried and you liked it. Really happy, especially as I didn't even have to push you or eat any of your food as a compromise. This is definitely a winning day for me."

I tried to muster a smile but instead I walked back to the counter to start stabbing the red onion I'd left.

"Do you want an omelette?" I asked, hoping that would change the subject.

"Don't you mean your version of burnt scrambled egg by the time it gets onto the plate?"

"Such smart talk for someone who trusts me not to slip arsenic into their dinner this evening," I replied.

"I think I should go back to work and keep you in the lifestyle you're accustomed to."

It was obvious that I couldn't tell him I hated Smug Club and I would never be going back. He was annoyingly enthusiastic about this latest development in my day.

I decided that in order to keep my sanity, for a little longer, it would be ok to fudge the truth a bit.

I'd keep Ben sweet and tell him I was going to the playgroup when really I could hang out with Joseph in his café.

It was a win-win.

Ben would feel better knowing I was out in the world, while I could awaken some grey matter and help a failing business.

One little white lie can't hurt, can it?

Chapter 6

I spent the rest of the afternoon wracking my brain in an attempt to come up with some ideas on how to help Joseph and then I realised I didn't even know the name of the café. I shared with him intimate details of my life and decided on this crack-pot plan without even asking the name of the business.

What a moron.

I decided to stick to researching the competition so it wouldn't be a complete waste of my time.

By the time Ben came home for the evening, my brain was running at 100mph. I served up the dinner and tried to concentrate on being present but I was a million miles away.

"Amy?" he asked, with the usual concern in his voice.

"Hmmm?"

"Did you meet anyone interesting today?"

"Today?"

"At the group, sweety," the edge in his voice had increased. I decided I should probably engage in the conversation properly or he'd have me sectioned before dessert at this rate.

"Oh, the group. Eh, yeah I guess - a few people."

"This chicken is delicious by the way," he continued.

"What? Firstly, it's fish pie and secondly, well I don't think there needs to be a secondly after that critique of my cooking."

"Yes, I thought that would get your attention. I'm trying to have a conversation with you and you keep zoning out. Apparently pretending to like your cooking gets you back in the room."

"I'm sorry, I have a lot on my mind."

"Anything you'd care to share with the rest of the class?"

"Not really. Just planning out the rest of my mornings with Arthur."

First lie

"That's a good idea. Remember to make them realistic goals, like the therapist said."

"Yes, Ben, I know. I was there, even if it was for one session."

"Half a session and I'm sorry, I'm just trying to help."

The conversation ended there. The only sounds heard were the scraping of forks off ceramic and food quietly being shoved around plates without anyone actually eating it.

This was the quietest part of the day in my house. Everyone grimly looking at the 'meal' in front of them, while I gathered the strength to start forkful negotiations that always ended in a screaming match.

That implies it was a two-way conversation. I'm generally just screamed at until I give up and let them go play. Thankfully, this evening, Ben took the lead and I got back to mulling over options for the café.

As we settled in our respective spots on the sofa for the night, my mind tried to kick-start into work-mode-Amy. That was easier said than done. Baby brain and depression to one side I was pretty much surviving on minimal sleep still and it had taken me seven attempts to spell the word "accurate" the other day.

"What are you thinking about so seriously over there?"

"Nothing, a new recipe," I replied, without looking up at him.

Second lie

This is never going to work; I don't even know the name of the bloody place let alone put together some master plan that can change the direction of this man's business.

My inner bitch had awoken to join in with my critical internalising of this ridiculous plan.

Why did you think you could manage something like this? Even before your crackpot breakdown, you were a dead weight in work, so what makes you think you could help this man? You can't even help yourself.

I put down my phone and stared at the television so I could pretend I was looking at whatever was on the screen. As much as I loathed that woman, I couldn't ignore what she was saying. I knew she was right. I had no idea what I was doing anymore.

***

When the day came to keep up the farce of going to Smug Club, I now felt like I had two places to avoid for the rest of my life in the same stretch of road.

Perhaps we could move?

"Have a great time at playgroup," said Ben, "I think you need the adult company today you were in great spirits after last week."

"Hmmm yes, I'm looking forward to it. There's definitely a couple of mums I'd like to talk to again," I replied.

Third lie

I mindlessly walked with Arthur towards Shame Street, (I decided that's what it should be called now) and started to pick up my pace. I practically jogged past the car park of Smug Club.

I wondered if I had judged them all too harshly and too quickly. It wouldn't be the first time, nor would it be the last. I walked back towards the scene of last week's debacle but no matter how much I tried I couldn't will myself to go in.

I couldn't sit and be the mother they wanted me to be, nor could I be the wife Ben needed me to be. I tried the therapy, I'd keep taking the tablets, I'd even try that mindfulness crap he was always harping on about, but I wasn't going to sit and pretend to be one of 'them'. I'd never be welcomed as part of the Smug Club elite. I take the kids to *McDonald's* and don't even feel a little bit guilty, I haven't registered the youngest with a dentist and more than once we've stayed in bed and had crisps for breakfast.

"I'll never fit in," I told Arthur, aloud.

His nod was all I needed to ensure me that I was making the right decision. I made sure no one could see me leave the car park and high-tailed it out of there. I left them, and all the doubts I was feeling, behind. With a smile on my face and a warm feeling in my tummy, I was more and more certain I'd made the right choice. Joseph's tacky little café would be my retreat for a couple of hours a week; perhaps just by getting out of the house more, it would help me remember the old Amy.

One who wouldn't be overwhelmed by a group of mums or afraid to stand up for a stranger being ganged up on.

First things first, I needed to tell Joseph I wasn't the woman to help put his business on the map. Instead, I would recommend a few people that would work their magic, but it definitely wasn't me.

I started to stride, with purpose, towards the café in order to let him down gently.

I was working myself into a frenzy and tried to practise a speech that was heartfelt, but firm. Unfortunately, I was that determined in my march I managed to barge through the door using my momentum as a type of battering ram and scared the bejesus out of Arthur and Joseph simultaneously.

"I'm sorry, I'm so sorry," was all I kept saying to both of them.

It took a good three minutes of me soothing Arthur while Joseph soothed me before I was able to sit down and actually let him know why I was really there.

As soon as I looked up at his kind face I lost my nerve. He told me to sit down and he'd be over to chat when he was finished with a customer. Arthur had already gone over to the toys and left me to keep my head in my hands and try to regulate my breathing.

"You alright, princess?"

The accent was unmistakable but still, I peered through my fingers to check if it was really her.

It was.

With one girl on her hip and a take-out coffee in hand, there stood Elle with pursed lips and a challenging look.

"Hi," I responded sheepishly, "I'm fine."

"You don't look fine."

"Well, I am."

"Fine, don't tell me. Aren't you late for your little club? Smug Club I believe you called it. That place that's too good for the likes of me?"

"I'm not going back. I don't think it's quite for me."

"No shit, babe."

The hostility in her demeanour subsided once she found out I wasn't joining the enemy.

"Mind if I join you?" she asked.

She had already sat down on the sofa across from me before I answered. She told her daughter to join her sister, who was already at the toys with Arthur.

"Maybe we should address the awkwardness you seem to exude from your pores right now," she continued.

Why does she have to be this direct?

"I don't know what you mean," I lied, badly.

"Oh, I see. You're repressed."

The nerve of this woman; it usually takes a whole three meetings with me before people can put their finger on what's wrong with me.

"I'm not repressed," I said as calmly as I could.

"Yes, you are. I've known you for twenty minutes in total and I've figured that one out, I've just saved you a fortune in therapy and you probably hate your mother. You lot always hate your mother."

"My lot?"

"Yes, the repressed lot. Do you hate your mother?"

"I'm not repressed," I repeated, firmer this time.

"That didn't answer the question. What do you do for you?"

"What do you mean?"

"To indulge yourself, to show yourself some love?

"I think it's very important that you indulge in something that's just for you. Something no one else knows about it. Do you want to masturbate with a huge black cock while listening to ABBA? Who cares? Go for it! Do whatever makes you happy, as long as it isn't some shit that you have to do as a wife or a mother. So, what's yours?"

I racked my brain for an appropriate answer to this that wouldn't constitute as sharing too much information. I couldn't think under the pressure of her gaze so I went with the first thing that came into my mind.

"Sometimes —" I started.

"Yes?" she asked, eagerly.

"Well, sometimes I buy the more expensive sanitary towels even though the cheaper ones are right there and they do the job. It's like they're my little luxury. I feel guilty about it because some weeks it pushes me over the shopping budget but the other ones are very... chaffing. You know?"

As soon as I said it I knew it was the wrong answer. It was out there like a steaming turd sitting in the middle of the table and we were both just staring at it, not knowing what to do or say. Finally, Elle broke the silence.

"Jesus Christ."

"What?"

"That's the most depressing thing I've ever heard. You show yourself love by purchasing fanny pads that don't feel like sandpaper against your minge? Amy, I was wrong about you, you're not repressed."

"I'm not?" I couldn't keep up with this woman's flippant assessments of my character.

"No, you're not," she replied, "The word describing what you are hasn't even been invented for your level of repression."

"Oh."

"Don't worry though, I've come along at the right time and we're going to drag your martyred arse into the light and I swear, if you ever attempt to buy the sandpaper pads again I'll burn down your house."

My face must have been horrified because she continued her tirade of 'help' with:

"Don't be scared! You and I are going to be great friends. By the time I'm finished you're going to find that inner assertive badass again."

"Again?"

I couldn't remember the last time I'd said something that wasn't a question.

"Yeah! I can tell you haven't always been this mousy housewife persona you've got going on. You've got secrets Amy and you're going to tell me in your own good time."

"Do you really masturbate with a huge black cock?" I asked.

"That's a bit personal for a first date don't you think?"

"Oh God, sorry."

"I'm screwing with you. No, I don't masturbate with a giant black cock while listening to ABBA. I hate ABBA. It's to Nirvana," she laughed.

For the rest of her coffee, I sat quietly listening to Elle DeBruyn talk about her life. According to her, growing up in South Africa was a much more liberating experience. Her parents were 'spirited' - as she described them – but, to me, they sounded like self-absorbed narcissists; dragging their daughter from one place to the next so they could 'experience the earth'.

For the first 12 years of their daughter's life, they didn't enrol her in a school and just went where the wind blew them; flitting from one 'experience' to the next.

"Dad was a writer and said the world was his muse," she explained, "One week we'd be camping in some remote woodland, then he'd crack up about the silence and needed to be back amongst civilisation. Never the same place twice. Mum would be working whatever shit job she could find in wherever we'd end up. By the time I was 12 she got completely fed up and took me out the door with her. Her sister moved to Ireland in her twenties and offered us a roof over our head.

"Even then, mum was getting restless and we still moved about quite a lot. I think she missed the road with dad, not that she would ever admit it. Never heard from him again and mum bit the bullet a couple of years back."

"You poor thing, I'm sorry. That all sounds quite traumatic."

"Don't get me wrong, it was a happy enough childhood but nothing I'd put my own children through. I never had a base to call 'home' and I think that really screwed me up. My husband, Keith, was the only person that could keep me interested long enough for me to stick around longer than six months in one place. I went to school and all that, did alright in that stuff but I was never going to be one for an office. I paint, by the way, people mostly. I think I'm quite good. Sell enough online but thank fuck I married a normal 9-5 guy. We balance each other out. What about you? Who is Mr Repressed?"

"Mr Repressed is nice. Sorry, I mean Ben. His name is Ben."

"Alright," she winked, "Tell me about Benny then."

"Not much to tell, really. We met in university, have been together ever since. Happy marriage, nice kids, nice home. Nothing too traumatic, or interesting when I hear myself describe my life."

"You sure about that?"

Oh God, she remembered.

"I…I… that's not something I want to talk about just now," I stuttered, with colour rising in my cheeks.

"That's fine. We can just keep things light and talk about the weather or the nice house and nice marriage you have, but remember: you and I are going to be good friends, great friends in fact. Starting from tomorrow."

"What's tomorrow?" I asked, anxiously.

"Ah, settle petal, you're going to be fine. Just maybe get rid of the kid for a couple of hours and wear something a bit looser."

"Looser?"

"Yeah, like stuff you can move in."

"I don't think I own any exercise stuff. Will jean shorts do?"

"Is that a serious question? No. You look like my size I'll bring you something."

I didn't feel it was necessary to point out to her that her boobs were at least three cup sizes bigger than mine, I hoped she would realise that all by herself. We agreed to meet back at Joseph's for midday. Adam would have school and Arthur could have his nap at my mum's house.

Although that meant I would have to go and talk to her. Something I could happily avoid from one Christmas to the next.

I thought about just sending a text, but she'd probably pretend she didn't get it and I'd have to show up unannounced. Visits with her were stressful enough without the added 'lost text' argument.

If I went now I'd have to leave to pick up Adam at school anyway, so there would be a reason to cut the torturous visit short. Excellent

At that moment, Joseph approached the table cautiously.

"Amy, are you and your friend busy? We can talk another time?"

"It's ok, Joe, I'm heading out," said Elle, "I'll meet this little lady tomorrow. I love this place, you'll be seeing lots more of me – starting tomorrow, isn't that right, princess?"

I smiled, shyly.

In a flurry of noise and exuberance, Elle and her girls were gone.

"She's quite a character, are you good friends?" asked Joseph.

"Not really, I'm just trying to get out to meet people, I suppose."

"That's a good idea, Amy. Just maybe don't let her eclipse you."

"Eclipse me?"

"Yes, you are your own sun. She's a bright one but you are just as bright."

"That's rather cryptic," I said with a wary smile.

"Not really, just an old man trying to butt his nose in. Now, what is our master plan for my beautiful café?"

*I was really hoping to leave without having this conversation. Maybe I **was** repressed?*

"Well, I've been doing a lot of research and there's a lot of competition out there, Joseph."

"Yes, but my coffee is better and so is my food – even if it is prepared by my halfwit son-in-law."

"Even so, I have an important question which I probably should have asked before now."

"Yes?"

"What's the name of this place?"

His laugh was loud and it made Arthur jump from the other side of the room.

"Yes, that is an important question. It's called 'Joseph's', my dear."

"I guess that's easy enough to remember then. I'll write it in my notes."

The only problem was I didn't have a notebook or a pen. He must have seen me looking awkwardly and blushing because he pushed forward the napkin Elle had left on the table and handed me the pen from behind his ear. Again, his smile was nothing but kind but the mortification was getting a bit much.

"Well, I can work on this again this evening and if I come up with anything I'll let you know tomorrow."

"That's no problem, Amy. You take your time. If we are going to get this right – and I have a feeling we are – it will take time. You can't rush perfection, am I right?"

"Yeah, of course."

I took my leave and decided to head to my mother's while I was on a roll for having awkward conversations with people I didn't really want to speak to.

Chapter 7

I argued with myself about the visit to my mother's the whole drive over and before I knew it I was in the driveway. The curtains had already twitched, which meant I'd been spotted.

There was no escaping her now.

I dragged a sobbing Arthur - who had fallen asleep in the car and didn't want to go anywhere but back to sleep – while he hit me over the head with his rubber hammer. We were a sorry sight by the time my mother opened the door.

"Do my eyes deceive me? Has the prodigal daughter returned?" she said.

I do admire how she manages to get guilt in right away before I've even got through the front door. It really is a talent.

"Hi, Mum," I said, wearily, setting Arthur at her feet so I could kiss her on the cheek.

"Mum? That's short for something, isn't it? Mother, perhaps? That can't be right. I only have one child and it's been that long since I saw her I've forgotten what she looks like. You may call me: Eloise."

"Mum it's been two weeks and during that time I have been on the phone."

Her stern eyes burrowed into me making me feel like an errant teenager, caught sneaking in after curfew. If I was going to earn a babysitter I had to change my approach, so I decided on a different tact.

"Eloise, please forgive the intrusion," I said, "Might a weary woman come and rest her legs for ten minutes. I don't have much in terms of payment, but please accept this offering of a tiny slave. Their small hands are great for chimney sweeping."

"You're a terrible daughter, Amy," she replied.

"I know, Mum. Now, let me in."

Eloise Galbraith was newly retired but an old world battle-axe. If she was being introduced on a reality tv show she would be described by the voiceover as 'straight talking'. I always felt that was just a nicer way of saying 'bitch'. This isn't a male/female thing. If my father behaved the same way she did, I'd call him a 'bitch' too.

She loved my children. I suspect more than she loved me, but that's another thread I'm not willing to pull at. She was doting, loving and patient with them. None of these traits made an appearance during my own childhood, nor did they extend to me, now.

I knew she loved me, I just think she didn't like me that much.

"Dad in?" I asked as I tried not to look panicked at the thought of it just being the two of us.

"Of course, your mother is only interested in her father. Poor old Granny would never do, would she Arthur?"

"Please don't passive-aggressively talk about me to my child."

"For goodness sake, don't be so sensitive. He's not here, he's in the garage tinkering with something or probably smoking again."

My father didn't smoke, my father has never smoked. He once found an empty cigarette packet in the back of his taxi at the end of the night and left them sitting on the bench in the garage, meaning to dispose of them when he finished cleaning out the back of the car.

My mother found them and has accused him of being a secret smoker for 17 years now.

"Don't roll your eyes at me, Amy. You inherited those from me when you came screaming into the world after 39 hours of excruciating labour - WITH FORCEPS - none of this namby-pamby, epidural nonsense in my day. Back then you were a *real* woman."

"Mum I'm 32, you're not referring to the dark ages when you talk about 'the good old days' of childbirth – it was the eighties - and I had two emergency sections, I hardly took a tablet and sneezed either of them out. Although I have been neglecting my pelvic floor exercises as of late, so if I was ever tempted to go for a third, then I could probably manage it."

"I'm doing mine now."

"What? Gross. Mum!"

"What? You'll never find your father straying because of a loose vagina at home."

"No, Mum he will be found wandering the roads to get away from the mad woman who keeps talking to him about her vagina – loose or not."

"Should I come back later?" My pale-faced father said as he entered the kitchen at the point of me saying 'vagina' a little louder than one should in polite conversation.

James Galbraith was a taxi driver and a saint. Yes, I was biased. During my teenage years, the house was like a battlefield in the never-ending war with my mother. He always played peacekeeper but I couldn't wait until the day I could escape to university and never come back. I still hated coming back now.

There was no familiar scent that made me nostalgic and took me back to a happy childhood. Even the thought of a bear hug from my saintly father wasn't enough to take me back here more than absolutely necessary. I don't know how their relationship worked, how could he keep warm at night with a stubborn ice queen as a bedmate. But, if I was honest with myself, the answer was obvious: they loved each other.

That, and her tight vagina, apparently.

These two people who were poles apart in every facet of their being had been married (happily) for over thirty years.

In the quiet, when she thought I wasn't paying attention, I used to spot her wipe a crumb from his face or gently fix a hair back into place. Any evening I stumbled home after a late night with my friends, pretending not to be drunk, she would be there with folded arms waiting for me. Or that's what she would tell me she was doing. The only thing is, she wouldn't go to bed when she heard me collapse into mine. She would still sit in a darkened living room and wait until she heard my father's car turn into the drive, then scuttle up the stairs before she heard his keys jingle in the door. Only when she was certain all the family was under the one roof would she go to sleep.

The next morning it was business as usual: her fussing and complaining about what I was wearing or who I was hanging out with. All glimpses of the protective, loving mother were buried again until it was necessary. Maybe one day I'd talk to her about it all, how I wished she'd just put her guard down once. Today was not that day.

"Can you take Arthur for a couple of hours tomorrow?" I said to no one in particular.

"Ah, the penny drops! This is why she's here, James."

"I think your mother means, 'yes we'd love to'. It's been an age since we've had him."

"I don't need you to answer for me, I'm a grown woman, I know how to answer my own daughter. Yes, we'd love to have him," she repeated.

My father sighed and smiled at me, while my mother glared at the traitorous camaraderie between us. It was always the same dynamic here. For as long as I could remember, the two of us would trade knowing looks - and in later years, text messages - warning of her mood if one of us was late home.

"Are you staying for some food, love? You're wasting away," dad asked hopefully.

"I can't, I have to get back and pick Adam up from school, and I'll ignore that snort of derision, mother."

"What?" she asked with mock innocence, "You're beautiful, just the way you are. A little cushioning looks good on you."

"Just put the kettle on and we'll pretend to be a nice normal family," I said, through gritted teeth.

"Normal?" asked dad, "Pfft, who'd want to be that. If you ever disappoint me like that we'll cut you off," He kissed my head as he finished the sentence and went to grab the usual three cups from the cupboard.

Once the three of us had settled onto the chairs surrounding the kitchen island I waited to hear who had died – the only conversation my parents like to have in my company.

When I was single it was informing me which of my classmates were getting married, but now that I've reached the grand old age of 32, and I have dependents of my own, I now only need to know about who has kicked the bucket. The more tragic the story, the better entertainment it was for my parents. A young mum who died in a freak accident could result in a week's worth of follow-up stories and hypotheses.

"Have you heard about Jihadi Paddy from up the road?"

Choking on my tea and hoping against hope that I had misheard my mother, I asked her to repeat the question.

"Jihadi Paddy," she said, "big brute of a fella that lives up the road with the woman who looks like she's been chewing a wasp her whole life – Cathy something, I think."

I stared blankly and waited for her to continue.

"Why are you looking at me like that?" she asked.

"I'm waiting to hear about the Islamic extremist who is living around the corner."

"What? There is? Who?"

"Jihadi Paddy?"

"God, no. He's not one of them, he belongs to the born-again lot. He used to be on the beer daily and had a bit of a gambling problem, but I don't think he's planning on blowing anyone up. Well, I don't think so anyway."

"I'm genuinely confused as to where this conversation is going, mum."

"Hush then. Well, he was doing one of his shouty sermons in the bandstand in the park on Saturday when your father and I were walking by."

"Did he threaten you? Or was he giving out about the freedom us pesky women enjoy in the Western world?" I asked.

"What? No, for goodness sake Amy he's harmless. Why are you being so awkward? Just shut up and let me tell you the story."

"If he's harmless, why are you calling him Jihadi Paddy?"

"The beard."

"The beard?"

"Yes, Amy, a beard. It's a great big bushy beard and it reminded me of those lot I keep seeing on the news. You know, the ones that do the horrible beheading videos on the internet? Anyway, his name is Paddy, it rhymed with 'Jihadi' so it stuck. His name is now: 'Jihadi Paddy'. Can I continue with my story now?"

"Please, do," I replied, still not quite sure where this story was going.

"Well, your father and I were walking in the park on Saturday and PATRICK from up the road –"

"Actually, I think his name is John," dad interrupted.

"Then why have you been letting me call him Paddy this whole time?"

He shrugged and said: "It rhymed."

"Well, now the story doesn't make any sense. Why didn't you tell me this before, James?"

"I don't know, it didn't seem important."

"It was important, there's no point in it at all, now. God, you're infuriating."

I never did get to find out what John was shouting at my parents about or why his wife looked like she was eating a wasp. Maybe it was because of his beard.

After an excruciating hour with my parents, I made plans to leave Arthur with them in the morning and ran for the door.

"Did you know that babies have a natural inbuilt fear of plants?" said Mum.

"No, I didn't know that."

"I saw it on a documentary. It's from when we were monkeys," she continued.

"That's nice, say 'bye' to granny, Arthur."

"I'm only bringing it up because that little boy of yours tends to either pee on mine or try and rip them up from the roots. Why do you think that is?"

I knew my mother well enough to know there was no right answer, so instead, I went for:

"Maybe he didn't evolve from monkeys, ask John up the road."

"You're a terrible daughter, Amy."

"I know, mum."

Chapter 8

The hike up the hill towards the school for Adam was never helped by Arthur. Some days he wanted to be carried, other days he wanted to walk on his own and stop to inspect every rock or weed that caught his eye. Today was a weed and unending question day.

"Why do I have a widdler?" he asked.

"All boys do."

I had learned, early on in this parenting malarkey, that it was best to keep my answers short and to the point with Arthur, but it rarely stopped the follow-up questions.

"Even daddy?"

"Yes, even daddy. I think. It might have dropped off because I don't remember the last time I saw it."

"What, mummy?"

"Nothing sweety, have a raisin."

I wasn't in form for thinking of my abysmal sex life. At this stage, the only time I remember even thinking about it was when I considered the possibility of having a third child. The notion lasted for thirty seconds, and even that was about four months ago.

Trying to conceive Adam was an awful period in our relationship. We tried for nearly three years. The whole time I panicked about being infertile so I incessantly took my temperature and urinated on an endless supply of ovulation sticks. Sex became a chore and it never went back to the way it was even after Adam arrived.

Every so often I'll have that extra glass of wine to help make me slightly more receptive to Ben's advances but even that had stopped. I used to make sure we didn't go longer than a month in between obligations but now I don't bother. I've told myself I'm much happier without the hassle.

With Adam in school and Arthur out of nappies, society – and by society I mean my mother – has now decided that it's time for another child.

Surely, I need to try for that girl I'm missing?

It's a question I never tire of hearing, every few months.

Instead of telling her, and everyone else, to mind their own business and to leave my vacant womb alone, I change the subject.

I am a wimp, especially when it comes to standing up to my mother.

It's not that I had completely ruled out the possibility of a third child, it's just the thought of it was about as appealing as a lobotomy.

I still fancied Ben, he was still as attractive to me as he ever was. I always found that time is a lot kinder to men than women. Men always seemed more distinguished with age, while everything of mine was getting closer to the ground with every passing year. Ben regularly tells me how beautiful I am, he does little things that make me feel pretty and loved as a woman. The problem is me. I don't see past the yoghurt and snot stains on my top, my bushy, greying hair scraped back into a bun. I don't remember the last time my face felt a little attention – I'm talking moisturizer, never mind makeup.

I don't remember when I stopped trying. I never had to try for Ben, I meant trying for me. Trying so I could look in the mirror and not hate what I saw. I just didn't care. What was the point? If I don't like who I was on the inside then what did it matter what I looked like on the outside?

So far, this 'not thinking about my abysmal sex life' idea wasn't going well. I figured I should probably hone back in again and see what Arthur was up to:

"Don't you think so mummy?"

Shit

"Hmmm? What was that?"

"It's ok mummy, I'll ask granny tomorrow," he mused

Well that's definitely going to come back to bite me

I hated the school run, apart from the obvious shitty parking and the trek to the school itself, I have the exact amount of social anxiety which makes me completely useless at every type of small talk that seems to come so easily to those around me. I know exactly one parent at the gates. Well, 'know' him is a bit of stretch. I don't know his name, his child or if he speaks English, but we do silently nod at each other while we wait for the teacher to release the hounds.

Our friendship was solidified the day I drove into a space that was miles too tight for my car and I heard the dreaded sound of metal scrapping off metal. His face said it all. I slowly backed out and parked as far away from the scene of the crime as possible. Scurrying over, Arthur on hip, I joined my silent friend to inspect the damage.

I recognised the car, it was the teacher's. I convinced myself, that because of this gaff, my son would never get into university.

"No! It's her's isn't it?" I said in an unhelpfully panicked tone.

He nodded

"Is there any damage? I can't see any, is there?"

He shrugged.

"I'm just going to tell her it was me and she can take a look herself to see if there's damage. Yes?"

He shrugged.

"You're right, what good would that do? There's no damage and then she'll just end up hating my son and he'll get all the shit parts in any of the school productions, stinting his confidence, making him underperform and then there's this big domino effect. So what if there's a tiny scratch? That doesn't mean being truthful about this is going to stop her ostracizing my child and leading him down a path of underachievement, poor self-confidence and hard drugs, does it?"

Nothing.

"Again, you're right, I just need to relax. This isn't a big deal, we're on the same page here aren't we?"

Nothing.

"Good talk."

Ever since that day, he just accepted that I'm going to stand next to him so I don't have to talk to anyone else. He just seems relieved that I haven't spoken to him since.

When Adam ran towards me, his cheeks were rosy and his sleeves were rolled up like he means business. What business that is I never find out because every day I ask him about what he did in school, and every day I get the same answer: "Nothing, it was boring."

I missed simpler days when the answer was: "I don't remember."

I had hoped there were at least another ten years before we were in the fully-fledged teenager mode but apparently it starts when they're five.

The drive home was a noisy affair, with the two of them arguing over who owned the colour 'green'.

I let my mind wander to the possibility of what tomorrow could bring. Would it be another coffee? Would Elle pry further into my mess of a life? Mess made things seem more chaotic than it was. There were no fights or tension at home. The house was kept clean, there was dinner on the table in the evening. It's just when the kids went to bed and Ben went into his phone to play a game, or whatever he was doing on the damn thing, I felt completely alone. I felt alone at the best of times but now I was beginning to feel despondent about it all. My life, my family, my future - it was a feeling that scared me and wasn't a totally unfamiliar one. It made me think about cold water that burned my lungs and -

"Mummy," cried Adam, "Where are you going?"

I was back in the car with the boys and we were nearly home, but I didn't even remember the drive here.

"What's wrong? We're going home, where else would we be?" I bluffed.

"You said we could go to the library. I'm tired of the bedtime books we have."

"Tomorrow Adam, I have a better idea for today," I lied.

I had no better idea. I just couldn't be bothered spending 40 minutes trying to find parking outside the library. I prayed the iPad was charged and there was some semblance of junk food in the house that would seem like I had a 'party' planned for them. My prayers were answered and with the building of a fort in the living room underneath some chairs and a bed sheet, my reputation as the not-so-terrible parent was saved.

Elle told me to wear something 'looser'. Did she mean like morally loose, or physically loose? I had neither so it was kind of a moot point. What would morally loose even look like? Nipple clamps on the school run? I tried to think of what constituted as 'morally loose' outfit choices and then I realised that I had turned into one of those townspeople from 'Footloose' who wanted to ban dancing.

When did I become one of those people?

I didn't have anything that would fit into the category 'activewear' saying as I'd been to exactly one spinning class in my life and decided it was like all the pain of anal sex and none of the pleasure. This was the exact explanation I gave to the instructor who made the fatal mistake of asking how I got on. After that conversation and judging by the horrified look on his face, I thought it would be better just to never return.

Ben was always pushing me to exercise, not because he was particularly enthusiastic about exercising as a whole, he just wanted to get me out of my own head for even a half hour a day. When I could feel my mood slip he was all but pushing me out the door for a walk and quoting some inspirational crap like: 'exercise is the most under-used antidepressant'.

I really wish he'd quit *Instagram* and quoting bull like that to me, but it keeps him happy and lets him think he has some shred of control over the mental wellbeing of his wife.

When he came back from work he found me sitting in the middle of our bedroom surrounded by the entire contents of my wardrobe. I'd found some leggings that had a hole in the groin and one of his t-shirts that said 'Be the Dream'.

"Does this look like loose clothing to you?" I asked.

"Morally loose or physically loose? I mean the hole at the crotch is sending out some definite messages, sweety."

"This is why I love you," I replied as I gave him a hug.

I told him about my mystery activity with the boho-chic mum in the hope he'd warn me of stranger danger and say I shouldn't go. Unfortunately, I'm an adult and he didn't think that I was being groomed for sex by a stranger so I had to go and make a friend in my thirties. He was annoyingly excited at the thought of me stepping out of my comfort zone. It was infuriating.

"So you've no idea what you're going to do?" he asked.

"Nope, just to wear loose clothing and we're meeting at a coffee shop."

"Did you meet her at the parent club?"

"Yeah," I stuttered, "I mean she goes sometimes."

"Not a veteran attendee like you, eh? See? I told you if you stick with it you'd eventually meet someone who you could get along with."

"I don't like people," I said, flatly.

"And yet, you're heading out with a new friend to do something which may, or may not, be approved of by the Church Elders should they find out. I'm proud of you," he said, as he kissed me gently.

The knot in my stomach gave another twist at the lie about Smug Club, but now wasn't the time to dwell on my lies. I decided to get on with my usual evening routine with the kids whilst I tried to ignore my building doubts about what I was getting myself into.

Chapter 9

As I pushed open the door to Joseph's I noticed Elle was already there waiting for me at the counter. She was animatedly talking to Michael who had a look of fear on his face. It turned to relief when he spotted me. Elle's attention was instantly drawn to me.

"Amy!" he half-shouted, "your friend Elle is here."

"Hiya Little Miss Repressed," she half shouted, "wow you look, bright..."

In my panic about what to wear for the mystery activity, I popped to the supermarket and bought the first two things I could see in my size at the 'activewear' section. Unfortunately, both items were neon yellow in colour.

"Fuck me, Amy, you look like the surface of the sun over there," she continued.

"Yes, well here I am," was all the reply I could muster.

"Here you are," she repeated with a smirk on her face, "Right, get us a cuppa to-go and we'll be off."

Joseph, who I suspect had been hiding out back in the kitchen, from the loud South African, popped his head out at the sound of my name.

"Ah, Amy. When will you be in again to make me money?"

"What's this now? You do some shifts in here?" quizzed Elle.

"No, this angel came in last week and has decided to help my business by getting us customers," explained Joseph.

"Amy, you dark horse."

"It's nothing really. Like really nothing, I have literally done nothing to help yet," I blushed.

The three of them were looking at me awkwardly.

I should probably sell my skills a bit more.

"Nothing yet!" I offered, "I mean I'll definitely be starting with the social media and website and do those modern photos to make –"

"To make this place seem less like a tacky shit hole and more of a knob jockey haven?" interrupted Elle.

"Something like that," I trailed off and avoided Joseph's gaze.

"How dare you? My wife decorated this beautiful establishment," he said.

"No offence intended, mate. I love this place. The coffee is the shit and I don't mind that there are freaky little gnome guys watching as I take a whizz"

Joseph stared at her for a few seconds, wondering if he was being offended further but he decided to keep things cordial.

"Knob-jockey haven," he laughed, "This is funny. Why do they want avocado with everything? Sometimes I think they don't know what hot food tastes like because they spend all their time taking photos of it. I don't understand this."

Michael laughed and was rewarded with a slap on the back of his head from his father-in-law.

"You shouldn't have time for laughing, get in the kitchen or I'll tell my daughter to divorce you," shouted Joseph.

"Shall we go?" I asked Elle, hopefully. I had a feeling this unpredictable mood of Joseph's was just the beginning of a horrible day for Michael.

"Sure, let's go. Can't be late for our first class. I'll drive."

"Class?"

"Yeah, we're going to get our hearts pumping baby. It's probably best if we get you somewhere dark for the sake of my corneas."

"Is it really that bad?"

"Amy, you look like a radioactive canary."

"Did you bring me something, like you said?" I asked, hopefully.

"Oh I did, but this is much funnier for me so you'll just have to make do. It'll be fine, we'll be in the dark soon."

If the fact that the word 'dark' kept getting mentioned wasn't enough to make me nervous, then pulling up to the local dive of a nite club at 10.30am on a Wednesday was really starting to panic me. Pulling down her visor to see her mirror I watched Elle take out a little pot of what I thought was lip balm until she started dabbing it across her forehead in a V shape and dotting some over each cheekbone.

"Want some?" she asked.

"What is it? Is it that aloe vera stuff my neighbour keeps trying to sell me on online?"

"Eh no, Amy, it's UV paint. It's not a prerequisite but its fun and fun is something you're sorely missing in your life."

I shook my head and got out of the car.

"What are we doing here? Is this like an illegal rave or something?"

"HA! That would be some chance, in this town. You're a laugh. It's an exercise class and to be honest, I think you'll fit right in with that outfit. Let's go."

I could feel the vibrations of the music in my chest as soon as she opened the heavy door into the club. My feet were sticking to the carpet and that feeling of dread I'd been fighting was beginning to come screaming to the surface.

Why am I here?

Judging my Elle's concerned expression, the obvious panic I was experiencing was showing on my face.

"Amy, are you ok? You look like you're about to shit yourself."

"I don't think this is really for me, Elle."

"Alright, no worries. Just let me go in and get your name off the list so I can free up the equipment for someone else."

"Equipment?"

"Yeah, it's a boogie bouncing class," she explained, "Come take a look, it's fun I promise. You can watch from the balcony if you want, it's just little trampolines, some music and you bounce. It's not hard."

"Why the paint?"

"Why not? It's a nite club, Amy, let's pretend we are having a social life?"

"Tiny trampolines don't sound that scary unless - I wee myself."

"That's the spirit!" She replied, with an unsure sideways glance.

We walked into the main dance floor and I saw the 30 evenly spaced out trampolines with very protective looking women standing next to each one.

I followed Elle to the front of the room and dreaded the thought of being stuck at the top with the instructor judging my terrible rhythm.

As we stood at the top of the room, Elle pointed out my tiny trampoline, right in front of a podium - which I assumed belonged to the instructor. I wondered what her job title would be. Master Trampoliner? I resolved to ask Elle afterwards.

I looked to either side of me and was horrified to find she was nowhere to be seen. Had this all been some horrible revenge for Smug Club? Was it too late to run out of there? My question was answered when the thundering beat of a new song began and I heard an all-too-familiar voice coming from the speakers.

"Alright, bitches, let's sweat!" The distinctive accent sent a shiver of fear up my spine. I looked towards the podium and there she was. Her megawatt smile was accentuated by the black light and the little touches of UV paint on her face made her look like some sort of formidable Aztec Priestess.

Not only had she dragged me to this bizarre early morning rave, she was the leader of it.

"Now, we've got a newbie at the front here ladies, you can't miss her she's the one that looks like a fucking *Simpsons* character in that beautiful ensemble. Everyone give a big, boogie bounce, welcome to Big Bird!"

A resounding 'Hi, Big Bird!' echoed through the room and I prayed that the ground would swallow me whole, or if there was a God he could see fit that I bounced through the ceiling and into an A&E Department.

"Now you know the drill, ladies, we're here to sweat and if you're slacking off, you're out. I've got a waiting list coming out my arse so EARN YOUR PLACE!"

Her words of encouragement, which sounded more like a threat, were greeted by a resounding scream from everyone around me.

What the hell have I got myself into?

"Amy! Shift your arse onto that trampoline or I'll call you Big Bird for the rest of your natural born life," she shouted.

"Oh, yes eh ok."

I can do this, it's just bouncing up and down after all?

I gave a weak smile to the woman on my left but she was already lost in 'the zone' or whatever these people call it. The gentle bouncing was nice, the rhythm was steady – not too fast – even I could keep up and was feeling a bit more relaxed with every passing second.

I didn't recognise the song but I decided to make up my own words to get me through the next three minutes:

Don't pee, don't fall, don't pee, don't fall, up, down, up, down, up, down, don't pee, don't fall. This isn't so bad.

The rhythm was hypnotic, the beat was strong and I was keeping up. I assumed there would be a break in between sets and a wind-down bit so it reassured myself that the whole thing would be over soon.

I am totally kicking ass

I could feel my shoulders loosen with the build-up of the music and it was fabulous. My ponytail came loose but I didn't care, I shook my hair free and kept up with the rhythm. It's amazing how freeing this all was and I wanted to kiss Elle for giving me this gift.

"Right, bitches, the beat is going to drop and you know what to do!" she shouted.

I found myself screaming with my boogie sisters in agreement and waited for whatever was next.

Then all hell broke loose.

This 'dropped beat' we were waiting for turned my oneness with the universe into complete anarchy.

What the hell were these people doing? Why are her arms like that? What is this? Jesus, they're all doing it. Does she seriously expect me to do a turn? Are you serious?

I am in hell.

I did my best to keep up but I was at least three seconds behind everyone else. I could feel judging eyes on me. Their zen was being destroyed by a rhythmically challenged arsehole in their midst.

I wanted to punch Elle for putting me through this.

The next 45 minutes continued along the same lines. I could feel my face burning with shame and general sweatiness. There were no breaks, there was no wind-down, there was just bouncing; so much bouncing.

I swore to do my pelvic floor exercises religiously if I could just make it out of this class without accidentally urinating on myself – that really would have been the crowning achievement of this experience.

"Right, guys, this is the last routine of the morning and I can feel the energy has been slacking in the last few numbers so just get your shit together and let's smash this!"

Her words were greeted with more cheering.

For goodness sake don't they ever get tired of cheering? What the hell is there to cheer about? I'm fucking dying here.

"I'm looking at you Amy, you're going to give this your all, ok?"

I managed a thumbs up while scowling at her direction. At least I think it was her, there was that much sweat in my eyes I just hoped I was facing the right direction.

All that stood in between me and freedom was this final routine, so I resolved to get through it in one piece.

The thumping of the electronic bass started up again. This time I recognised the melody – or what it used to be before some 20-year-old DJ tore it apart and stitched it back together in some Frankenstein's monster mash-up of an eighties classic.

My hair was matted with sweat and kept sticking to my shoulders or my face when I tried to copy the turns of the others. The song was marginally slower so I could just about keep up. I couldn't decide if I was starting to enjoy this or if I was starting to hallucinate due to dehydration.

I attempted a type of high kick, bounce combination and felt a sharp sting of pain against my hip.

Great, not only have I endured this, I may also need a hip replacement at the end of it all.

I made my bounces less enthusiastic after that but caught a glare of disapproval from Elle when I wasn't 'giving it my all'. Out of fear, I upped my game again in the hope she would eventually get bored and look away.

Keep going, you can rest when she turns away.

Her gaze remained firmly on mine and I worried she was taking this drill sergeant routine too seriously.

She kept bouncing and then she added in a few new moves to the mix. Something involving her arms reaching down - the sweat in my eyes was making it ridiculously hard to see. It looked like a move I was never going to be able to do without falling head over heels so I ignored her and kept to the simple, safer, bouncing.

She kept this up for another ten seconds before finally flinging her arms in exasperation and shouted into her headset:

"For fuck sake, Amy, pull up your drawers! This isn't that kind of party."

It took a few seconds to register that I was actually living a recurring nightmare of being naked in public. In my rush to regain some dignity, I managed to smack my lip off the handrail of the trampoline and fall over onto the woman on my right.

"AMY!" Elle shouted as she bounced elegantly off her trampoline and rushed down the steps of the podium.

"When I said give it your all I didn't quite expect this?"

"Cuth you full uf my trofthers?" I pleaded.

"What?"

"UF, UF!"

"Do you want me to help you stand up? Hang on, you'd better get your trousers up first. You're a little rebel, Amy, I'm well impressed with this free body vibe you've got going on but maybe ease the rest of us in first, yeah?"

"You're noth finny!"

"Ah, you're all right, princess. Let's get some ice for that lip."

I watched as the other 'sisters' of mine left the class, trying not to laugh in my direction. I sat on a barstool with a towel full of ice on my lip feeling very sorry for myself and glaring in Elle's general direction. My lip felt puffy but wasn't bleeding and I managed to regain my speech so I didn't feel like a complete idiot by the time she was locking up the door after the last of the boogie bouncers had left.

"Alright, Lady Godiva, how are you recovering over there?"

"Piss off."

"Ok, I think I deserve that one but seriously Amy, you did really well for your first class and now you should feel happy you were able to share so much of yourself with others. I mean, maybe a bit too much."

I groaned and replied: "I want to go home and bury myself under my duvet for the next year."

"Wise up, I'm kidding. Honestly, no one noticed."

"No one noticed? You announced it over the sound system!"

"I had to! You were looking right at me when I was trying to get your attention and warn you, your pants were on show, but you just kept bouncing."

"The elastic went," I explained, "I'm not a flasher."

"Well, I figured that, I didn't think you were into public nudity."

"I thought you were a painter?"

"I am. I do this to keep the old bank account ticking over. It's a fad, but I'll make hay while the sun shines. Now, let's get you something to eat, at Joseph's, and you can scowl at me from across the table."

I attempted a smile but my lip felt like it was going to burst.

"I could sue you know."

"I know, but what the fuck would you to do with art supplies and thirty tiny trampolines? I'll give you one of the twins if you like, they're doing my tits in at the minute."

"No thanks, I don't know what to do with girls. I mean, what do you feed them?"

"Mostly unicorn piss and marshmallows," she said, nonchalantly.

"Sounds about right."

We both laughed and suddenly my lip didn't hurt that much anymore.

Over carrot cake and coffee we chatted more about our lives.

Her husband was her first long-term relationship and they fell in love at a music festival in Dublin.

"He was there trying to pretend he wasn't so fucking uptight and I think I was meant to be some festival fling that he forgot about when he got back to civilisation, but we ended up just staying in this shitty tent for like three days, barely coming up for air. It was pretty hot when you look back on it. Now it's all chaos and work and adult bullshit but I still make us go camping on our anniversary. He pretends to hate it but I know it's the only time he lets himself breathe. I love him, but he is wound so tight I think he might keel over and have a heart attack. The life insurance money would be handy. Oh! I could open a studio that has the right kind of new age vibe that's bordering on pretentious."

"I think you've gone a little off tangent."

"Have I? That tends to happen when I think about getting rid of my husband. I have the whole funeral planned, even my outfit. Is that a bit mental? Fuck it."

"No, it's ok. I've written Ben's eulogy a few times."

"Oh really? What does yours die of?"

"It depends on whether or not he's pissed me off that day. Good days, it's like some lingering disease that just sort of makes him sleepy – no pain. He gives this lovely speech about what a wonderful wife and mother I am before he goes to sleep and doesn't wake up; it's all very moving."

"That's some romance novel shit right there. What about the bad days?"

"Meh, that changes too. The other week, when we hugged and our bellies touched he said we were starting to look like sumo wrestlers because of all the takeaway food we'd been eating. I think he meant in a cute, cuddly way, but it didn't come across like that. I wouldn't speak to him for the rest of the night and just imagined tiny fish – the ones people use to eat the dead skin off their feet - just going to town on his junk."

"Well… that's dark."

"Yeah. Just all up in his penis."

"I like you, Amy. You're weird."

"I like you too, Elle."

Chapter 10

I got back to pick up my youngest cretin later than agreed but Arthur was busy helping my father in the garage. I came in to see him hand tools over that dad never asked for and generally messing up any system of organisation that was previously in place.

James Galbraith did not like a mess, especially around his car. While other families went to the seafront in the summertime to enjoy ice cream and a view of the water, mum and I had to stand outside the car on a windswept beach until all remnants of ice cream were gone. To this day I don't let ice cream in the house because it brings back memories of hypothermia and tension.

"How are the men?" I asked

"We are grand, love. Oh. That's a nice outfit." he said, blinking

I'd gone a whole half hour without hearing about how hideous my outfit choice was.

"Eh yeah, it's just activewear; all the young ones are wearing it."

"Hmmm, that's nice, love."

He wasn't convinced but turned his attention back to Arthur who was getting suspiciously close to an electric saw.

"I'll just go in and ask Mum to put on the kettle, are you coming Arthur?"

"No," he replied with utter conviction.

"There might be biscuits?"

"Bye, granda."

I smiled at my fickle child but realised I would probably follow anyone who offered me biscuits too. It wasn't a habit I grew out of after childhood.

I once dated an awful boy for six months longer than I should have because he worked in a corner shop and would bring leftover buns to my house after work. He dumped me when he noticed I was getting 'heavier' and accused me of eating my feelings.

I think he was just more pissed off that I was more interested in eating his baked goods more than eating him. I don't even remember his name.

"Mum?" I said

"Yes?" She barely took her eyes up from her computer as I came into the room.

"Can you remember the name of the boy I used to date? The one who worked in the shop, up the road."

She peered up from behind the computer, suspiciously.

"Why?"

"He popped into my head, that's all. Couldn't remember his name, I thought you might."

"Why would I? Do you think I've nothing better to do than be interested in your dating life?"

"It was just a question."

"Well, I don't know. Ben perhaps?"

"No mum, that's my husband."

"Oh. Thought I had it there. Anyway, how was your time off from your motherly responsibility?"

"It was great, I busted my lip and flashed a room full of strangers."

"I thought your mouth looked a bit puffy but you know me, I'm not one to pass remarks on others."

The incredulous silence was lost on my mother and I decided to let it slide while I hunted for biscuits for Arthur.

"So?" she asked.

"So, what?"

"How was it? What *are* you wearing?"

"Oh, for god's sake!"

"Language, Amy!"

"Sorry, I'm just going to burn this bloody outfit when I get home."

"Yes, that's probably best. I don't even think the homeless would want that. Where were you?"

"I was at an exercise class with a mum I know, then we went for a coffee after."

"That sounds pleasant."

Apparently, that was all the conversation she fancied so she got back to her computer screen and returned to ignoring Arthur and me.

"I think we'll just head on home, mum. Thanks for having Arthur."

"Hmmm? Oh, yes. He's a darling. Out helping granda and making sure he wasn't smoking, weren't you poppet?"

He didn't answer, he was too busy shoving the third biscuit in his mouth before I could wrestle it out of his hands.

I popped my head into the garage to say 'bye' but dad was busy trying to reorganise the tools that Arthur had 'helpfully' mixed up, I decided to leave him to it before he realised there were more tools on the ground beside the door

By the time we made it home, Arthur had fallen asleep in the backseat of the car and I managed, successfully, to get him onto the sofa so I could enjoy the silence for a few minutes. Silence, in this case, meant scrolling mindlessly through my phone. By the time I rummaged through my bag to find it, there was already a missed call from Ben and two messages from Elle.

Elle: What are you doing tomorrow night, bitchface?

I assumed that was a friendly term on this occasion. I clicked on the second one.

Elle: I have a great idea for us to do and it's totally going to help you be your old badass self.

I didn't like the sound of this already so I decided to ignore it for a while and hoped there wasn't some 'read' notification attached. I decided to phone Ben instead, I was certain he would be on edge waiting to hear about my 'date' with another actual adult.

He picked up within two rings.

"Well? How did it go?" he asked, eagerly.

"It was fine."

"Fine? Oh, that doesn't sound too good. I'm sorry, sweety. There's always plenty of other mummy fish in the sea for you to hang out with."

The sympathy in his voice was enough to help me make my decision a lot quicker. I would not be pitied by my husband. Yes, I had been injured and lost some dignity, but that's what 'getting out there' was all about – or that's what I told myself.

"No, I liked her fine. We're going out on a girls' night tomorrow in fact."

"Really?" he said in a surprised tone, "that's great news. You know tomorrow is my gym night don't you?"

"I forgot, I'll reschedule."

"No, sweety, it's fine. You never go out and do things for yourself. One week off the gym won't kill me. Just don't make a habit of it, little lady."

"Please, don't ever call me that again."

"I know, I'm sorry. Don't tell the kids of the shame I've brought on the family," he replied.

"Go away and earn money, I want to eat chocolate without sharing before Arthur wakes up."

I spent the next while trying to word a breezy-sounding friendly message. It was harder than I thought. I've never been a very 'breezy' person. I'm more bare-minimum-to-get-through-the-conversation or I give far too much information within the first sixty seconds of meeting someone, there is no in between.

Amy: Hiya babe

Babe? Who the hell am I? delete. Keep up the banter, Amy. She called you 'bitchface'.

Amy: Hiya cunt-arse

Seems unnecessarily harsh. Delete.

Amy: Hi Elle-belle

No, we're not at the nickname stage of our relationship yet.

Just as I was deleting my fourth attempt at an opening line, the phoned buzzed.

Elle: What the fuck are you doing over there, writing the Magna Carta?

How did she know? I didn't have to wait long for an answer to my question.

Elle: Those three fucking dots keep popping up like you're writing something and then

disappearing. It's doing my head in. Are you in or out for tomorrow? Just say 'yes'. It's easier that way.

Even in text form she was bossy.

I weighed up the pros and cons of the situation. Did I really want to go with the pushy stranger to something I know I'm probably going to hate, or should I just sit with my husband and endure an evening of sympathetic looks?

Amy: I'm in.

Elle: Good on ya. I'll pick you up at your place at 8 pm. Wear something nice and not something that's visible to the naked eye from space, you twat.

I replied with my address and decided to forgo any type of emoji or well-meaning profanity. It was better for everyone if I kept it short and sweet. The next obstacle was trying to figure out what to wear on my next outing with this formidable force of nature.

Dinner was the usual affair of forkful negotiations with the boys. I don't know when I became a hostage negotiator but dinner was always stressful.

"Just four more Arthur," I pleaded.

"No. It's yucky."

"You liked it last week?"

"No. It tastes like poo."

Laughter erupted around the kitchen table, including from Ben. He received a swift kick to the shin under the table.

"What?" he asked, shocked at the unexpected violence, "You live in a house of boys, and to boys, the word 'poo' is always going to be funny. Poo, poop, poopy pants, poo head."

More laughter erupted from the kids.

"I give up, I'm going upstairs to read. You can deal with the rest of this."

I was satisfied there was enough panic on Ben's face as I left the room that I knew the poo conversation would be at an end, now that he had to be an adult in this 'house of boys'.

I lay down on my bed and picked up the book that had been lying on my bedside table for the guts of eight months. I used to devour books; now I was lucky to get through two a year. It wasn't for all the time I was spending with kids it was more to do with just being bloody knackered at the end of every day and it was much easier to scroll through my phone that to read something that required actual brain cells. Before I even found the bookmark, my phone buzzed.

Elle: I've had a think about it and I've decided I don't want Keith to die of a heart attack that's too good for him. He brought himself home a takeaway without any for the rest of us because he felt like eating something 'nice'. He's such a moron.

Amy: That's a dead-skin-eating fish offence.

I smiled at my witty reply and hit 'send'

Elle: Too good for the turd, I'm going to train a bunch of Chihuahuas to gnaw off his gonads at my command. Now the house smells like glorious fried food and I'm dying for some fast food but I can't or that means he's won. Currently in the kitchen trying to chew down this bloody salmon and couscous. Fucking, men.

We continued to trade tales of woe about our useless husbands and had a competition on who was worse off. I clinched the title by explaining that her girls would eventually grow up and come back after the horrible teenage years to love her like a cool best friend, whereas I would be replaced by whoever my sons chose to spend their life with and I would be left with Ben, by myself, in my twilight years, while she was clubbing in Ibiza with her cool daughters.

Despite that depressing realisation, I enjoyed the conversation with another female and it put me in a good enough mood to rejoin my family.

They were gathered in the living room playing together when I came back into the room. I liked to watch them play together. Ben was definitely the fun parent, the boys adored him and he knew it. For those few minutes I loved them unconditionally. They had to ruin it by speaking to me.

"Mummy, can we get a dog?" asked Adam.

"No," I said, curtly.

"But whhhhyyyy?" my darling children wailed in unison.

How I hate the sound of whining children.

"Because kids, I would be the one looking after it. Walking it, feeding it, cleaning up after it and when you get bored of it, I'm stuck with it. Just like the goldfish."

"What goldfish?" asked Ben.

"EXACTLY!"

The goldfish had died two years ago but I still liked to bring it up as an example of how irresponsible we are, as a family, when it comes to animals. The dog debate came up at least once a month. I blame that stupid cartoon about the rescue dogs. It gives kids an unrealistic view of dog ownership. They won't go around rescuing people in cool vehicles. They'll shit everywhere and chew the crotch off my underwear. I thought I'd put an end to the conversation but then my third 'child' decided to bring it up when the boys went to bed.

"Why don't we get a dog, babe?"

"Firstly, we decided to never call each other 'babe' because it's creepy, and secondly I don't want a bloody dog."

"But whhhhyyyy?"

How I hate the sound of a whining husband.

"Are you doing this in order for the compromise to be: no dog, but I'll give you sex?" I asked.

"I hadn't thought of that, well can it be?"

"No."

"Worth a try," he conceded, "I'm serious about the dog though, it would be good for you to have a reason to properly exercise on a daily basis."

"I'm chunky and you're stuck with me."

"This isn't about weight, Amy. It's about mental health. You know exercise is a great antidepressant."

Ah, that old chestnut again.

"Yes, but so are antidepressants and they're working fine," I replied, "Can we just stare at the television now?"

"What about talking to someone again, you liked it after…"

"Stop, Ben. I'm asking you to stop and I'm asking nicely."

"Ok. I'm sorry, you know I just like to make sure we've got all the bases covered. Don't want anything slipping through the cracks like last time."

"Last time, as you so elegantly put it, was a breakdown. I'm fine. We're fine. I just don't want to walk a dog to keep you happy."

"Will you at least think about it?"

"Fine, I will think about it if puts an end to this conversation so I can watch the television for an hour without getting a lecture on my mental health."

I had every intention of thinking about the possibility of a dog. A whole crowd of them, more specifically: trained Chihuahuas that could gnaw the gonads off an irritating man at my command.

Chapter 11

It was 7.55pm the next evening and as I nervously checked my reflection in the mirror I had the overwhelming sense that someone was watching me. It was Ben, of course. He'd been following me around 'casually' all evening. I was nervous about what fresh hell awaited me but by the looks of things, not as nervous as my husband.

"You're doing it again," I said.

"What?"

"Stalking me like a Komodo dragon waiting for the poison to kick in so I'll keel over."

"No I'm not, I just want to meet this woman," he replied, sulkily.

"Are you going to be weird?"

"No, are you?"

Touché

"Probably; actually, it's pretty much a given."

The doorbell rang and we both looked at each other.

"Will you answer it while I get my handbag together? Please don't say anything embarrassing."

"Of course I won't, that's an impossibility. I can see you rolling your eyes, Amy."

Right, what do people bring on a night out anyway? I'm pretty sure I won't need a dummy or the nappies, but maybe the wipes – God knows where she's bringing me.

Should I bother bringing make-up? After two glasses of wine, I'm never that bothered with how I look, anyway. Maybe I should bring some, just in case we are in that horrible female-bonding situation at the bathroom and she wants to talk about something deep and meaningful. I can pretend to put on mascara so I won't have to look her in the eye when she's talking about emotions.

I heard the laughter from the two of them in the hallway and decided to check it out. When I peered over the bannister I could see Elle in a floaty ensemble with her hair clipped up with a large, exotic-looking flower pinned in it. She laughed heartily again and I realised that she must be being kind, Ben was definitely not that funny.

"There she is," Elle called up with a wink, "ready to paint the town red?"

"I'm not sure how to answer that."

"Just get down the stairs. Is she always this uncertain?" she asked, Ben.

"Yes!" He agreed with too much enthusiasm, "I mean no. Well, maybe… just sometimes."

Poor cover, Ben.

"Indecision runs in the family, eh?" she laughed.

She hooked her arm in mine and I instantly had to try to keep up with her stride out the door.

"Right, Benny, don't wait up!" she called from over her shoulder.

I didn't get to give him a kiss 'goodbye' but he was too busy waving enthusiastically from the door to notice my panicked look as I was dragged out to her car.

"Don't worry, I'm going to leave this piece of shit car in town and we can get properly rat-arsed, ok?" she said.

"Well, I mean I have the kids tomorrow so not exactly rat-arsed. How about like… hamster-arsed?" I asked, in way of a compromise.

"Hamster-arsed? Alright, but before you decide on a night of sobriety I think you should find out what we're doing first."

"Going to a bar?"

"Correct, but there's an event at the place we're going to and I thought it would be fun."

"Like a pub quiz? I haven't been to one in years and I'm pretty sure my specialist subject is kids' cartoons, at this stage. I'll give it a go though."

"No, not a quiz. Before I tell you, I want you to just hear me out; before you inevitably flip out, that is."

"You're making me nervous."

"That's not hard, let's be honest. Anyway, I think you need a bit of a confidence boost. You're in this little bubble of your family and you just seem so fucking deflated. Like 'what's the point in even trying' type aura around you.

"Look at you tonight, you look great. Why don't you make that type of effort all the time? Now, before you get all indignant and start shouting at me, just remember what you thought when you looked at yourself in the mirror this evening compared to this morning. Did you get a little lift from taking the time on yourself? This isn't about dressing up for Ben or anyone else, I mean do it just for you.

"Bitta lippy can go a long way to helping you face the day. My make-up is my war paint and I'm ready to kick arse in the day ahead. It's a little thing, but confidence is key. You're the least assertive person I've met and I think a little confidence boost could do you wonders."

"What's the point in putting on make-up? It takes up time I'd rather spend sleeping."

"See? 'What's the point'? That defeatist attitude has got to go. You're amazing and I'm going to shake you back to life even if it kills me."

"So what? I should shove on some lipstick and sing a power ballad at some cheesy karaoke bar? I'd rather throw myself from the car now."

"No! I can't stand karaoke bars. They're really depressing. There's always some group of women singing *'I will survive'* or an ageing crooner, who thought he was a 'star' in his youth, massacring a *Meatloaf* song. My idea is much more sensible. All you've got to do is trust me and keep an open mind. We're here."

She had pulled up to a trendy bar on the other side of the town. I hadn't been there before, but that wasn't hard. Bars and bistros were always popping up and disappearing before I had a chance to even know they existed. I could see a group of women, younger than us, heading in the same direction and I outwardly groaned. Elle noted my reluctance and hooked my arm again, half dragging me through the door behind them. This was going to be a long night.

A very cheery-looking hostess greeted us at the door. Her teeth were unnaturally white and I felt unnerved when she smiled at us.

"Hiya, ladies!" she said, "If you want to pick up a wee form over there and pop on a wee name sticker we'll be starting in a wee while. Any questions?"

"Yeah, can you stop smiling at us for a *wee* while, because it's really freaking me out?" asked Elle, nervously.

The hostess immediately dropped her act and nodded her head towards the pens.

"There are the wee pens, move the fuck along. Thanks, ladies."

I pulled Elle away from the, now glowering, hostess towards the group of women already filling in their 'wee questionnaire'. I didn't need to wonder any longer what the evening held; it was in bold print at the top of the page: *Speed Dating*.

"No. I'm out of here," I said.

I spun on my heels and headed to the front door, past the confused looking hostess, when Elle managed to get in between me and the exit. She forcefully clotheslined me into a booth, where an unsuspecting couple were sitting. She then proceeded to wrestle me into an awkward lying position, taking over half of the booth. Eventually, she managed to pin my arms across my chest and sit on my legs.

"I told you to keep an open mind, princess. This doesn't seem like you're being very receptive to this idea."

"One: I'm married, two: I can't imagine if I were single that I would remotely be interested in meeting people this way, three: I'm married and four – "

"Let me guess: you're married?"

"YES!"

"Sorry, we're trying to have a romantic meal here can you girls please just take your domestic somewhere else?" said the male half of the disturbed couple.

"Shut up, arsehole; she would be so lucky to have me as her woman."

Turning to me she continued: "Now if I let you up will you promise to hear me out?"

"Like I have a choice, you drove me here and assaulted me when I tried to leave."

"Great!" She turned her attention to the couple once again and said: "Sorry about the 'arsehole' comment. Can you two, shove up? I need to give this one a pep talk."

They stared dumbfounded and eventually shuffled up allowing us both to sit in the booth with them. This did not make things less awkward between us.

"Now, as I was saying in the car I think you have a self-esteem issue and I want to help. The make-up is all superficial nonsense, I grant you, but I thought if you could see yourself through someone else's eyes – particularly someone who wasn't looking at you as their wife or mother - you'd be able to see you're not dead yet."

Was I spending too much time with this woman or did this make sense?

"You deserve to feel desired and attractive and from what I gather by your put-upon demeanour you're not exactly feeling that within yourself. This isn't about the men you talk to it's about the feedback after. Personally, I could live without men – no joke – but I couldn't find an all-female empowerment conference for this evening in this shitty town so I'm improvising. I just want you to see yourself from another perspective. If you take nothing from this experience, so be it; at least there's wine."

I don't know how long I stared at her saying nothing.

"What have you got to lose?" said the female half of our booth companions.

"See? She agrees with me and she knows what she's talking about - I just know by the look of you. You're totally in the know."

Female booth companion seemed pleased by this ridiculous compliment and blushed while her partner stifled a laugh.

"You are buying all the wine," I said in a defeated tone, "and we don't say a word to Ben about this."

"No problem, I agree to both those conditions, you're not going to regret this."

"I already am."

Chapter 12

Despite going along with her plan, I fell at the first hurdle: the questionnaire.

"What the hell am I meant to write in this?" I said.

"Just make it up, I mean we're never going to see these people again so, fuck it. Just say you're looking for friendship but open to more and go from there."

"I shouldn't put my real name then?"

"No! Not unless you want them looking you up on *Facebook* to 'connect'. How would you even explain that to Ben?"

"How do I explain ANY of this to Ben?"

Cheery hostess shot me a look similar to that of a pissed off librarian for talking too loudly.

"It's not that hard, have a look at mine." She proudly showed off her handiwork and to my horror, she was already finished her one.

"You're an astrophysicist named Lulla?"

"Yeah, don't you think I look like a '*Lulla*'?"

"What if they pair you with an actual scientist and you've nothing to say to them."

"That's a very ignorant viewpoint, Amy. I mean how do you know I don't have the basic knowledge that I could pass as this persona for the three minutes I'll be speaking to them? I could know stuff. I've watched movies about space and shit."

"You're right, I'm sorry, that's exactly the same as being an actual astrophysicist."

The sarcasm wasn't lost on her and she gave me a playful dig in the ribs.

"Right, well I'm Eleanor and I'm an air hostess."

"Nah, that's too unbelievable," she replied.

"What? How is me being an air hostess more unbelievable that you being an astrophysicist?"

She took the paper out of hands and started to fill it out for me.

"I dunno, it's just this *air* you have," she mused, "Oh, I know – be a travel agent. That's pretty much the same and you don't look like an Eleanor. Why don't you try like 'Aimee'."

"That's my fucking name," I hissed, through gritted teeth.

"No, I spelt it differently, see?"

"Get me some wine and stop talking to me for three minutes. Consider this our speed date."

"Righteo, wine it is."

Elle didn't know what she was talking about. I could be an air hostess, I could be happy and helpful and wear those nice uniforms and brush my hair. For all these people knew I was the best goddamn air hostess in the world.

'Lulla' came back with red wine without offering any further explanation about what kind it was. Not that it mattered at this stage, I decided needs must and gulped down half the glass.

"It's that type of night, is it? Awesome, I'll catch up," said the over-enthusiastic astrophysicist.

"Yes, *Lulla*, it's that type of night saying as I've been taken speed dating for some reason that kind of made sense a half hour ago but now I'm beginning to think I've Stockholm Syndrome."

I knew she wasn't listening.

"What was that?" she asked, "Never mind, I'm sure it was something unnecessarily aggressive. Oh, look! We're heading in, give me your questionnaire and I'll leave it in with the not-so-happy hostess. She's going to send all the weirdos our way anyway, because of that crack I made about the smiling. You're sticking with Eleanor the air hostess I see?"

"Yes, I'm a fucking air hostess. I'm a bloody brilliant air hostess."

"Alright, alright; keep your knickers on *Eleanor*."

She disappeared into the crowd of women vying to get their questionnaires in while I hung back and took another big gulp of wine. I prayed to the universe that I wouldn't run into anyone I knew, or worse, Adam's teacher. How would I explain that one?

I need more wine.

"Fuck me, those lot are thirsty for some dating action if you know what I mean?" she chuckled, mischievously.

"I need more wine."

"Already? Right hang on and I'll get you more. Just pace yourself, will you? This is meant to be a positive exercise, how shite are you going to feel when the feedback you get is 'she was too pissed to speak'"

"Wine, Elle; now."

"See? You're becoming more assertive already and this is only the second time we've hung out. I'm telling you: it's onwards and upwards, princess."

I had finished my third glass of wine before the hostess reappeared and ushered us into a side room to discuss what would be happening in the evening ahead.

My head was already swimming and I wasn't paying much attention but from what I gathered I just had to sit there and every three minutes a different 'match' would come and chat with me. I severely doubt there was any science behind these so-called matches. I was certain we would just be talking to every man that signed up – compatible or not I had a feeling that the women outnumbered the men anyway.

Cheery, the hostess, was clapping her hands for our attention and the excited women at the front finally settled down to hear how they were going to meet their Prince Charming. I decided I should keep my eye-rolling to a minimum or Cheery would murder me.

"Alright, ladies! I just need your attention a wee minute more. Thank you. Now, once you've met all your suitable matches, you just put a wee tick beside their name if you want to chat more or a wee cross, if not. There's plenty of eligible men here tonight ladies and if you just bear with me a wee minute more we are going to get you all sorted."

I decided that if I had to listen to her *wee* voice for the entire evening I was going to use one of the tea light candles they were passing off as romantic ambience to set the curtains on fire, or her hair extensions, no that's too much – just the curtains.

I wobbled back out to the bar to find Elle talking animatedly with the bartender.

"Where's my wine?" I said with a slight slur in my words.

"Jesus, Oliver Reid lives. Here's your wine, although by the looks and sounds of it I should cut you off already."

I smiled as sweetly as I could and took the glass from her.

"Your teeth are grey. Now, you're never going to get married. Your true love could be next door filling out a questionnaire looking to meet an aggressive air hostess as we speak."

"If he's my true love then he won't mind about my grey teeth. Do you ever think about teeth?

"No, Eleanor I can't say that I do," she replied.

"Like, aren't they just tiny, explosed bone?"

"Explosed?"

"You know what I mean."

"You're spilling your wine. Next drink is water, lightweight."

She took me by the hand and we walked back into the side room to meet our soul mates.

Chapter 13

I can't remember if I felt the pain of a headache or the wave of nausea first. All I knew was that I was waking up to the mother of all hangovers and I needed Ben to get me water because there was no way I was making it down the stairs anytime soon. With eyes still closed, I blindly felt for his chest to tap him so he'd wake up.

I eventually felt the warmth of his skin under my fingertips. I started tapping and mumbling his name to try and get him to stir. When he didn't move I poked him more violently until I heard a protesting voice that did not belong to my husband.

"Fucking hell, Eleanor!" said Elle.

It all came screaming back to me: the wine, the speed dating, the wine, the booth, the wine, something about teeth…

Fuck, where am I?

My eyes shot open and I did not recognise the bed or the bedroom I was in. I sprang into an upright position and instantly regretted it when the blood pounded faster through my head and my stomach flipped like it was readying itself for an immediate evacuation. I lay back down with my arms across my eyes hoping to keep them from popping out of their sockets.

"Ugh, it feels like my brain and my eyes are too big for my skull and they're both trying to get out," I lamented.

"You? Brain too big? Nah, love. After your display of – what I hope was you on drugs – no one could ever think your brain was in danger of being too large for that head of yours."

She lay on her side and rested her head on her elbow.

"Are you ready to dissect that absolute car crash?" She asked, knowing I wasn't.

"Water, first."

"My days as your drink enabler are done. The kitchen is downstairs, the door at the back of the hall. Grab me one while you're there."

I assumed I was in no position to argue and shuffled my sorry frame out of the bed. It was only now I looked down to see that all I was wearing was my bra (a crappy one at that) and my jeans, which seemed to be on back to front.

How is that even possible?

"Water, first," I repeated, aloud.

"As much as I enjoy the sight of you in a greying bra that you've clearly had since the dawn of time, can you shove on your top before you flash more members of the general public?"

"I've never as much as *owned* a bikini and yet you've now seen my underwear for the second time in less than a week."

"Thank you?" she said, completely unsure if it should have been an honour.

I shuffled down the stairs and crept into the kitchen, hoping that I wasn't about to walk in on her husband and children eating breakfast, like I was some dodgy one-night stand. It was empty and I thanked the universe for one bit of good luck. I filled two pint glasses that were already in the sink. I gulped mine down straight away and refilled it while mentally trying to put the night together. As I reached for the tap again, I noticed smudging on my arm. It was a phone number.

Oh, sweet mother of God.

I began to spiral and the panic in my chest was wakening up. I ran up the stairs spilling most of the water out of the glasses and kicked open the bedroom door, startling Elle.

"What the?" She exclaimed as she sat upright on the bed.

"TELL ME EVERYTHING! WHAT IS THIS NUMBER? DID I CHEAT ON BEN? WHERE DOES BEN THINK I AM? DID I TELL HIM? AM I SINGLE MOTHER?"

Her blank expression was all I could look at while the rest of the room began to spin.

"They are a lot of questions," she replied, evenly, "Give me the water and sit down, before you fall down.

"This is called hangover anxiety, and judging by the amount we put away last night you can expect to question all your major life decisions for the next three days.

"Do you remember when you were younger and you didn't have to deal with that type of crap? Like physical hangovers are completely fine for me, I can deal with that type of shit but the anxiety stuff that catches you when you're trying to sleep is the worst, isn't it?" she pondered.

"Are you seriously talking to me about the different type of hangover when my marriage hangs in the balance?"

"I can see you're not in form for chit-chat."

I watched as she dug in her handbag that had been lying at her bedside. She pulled out her phone and read a text message out:

Ben: Hi Elle, yeah Amy was never great at handling the red wine! That's no problem; I'll leave Adam to school in the morning and take Arthur to my in-laws. Get Amy to give me a call in the morning. Good luck with research!

"Now, you can stop looking at me with that bemused look on your face. I covered for your drunk arse," she said, smugly, "I told him I was researching a book about the lives of the single millennial and one of the chapters was about dating so I 'dragged' you to this speed dating evening, where you drank three glasses of wine and didn't talk to anyone. Your conscience is clear and you don't have to lie to Ben about where you were because clearly, you are shite at lying."

"But you did 'drag' me. You literally ambushed me with the evening and then physically restrained me until I agreed to go," I protested.

"I see it very differently, besides my point is still valid. I saved your arse. If I had sent you home in the shape you were in, you would be getting the guilts from a grumpy husband and trying to function as an adult for the school run. I'm a fucking saint, Amy."

"Right, I'll send off the official notification to the Vatican. Just tell me why I have my trousers on back to front, I have someone's number on my arm and what exactly happened after we got there?"

"What do you think I would be the patron saint of?"

"ELLE!"

"Fuck, alright, alright. So 'Cheery' as you insisted on calling her let us into the far room after they finished tallying all our answers on that questionnaire so we could get the 'very best speed dating experience' by being paired with people that met our wants, or whatever. Complete bullshit of course because I asked for an academic with a trust fund, mummy issues and a tendency to prematurely ejaculate."

She took a large gulp of water and continued.

"You wrote 'non-applicable' in that box. Talk about not playing ball, so I crossed that out and wrote down 'someone with a pulse'. Don't you roll those eyes at me, Eleanor the air hostess. Now, where was I? Right, so you were already bladdered before anyone even came to sit in front of you. No judgement here, love, I'm actually quite impressed. I tried to keep up; I gave it a good try with the wine but failed miserably. I went onto Sambuca instead. That stuff is rough.

"I remember one night I had crap-all money and there was a promotion on in the bar, meaning Sambuca were £1 a pop. I had 23. Actually, I think I'm lucky I didn't die. I did miss a presentation at art college the next day but at least I wasn't dead.

"ELLE!" I interrupted. I didn't have the time or patience for her trip down memory lane.

"Keep your clothes on – for once. Ok, so this is when things get a bit fuzzy for me too. I remember you talking really animatedly to some tree surgeon. This was apparently the funniest thing you'd ever heard. You kept telling him if you guys got married your mum would finally be proud of you because you married a doctor.

"I tried to make things better by making a few bush trimming jokes but he got up and left your table before the bell went for time and completely blanked my table next to you.

"The next guy was a 'nerd' according to you but when he didn't like your alleged compliment about nerds being totally 'in' this season you cried because you'd hurt his feelings. He spent the rest of the date on your side of the table comforting you. You used his sleeve to wipe your nose. He also walked past my table and decided to stay on the far side of the room for the rest of the event.

"Then there was my favourite of the night," she said, straightening up as she spoke, "You started off pretty shaky, I mean you were still snivelling about the nerd but you perked up when you had another few sips of wine. The guy was trying to ask you questions but you were too busy asking me about your mascara. I'm not joking, it was a complete mess. You looked like a panda with hay fever at this stage. Any normal person would have just kept walking past that table, but fair play to number three, he stayed. He only started to panic after he told you he was a dentist and you flipped out. You kept showing him your teeth and talking about them being 'exposed bones'. You were really freaking him out. You said something like: "We're soul mates; you have to love my grey teeth." That was the tipping point for him.

"He must have said something to Cheery because we were kicked out after that. I didn't even get to talk to anyone; you kept scaring them off before they got to my table. We just went to the main bar and had a couple more drinks. You were so panicked that you were going to get lost and never be found again so I wrote my number on your arm in eyeliner so you could go to the toilet by yourself like a big girl."

"And my trousers?"

"What about them?

"They're on back to front."

She shrieked with laughter.

"I'd forgotten about the trousers! You went to the toilet by yourself - to prove to me you 'weren't that drunk' – and when you came back they were on that way. Again, that is pretty impressive stuff; I can barely get my jeans closed when I'm that pissed, never mind get them on backwards. I'm telling you, Amy, you were a legend. Bloody, crazy person when you're drinking, but I don't think I've laughed that much in my life. Come on, I'm bound to have something that fits so I can burn those clothes for you. They're bound to completely saturated in spilt drinks, sweat and regret."

She left some leggings and an oversized t-shirt on the bed and left me to get changed. I remembered the baby wipes in my bag and thanked myself for being such an intelligent and well-prepared person. I was clearly still drunk if that's what I took away from hearing everything that I had been up to over the last 12 hours. The inner bitch was going to have a field day on this drunken behaviour for months.

By the time I got down to the kitchen, there was dry toast and a fresh coffee waiting for me. Elle was busying herself around the room and not paying attention to her hungover guest.

"Where's the family?" I asked.

"They stayed in the in-laws last night."

"Oh, that's nice. Is that a regular thing so you have a night off?"

"Something like that."

It was the slight shift in her expression when she answered that aroused my suspicion.

"What does that mean?"

"It means me and the old man aren't getting on so great these days so he's living with the folks while we get our shit together. The girls stayed with him last night, I'll pick them up at dinner."

"What? When did this happen? Why didn't you tell me?"

"Yesterday morning, and before you ask: no it wasn't because he brought home that take-away. It's been coming for a while. I just need a breather, you know?"

"Yeah," I answered half-heartedly. I really didn't know. I didn't know her husband, their dynamic, their history, I barely knew Elle and now I'm in the middle of a marriage breakdown. I was starting to feel really conscious that I was in too deep with this friendship. I wasn't even sure it was a friendship. I just wanted to go home.

"Do you want to talk about it?" I asked, inconvincibly.

Please say 'no'

"No thanks, not right now."

Oh, thank goodness.

"Well, I'd better get a taxi home and get myself sorted for picking up Adam from school and all that other nonsense."

I tried to keep it light but I could see her mood had crumbled from the jovial one she had woken up with. Maybe I was overthinking it, she could just be hungover.

"I'll phone you a taxi, I won't go with you for the car, I'll walk in later; could use the exercise."

I was so grateful by the time the taxi beeped the horn outside. The conversation was uneasy after the revelation about her relationship and I knew I was becoming more awkward by the second. I promised to text her later on but as I sped away in the taxi I knew I had no intention of ever seeing Elle or being caught up in this whirlwind for one second longer.

Chapter 14

Elle was right about one thing: hangovers in your thirties were the worst.

I felt ill for days after my night of drunken stupidity, with Elle, and all I wanted was food that was deep fat fried.

I decided not to be a complete monster and text her – albeit two days later than I had said I would.

I didn't have the nerve to cut her out of my life but I still felt that I needed distance from the drama of someone else's marriage woes. Still, even though I tried to convince myself I was doing the right thing, I felt like one of those horrible fuck-boys your mother warns you about. I spent the night with her and then refused to see her again. I justified my behaviour by telling myself I had my own family to handle, a brain verging on the dangerous side of depressed and I really should be spending my free time to helping Joseph and his café.

Ben asked minimal questions about my night on the town and he gave up asking when I was meeting Elle again after my third shrug as an answer. I felt reassured that life would get back to normal soon enough and in the meantime when I felt guilty I could just pour my energy into raising the children – or, realistically, my phone.

Tuesday came back around and that meant facing Joseph. Yet again, I had very little to offer him. I had been playing around with some marketing ideas based on the phrase: "a cuppa Joe at Joe's" but it was all just flat and I really didn't want to be on the receiving end of one of Joseph's scathing looks, like poor Michael.

I decided to drive, simply so I could make a quicker exit from Shame Street should he start shouting at me. I put the radio up loud enough to drown out my inner bitch – who had been living it large, thanks to my residual hangover.

The street seemed to be busier than any other day I'd been down this way. By the time I got parked, I managed to build up some courage in order to face Joseph. I hated the thought of coming back empty-handed again.

I had hoped to sneak in and have a few minutes alone, so I could compose myself and put together a speech, but as soon as I walked through the door I was face-to-face with him.

There was nowhere to hide and my rabbit-caught-in-the-headlight look didn't go unnoticed, but instead of looking at me in anger he bundled me up into a huge hug. I could barely breathe and I was feeling more awkward the longer the hug went on. By the time he released me my head was dizzy from the lack of oxygen.

"Ah! Amy, you little angel," he said as he tried to come in for another hug – which I managed to sidestep.

"Thank you?" I said, completely unsure as to what I had done to deserve such praise.

"No, Amy, thank *you*."

I finally caught my composure long enough to realise that the café was packed. I was completely confused, I had done nothing – less than nothing. I'd spent a week trying to regurgitate a tired phrase about coffee.

"But Joseph, I didn't do this," I confessed.

"She told me you'd be modest, but you can't lie to me. This has been the best day of business we've ever had and it's because of you. I thank you, from the bottom of my heart. Today, I don't even mind Michael, eh?"

I smiled but felt no less confused, and then I saw her: Elle.

Fuck

I was in no way equipped to have an actual showdown with this woman. I knew I couldn't grab Arthur and make a bolt for the door without seeming like an utter shit and she was already making her way from the counter towards me.

"Hiya, princess," she said as she raised her right hand. All I could do was brace myself for the slap across the face, but it never came. Instead, I was bundled into my second hug of the morning.

"What do you think?" she asked as she gestured to the women around the room.

"I'm confused as to what is going on right now. Have I been in a car accident and this is all some comatose scenario?"

"Fuck me, you really do just jump into the dark stuff, don't you? Come over and sit down with me, I think we should have a chat."

She led me to the lumpy, old sofa – which was fast beginning 'my spot' in the café - and I waited to hear an explanation of what was going on.

"I'm sorry," she said.

I was completely caught off guard, I never imagined that I would be the one deserving of an apology.

"What's going on with me and Keith isn't your problem. I shouldn't have just landed you with that, especially with a hangover. I know I've come across as some mad bint who is desperately trying to change you, but that's really not the case. I like you, Amy. I like you broken and fucked. In fact, I don't think you're anywhere nearly as messed up as you think you are, you just need a friend.

"I thought if I could have you as my little pet project and make you see exactly what kind of awesome person you are, it would take my mind off the crap-heap that is my own life. I guess that's why I've been so pushy. I didn't mean to scare you off. This was my way of an apology."

"What is 'this' exactly?" I asked as I gestured to the café full of people.

"I offered everyone in my boogie bounce classes a ten percent discount if they came in for coffee straight after the class, I know it was cheeky but I don't really know how this marketing or PR stuff works so I thought it was start?"

"As long as Joseph is happy, I'm happy. Thank you."

I confessed to her I had no clue how I was going to turn things around and I was really a fraud. This man was putting a lot of trust in a woman he met for a half hour once and the pressure was a little daunting.

"Were you good at your job?" she asked.

"At one time, yes," I admitted.

"Then everything else, every excuse you're coming up with is bullshit. You can do this Amy, I'll have faith in you until you're able to prop yourself up."

I was touched, more than touched. I had been the one in the wrong in backing away from this friendship and, instead of being a complete bitch about it, she took my cowardice as a blemish on her character instead. Joseph was happy with me – although this had nothing to do with me nor was it down to any type of PR. I had to say something.

"I'm a wuss," I blurted out, "I was just hoping to disappear and not have to run into you again instead of just texting you and letting you know I was scared about getting in too deep with this friendship."

"I get that, although you are making this seem more like a dodgy relationship than just two women hanging out?"

"Yeah, I realised that as soon as it came out of my mouth. I don't know how to make friends now, I'm pretty useless at this. I am sorry though. I want you to know that, and you certainly didn't have to do any of this."

"I know, but I take four classes a week and that lot are always going on about never being able to find a decent cup of coffee. I figured I might as well push them in the direction of somewhere nice. I told them it was like a haven for fuck-ups who just need a good caffeine hit and some time to zone out."

Suddenly, I was hit with a lightning bolt of inspiration.

"That's it!"

"What is?" she asked, confused.

I explained that we could market the cafe as a haven for the 'fuck-ups' of the parenting community. I wagered that the two of us couldn't be the only ones that didn't fit in with the Smug Club brigade, and anyone else who felt that way could find their tribe (and get a nice coffee) within these walls.

"We can change the layout a bit. Give over more room for the kids to play, safely, in their own space and parents – or whoever – can come relax over here. It's not exactly reinventing the wheel but it's a start," I said.

"I think it's a great idea," replied Elle, "Anyone that needs a place to just 'be' can come here and have zero judgment about their lives and how they're raising their family.

"I'll start getting the word out, today, but you'll have to convince Joseph to be prepared for a lot more chaos around here."

"We could even have an official launch party and invite all the regulars that will start coming in. Stressed parents can pretend they have a social life again," I added, enthusiastically.

I wasn't looking forward to selling this idea to Joseph but, thankfully, Elle was on board.

I was mostly relieved to finally have an idea to present to him.

To say that Joseph wasn't enamoured with my plans would be an understatement. Feeling deflated, I told him to have a think about it and we could discuss it another time.

I was already starting to doubt that I could pull this off but Elle was on hand to stop my spiral in its tracks.

"Look here, Joe, are you going to trust my girl or not?" she demanded.

He was a little taken back but before he had the chance to reply she continued:

"All these people are here today because of her and there will be more tomorrow and the next day. She's a smart cookie, with a good head on her shoulders, and if she says this place can work as a haven for fuck-ups then we'll make sure every parent in town – that doesn't already have their head stuck up Mrs Clunting's arse – comes through your door to buy coffee.

"Parents need this. We need a place to come to so our kids will leave us in peace for twenty minutes, but we also need a place for us to relax in too. We're all losing our minds trying to be decent bloody parents and emotional compasses to these little turds, and all we're asking for is a child-friendly café with a decent coffee."

"Decent? There is no 'decent' coffee sold here, only the best," he replied.

"Right on, Joe, it's epic. Look, you've already opened your doors to the two of us and we're basically as bad as it gets. The calibre of customer is only going to get better.

"Now, tell me you're in and we can all get to work freeing the fuck-ups from the terrible instant coffee they've been subjected to at home because they're stuck there with their horrible children."

"Alright, I'm in," he said, with a clap of his hands, "You do this, Amy, I trust you.

"Michael," he shouted, "We're going to free the fuck-ups."

"Is that a new recipe?" asked Michael, as he popped his head out of the kitchen.

"No, stupid boy! See? This is why I keep him in the kitchen."

Joseph left the conversation in order to help his son-in-law finish prepping for lunch, and insult him some more.

Elle put her arm around my shoulder and hugged me tightly.

"We're going to free the fuck-ups, Amy. Get your excited face on."

I really hope that catchphrase doesn't stick, there's no way I can market that.

Chapter 15

In the weeks to follow, Elle's help was invaluable and our friendship blossomed.

I opened up little by little about my miscarriage and how I was spent my energy running away from ever having to think about it, as well as avoiding Ben's attempts to get me back into therapy.

Despite my attempts to get her to share her tales of woe or update me on her relationship with Keith, she managed to side-step my interrogations.

We were both avoiding the realities of our home lives and Joseph's provided the cover that we needed.

She was unbelievable at word-of-mouth promotion and knew people from all walks of life. They were all sold on the idea of a new place to escape to with (or without) their kids and they couldn't get enough of the bizarre-looking garden gnomes and grass for wallpaper.

I was busy with the social media end of things and trying to put together some sort of presence in the business scene. The local papers had been contacted, telling them about this newly opened haven for parents to get away from their daily stresses - and for those who just appreciated a good coffee. They were reluctant to run anything without advertising but I managed to persuade one journalist to come and see for herself what made this place something entirely different. My big selling point was Joseph. His welcoming nature, his genuine interest in every customer's story and his ability to make you feel at ease, within moments of coming through the door. Elle coached him before the interview to make sure our message was drummed into him.

"We need to let them bitches at Smug Club know that the average, rubbish parent is coming for them," she said.

"I will not incite violence, I just want to sell coffee," Joseph firmly responded.

"I'm not asking you to start a gangland war here, Joe. Now is the time for the slummy mum to fight back! The mum who tries her best every day and the dads who do just as good a job but get completely overlooked because they didn't birth the fuckers themselves. Parenting is a damn privilege but there's no *one* right way and we are here to help them realise they're doing a bloody brilliant job. They don't need the Smug Club seal of approval."

"Amy?"

"Yes, Joseph?"

"I don't want to curse like that woman. Do I need to in order to sell the coffee?"

"No, Joseph. You just be you and she will love you."

She sat with him for over an hour and was sold. Her feature appeared the next week over two pages, filled with pictures of all the oddities and wonderments that the café held, along with a smiling Joseph. The story welcomed all who appreciated a good cup of coffee and wanted a place to belong.

It was perfect. He was presented as a hero of the people and with that, more and more customers began making their way to this little coffee shop of chaos. They came, they got their coffee, they shared their stories and they stayed for as long as they needed. Joseph was happy, which meant Michael was happy, Elle was happy because she felt like every time the chimes of the door went it was another two fingers up to the Smug Club - and me, I was happy to feel part of something again.

Despite the success the café was experiencing, I was getting the cold shoulder at home. Once the feature came out there was no denying that I was part of this little band of parenting mutineers. Joseph talked about Elle and me several times throughout the interview. I had to come clean.

"Why didn't you just tell me?" Ben asked.

"Because you were so happy when I decided to leave work and all the stress of it behind; I didn't want to worry you about this."

"I don't think that's true. I think you prefer to shut me out."

"That's not fair, or true. You know everything."

"I didn't know you were part of some anti-mum-club gang."

"Ok, but now you know everything. I promise. I'm proud of this, I've helped someone with their business and in turn, he's helping a lot of isolated people feel like they have a place to be on crappy days. There are community groups and all sorts getting in touch. They want to rent a space for proper weekly meetings, I've even convinced him to turn one of the junk rooms at the back into a type of function room for things like that. I did this. Elle and I did this. I feel like I'm a functioning member of society and, more importantly, I don't feel like the weak link of the family."

"How can you think that? You're the most important part of this family. We don't function without you. That was the point of taking this break from work. Really being here for the kids and taking the pressure off."

"No, Ben. This wasn't taking the pressure off, this was me hiding. I had a very public, very traumatic breakdown and I was ashamed. I don't want to be ashamed of me anymore. I might not be the best mum in the world, but I'm trying, and part of that is me being involved with a project like this."

"It's too much. You can't handle this again. It's just too soon," he said.

"Who do you think you're speaking to here? You don't get to decide this for me. This is *my* life."

I know he meant well, I know this was all coming from a place of kindness, but right now he just seemed like the enemy. We stopped speaking to each other after that.

It's exhausting not speaking to the person you love. The first few hours were ok, I mean I quite enjoyed the quiet, but after the second day, it was really wearing thin. Unfortunately, we are as stubborn as each other and there was no end to this stalemate in sight.

Internally I was in a constant state of rage. I didn't understand how he refused to see how much better I was doing. It felt like I was always going to be the fragile little woman he had to protect. I couldn't bear the thought of that. I decided I would just have to keep going and show him I can handle it.

I'll show him. I'll show them all.

I didn't know who 'them all' was referring to but I felt like that was a nice dramatic way to end that train of thought.

If my home life was bad, Elle's was much worse. I
would get snippets of information on how the separation
was going.

"Shite," she said, "it's really shite."

She was nothing, if not succinct.

"Before this, when we would fight, I used to
daydream about being a single parent. I felt like they had
the right idea. They didn't have to stay with each other
for the sake of the children, had a few nights off when
the other one had the kids and then got to be a good
parent when they were back because they missed them.
It's not like that at all. I'm just fucking sad when the kids
are gone. Who wants to party with a sobbing mess? *I*
don't even want to party with a sobbing mess. I've even
set up another evening art class to have something to do
when they're away. I'm offering them the same discount
as my bouncing babes, by the way."

"I can't even draw a stick man, I've always wanted to
be able to paint," I mused.

"Come tonight then. It's better than sitting in silence
with Benny boy, isn't it?"

"I've just said I can't draw."

"So, what? You can wash the brushes or something.
Just get out of the house."

She was right; I don't think I could stand another
evening of silence with Ben.

When I told him he'd have to sort bedtime on his
own, this evening, because I was starting a painting class
he didn't even look up from his plate. He mumbled
under his breath and I decided not to rise to the bait.

This act of restraint lasted about twenty seconds
before I shouted: "What? Have you got something to say
about this as well?"

"I didn't say anything," he replied, still keeping his eyes fixed on the food in front of him.

"Can you stop this, please? I don't see what the big problem is, you wanted me to meet people and get involved with something outside of the house. I've done all that and it's still not the right thing."

"Is that what you think this is about?"

"What else is there to be fighting about?"

"This is about you not trusting me enough to share how you're really feeling. It's terrifying to think you're keeping secrets again. I thought we were past all that and now you're interested in painting? I don't even know you these days."

"It's a beginner art class; it's not a big deal. Elle is the teacher. I thought I might as well go, saying as we are all picture, no sound this week."

"It's not about the class."

"Then for fuck sake Ben what is this actually about."

"I've been trying to tell you what it's about. We are drifting away from each other and you're not helping by keeping chunks of your life a secret. I don't remember the last time we kissed let alone had sex."

And there is was: sex.

"That's what this is about? Seriously? You just want sex and we can feel like we're one entity again? Well drop your trousers then and let's get this over with."

For a second I thought he was seriously considering it, but then he shook himself out of his train of thought.

"Look, I was trying to give an example of how things haven't been quite right between us. It was the first thing that came to mind," he said, sheepishly.

"I'm late for class, we'll talk about it later."

I gave the boys a kiss goodnight on my way out the door and ran away from the house, as quickly as I could. I knew there was no way in hell I was going to talk about this later with him. He'd pretend to be asleep by the time I got home and I would let him.

On the way to the class, I was lost in my own thoughts, about how I could deal with this new bump in the road.

It's not like I didn't want to have it, it was always fun I just hadn't really felt like it. They warned me it could be a side effect of the antidepressants and I accepted that.

I could deal with non-existent sex life, as long as the tablets kept me from throwing myself into a lake again.

It seemed like a fair compromise. Up until now, I thought Ben understood that.

Apparently not. Did he really think all this could be sorted by a roll in the sack? What a funny creature.

My life was becoming a poorly executed balancing act. Once I'd got one aspect of it off the ground, something else would fall spectacularly off a cliff and catch fire. This particular fire, however, couldn't be ignored anymore.

I had to take action to put it out, or I could end up alienating my husband for good.

Chapter 16

"Of course it's about sex," said Elle, ensuring that everyone in the room stopped what they were doing and turned to look at us.

"What?" she asked, to her shocked classroom, "Get your stuff out and get ready to paint, you nosey bastards."

I really should have known better than to try and confide in the loudest person on the planet, but I needed a soundboard and she was all I had.

"Just screw the man and we can get back to our world domination with a chain of coffee shops to destroy dictator-mum-types," she continued.

"It's not that simple," I hissed.

"Have you forgotten how to do it? Have I awakened some dormant bisexuality? You think he's repulsive? Let me know when I'm getting warm."

"Please, stop talking."

I hated talking about this type of thing. I was always embarrassed at the thought of anyone asking me about my sex life, or worse still, anyone asking me for advice on it. I was never comfortable in my own skin and although I was finally kind about my body (mostly) I would never dream of a world in which I would gladly step into a lingerie department and kit myself out for a night of kink with the husband.

"When's the last time you fooled about with him, or anyone?" She quizzed.

"Anyone?"

"Yeah, maybe you can't be bothered boning him because you're doing the nasty with someone else."

"Just so I know, how many euphemisms for sex should I expect in this conversation?"

"Few hundred I suspect."

"Excellent," I replied flatly.

I explained that I wasn't sleeping with my husband because the sheer effort to shave my legs was enough to put me off the notion completely, never mind shave anywhere intimate to impress a new man.

"What has shaving got to do with it? I once let my underarm hair grow so long I was able to dye it violet. I couldn't deal with the upkeep though, the dye kept sweating off and ruining my bed sheets."

"Can we stick to my problem please?"

"Well, no, actually I have to teach. The world doesn't revolve around your little-repressed arse. Now, sit over there. Here's a pencil and try to keep your clothes on during this class."

I snatched the pencil and glumly walked over to a free space. I had no idea why I agreed to this class. I can't draw nor do I want to learn how to draw a bunch of grapes in a fruit bowl. I decided on doodling on the paper until someone needed their brushes washed. I didn't need to wait long before hush descended on the class and Elle commanded yet another room she was at the centre of. I was starting to see a pattern here.

"We have a newbie tonight guys, this is Amy and she can't draw for shit. Everyone say 'hi'."

I glared at her direction as I heard an unenthusiastic welcome from my classmates.

"Right, you know the score. The model will be changing position every five minutes so you guys have to get used to the movement and the change in shadows from every angle. Let's get to work then."

Model? Great, now I get to stare awkwardly at anywhere but the direction of this poor shmuck student, who is so broke they need to get their kit off in front of a room full of strangers.

The first thing I noticed about this stranger was that he wasn't remotely young. He was old, not death-knocking-on-his-door old, but still old enough to know better. He was balding at the back and was wearing a cosy looking gown. As he turned to face us and bare all, as it were, I looked at the man and quickly realised he wasn't a stranger at all. Instead, I saw the man I respected more than anyone else on the planet, the man who I measured all other men up against, the man whose penis was eye level with me and I had nowhere to run.

"MOTHER OF GOD, PUT IT AWAY!" I screamed as loudly as my lungs could manage.

"Amy? Oh, Christ what are you doing here? You can't draw. Oh Jesus, don't tell your mother. Givemethetowel, givemethetowel!"

In his hurry to grab the robe he managed to tumble sideways giving me – and the rest of the class – a full view of his anus. I was tempted just to gouge my eyes out with the pencil just so this horror would end.

Elle was busy trying to help my dad up, whilst shooting daggers at me for interrupting her precious class. I sat wringing my hands as if I were Lady Macbeth trying to get that damn spot out and I hadn't realised I was muttering to myself until I felt someone's hand on my shoulder trying to shake me back into the room.

"What the fuck is happening, Amy?" asked Elle.

I couldn't manage words yet, I was still trying to process what had just happened.

"Damien you don't have to raise your hands if you want to ask a question, this isn't a classroom. Well, it is but you don't need to be such a brown-nosing little twat," she said.

He sheepishly put down his hand and said: "Was that one of his poses? Should we be sketching now?"

"No, Damien," I said in my best attempt at keeping my voice steady, "I would prefer if you didn't spend the next two hours sketching my father's arsehole from memory."

Unfortunately, by the time I reached the end of the sentence I was screaming again. My fingers rubbed at my temples and I was waiting for the room to stop spinning. By the time I looked up my dad was nowhere to be seen and I could see Elle struggling to contain her laughter. I shot a look which seemed to convey 'I dare you to laugh, I double dare you' and it seemed to do the trick because her cheeks dropped and her face was serious once more.

"Where is my father?" I asked.

"He must be getting changed in the storeroom; maybe you should go have a chat with him?"

"You think?" I replied as sarcasm dripped from my voice.

I picked up my jacket and bag and headed towards the storeroom in order to confront my exhibitionist father. I knocked the door deliberately and louder than necessary to ensure that I wasn't going to be walking into anything else mentally scarring.

He opened the door, just a fraction, so I could see one eye peering out from his cupboard of shame.

"Are you kidding me, dad?"

"Amy, just meet me outside. We can go grab a drink and have a chat."

I thought a stiff drink was the best idea I had heard all evening. I nodded, turned on my heel and walked out into the evening air to wait for a completely unsatisfactory reason for why my father was getting his kit off in front of strangers once a week.

By the time he managed to get his clothes back on and come find me, my rage level had built back up to a fury but I decided not to start screaming at him in the street. The thought of a large vodka kept things on the inside and we walked side by side in silence to the nearest bar we could find.

It was a relatively old one, with three men sitting at the bar quietly watching football on the obscenely large flat screen that didn't fit in with the decor of the rest of the bar. The bartender was young; he looked like a schoolboy and also didn't fit in with the rest of the antiquated feel of this place. I ordered a vodka and tonic and left dad at the bar to order his while I skulked over to a seat. The table was sticky and I had a feeling that there was more than one mound of chewing gum – or worse - lurking underneath this table.

"Vodka for the lady," dad attempted jovially.

I said nothing and waited for him to start explaining.

"What a night, eh?" He tried again.

"Yes, it was full of surprises like I didn't realise that my dad's arse was quite so hairy."

"Keep it down, love," he pleaded as he sipped his pint.

One of the barflies must have overheard my sentence because he began to readjust himself on the stool to hear what we were saying, whilst pretending to still watch the football. His curiosity was betraying his nonchalance as I saw him nudge his companions and whisper to them.

"I think you should start explaining things and do it now," I continued.

"Well, there's not much to explain, love. It's nothing seedy or dirty – it's art."

"Art? Since when were you such a champion of the arts? I wanted to take a dance class when I was little and you told me you'd might as well just 'throw money directly into the bin, dancing won't get you a job.' I never bothered to ask you permission for any type of 'pointless' artistic hobby ever again."

"Well, it didn't crush your dreams and, let's face it, you really don't have any rhythm. It would have been a waste of money."

His attempt at turning this into a trip down memory lane wasn't going to work. I wasn't letting this lie.

What else don't I know about him? Who is this man?

"I can see that head of yours working away, pet. Questioning your very existence over there aren't you?" He asked with a smile.

"No," I lied, "You're a grown man, you can do whatever you want but if it's not 'seedy' then why haven't you told mum yet?"

I knew the answer already of course. Mum would probably have a fit and accuse him of fancying someone in the class. He would have to spend the rest of his life trying to convince her he wasn't giving another woman a 'free show'.

Now, my father wasn't an ugly man but the thought of another woman being impressed by his middle-aged spread was really more disturbing than anything I had thought so far. Even my inner bitch was remarkably silent; apparently, she was off pouring vodka straight into her eyeballs and leaving me to deal with this on my own.

"I saw a leaflet on the notice board at the pool, you know how I like to have a read of them when I'm waiting for your damned mother to get out of the changing rooms," he said, "It said they were looking for a live art model of any age, no experience and I decided to give it a go. It wasn't some big plan to dip my toe in the world of naturism. I thought if there was a nice picture at the end of it I would buy it from them and get it framed for your mum's birthday. See? I was planning on telling her, just in a more indirect way.

Mum's birthday is always a stressful time for both of us. Presents are ridiculously hard for us to think of; simply because she's never once liked anything we've gotten her. I still remember, when I was little, most other mother's fussed over the handmade card they were handed by their children, my efforts were greeted with 'what *is* that?' along with other such soul-crushing retorts. I was starting to think that maybe the pressure of gift-giving had finally got to dad. After decades of eye-rolling at his efforts, he'd finally cracked and this art class was the repercussion.

"When were you planning on presenting this masterpiece to her?" I asked.

"Well, I need to see if there's one that would be nice and get it framed. I don't know, at her birthday meal."

Ah, the birthday meal.

I dread this spectacle every year. It's usually in an uncomfortably posh restaurant which makes my blood pressure skyrocket as I try to keep the children in their seats for an unbearably long time. Sometimes I think she chooses these places on purpose, just to watch me crumble under the pressure. Now I can add the prospect of seeing my dad naked again, on canvas.

"It's not for another eight weeks, so I'm sure there will be something finished by then," he said.

"Are you sure she would want that?"

"What does that woman ever want other than to accuse me of smoking and write letters of complaint to the local council about the bin men. She's taken to calling them the mafia, you know?"

"The council?"

"No, the bin men. They're threatening to bar her from the dump altogether if she keeps making trouble."

I resisted the urge to ask why, or even how, her relationship with the weekly refuge collectors had come to this. Knowing her, it was down to some larger, social issue; but I was in no mood to find out what.

We finished our drinks, and as the warm glow of the alcohol hit my cheeks I started to view my nudist father as more of a rebel and pretty adventurous for a man of his age. I promised to keep his secret, but he declined my invitation to go back to the class.

I returned to the art studio to face Elle and the rest of her students.

I climbed the stairs and wondered if I would ever be brave enough to try something like that.

Maybe that's what I need to kick-start my love life again. I could do one of those boudoir shots. Editing could erase the damage from under my eyes, caused by years of poor sleep. It could even get rid of the cellulite that's taken up permanent residency on my ass making it look like cottage cheese.

I peered into the classroom and found Elle clearing up by herself. I was thankful that I didn't have to face her students after screaming the word 'arsehole' at them. She looked up and relief washed over her face.

"There she is," she beamed, with her arms outstretched for a hug.

I reluctantly walked over for the embrace and breathed her in. She smelt of white spirits and coffee.

"So, have you banned him from my class and told him you're the only one in the family that's allowed to get their kit off in front of strangers?"

"Hardy har har. No, actually, I'm quite the free thinker since I almost had a heart attack whilst faced with my papa's prostate. I figure he can do whatever he wants. Although I don't think I'll be joining your class anytime soon."

"Fair dos," she conceded, "Anyway, we've got a more important project to get on with."

"Which is?"

"We are going to make you sexy, Amy."

Chapter 17

As I ruminated on the school run the next morning, I could feel myself thinking my way into a bad mood.

Make me sexy? I'm plenty sexy

Yes, I was a bit rough first thing in the morning, but I bet even supermodels had morning breath - although theirs probably smelt of angel sweat not of garlic dip with cheese and onion crisps. This particular combination was caused by a midnight pit-stop at the fridge before bed, last night.

Things were still not great with Ben so I was comfort eating, which was best described as my normal level of snacking but with an extra side of guilt.

I resented that Elle condensed the problems in my relationship down to 'not having enough sex' and worse, that it was my fault. I used to have a perfectly healthy libido and our love life, in general, once verged on vulgar. I could have blamed the pesky mental breakdown and subsequent antidepressant intake, but in truth, I knew it wasn't that. Most of all, I resented that she was right.

I couldn't quite put my finger on the exact reason why I couldn't bring myself to sleep with my (mostly) charming husband, but I knew that slapping on some lipstick wasn't going to kick-start my desires and suddenly make me want to hump all over the house.

159

"Mum?" my self-destructive train of thought was interrupted by a panicked-looking Adam.

"Hmmm? Yes, love? What's wrong?"

"You have to unlock the door, people behind us are beeping for us to go."

Fuck.

I flustered with the unlock button and shoved an apologetic hand out the window to the car behind, who was staring a hole into the back of my head for making her wait. My mind was too caught up to sit in the house, or even to have a normal conversation with someone to take my mind off my, self-diagnosed, failings as a wife so I kept driving.

I drove until I heard Arthur start to snore and only stopped when I reached my lake. *The* lake.

Despite what associations this place had for me, it was still my only secret place to come and be alone. This was another secret I kept from Ben. As far as he knew I hadn't returned, not since my rubbish suicide attempt.

The truth was I had been here countless times since it happened. At first, I came to find Malcolm. I had hoped that one day he would be out walking his dog and he'd be able to see I was (relatively) happy and (relatively) healthy but I never managed to orchestrate that meeting.

I left the car doors open so I could hear Arthur snore, while I sat on the bench facing the lake. It was peaceful yet cold, and the horrible swans decided to leave me alone for a change.

What does sexy even mean at this stage in a relationship?

That seemed like a cop-out of a question. Just because we'd been together for 15 years shouldn't give me an automatic 'out' for making an effort. I know that. That was the curious part of my depression: I knew the things I should be doing and how I should be acting towards those that love me, but I couldn't. I had created this wall surrounding me which let me function as a 'normal' person in my day-to-day life but I had no desire to break down that wall and let someone get close to me again, even Ben.

Self-preservation? Maybe. Self-loathing? Almost definitely.

I had been on a path of self-destruction for so long that I didn't even know when I was doing it. Even with Elle pointing it out, I was still in denial.

She was wrong about one thing though: I already knew how to be sexy.

I knew how to fake the cheekbones and straighten the unruly hair and even what my legs looked like without four months' worth of hair growth on them.

I knew I would enjoy the feel of his stubble brushing up against my skin and even when I thought about the last time we were together my hand instinctively touched the right side of my neck, where he liked to bite.

I smiled at the thought of him nibbling at my left ankle like he used to. Lazy weekend mornings, before the kids were likely to come bounding into the room, were a particularly pleasant place for my mind to wander to.

I remembered a time when I used to call him 'gigil'. Apparently, it's a word of Filipino origin which means: the urge to pinch or squeeze something that is unbearably cute. I read it out to him from a Sunday morning newspaper because I thought it described him perfectly. I hadn't called him that in years. The days of adorable nicknames were long gone.

I still loved his smell. After a fight, when we hugged, I would breathe him in as deeply as I could – it was like a healing balm and the ultimate aphrodisiac.

It was the scent of home.

I don't remember the last time I was close enough to breathe him in; sure we slept beside each other but I tend not to sniff him when he sleeps. I had a feeling it would be considered a bit odd.

I knew I wouldn't be able to shake myself after twenty minutes on a bench and just snap out of this, but if I wanted to prove Elle wrong and get my marriage back on track I would have to, at least, fake it for one night. The answer to my immediate problem was simple: wine.

I decided to ignore the niggling worry that I was starting to depend quite a lot on alcohol to get me through any type of awkward situation and power through with my plan to inject instant confidence into my system – for the greater good and all that.

Before I changed my mind I dug out my mobile from the bottom of my bag and rang the one person I definitely wasn't in form for talking to about the problems in my personal life.

"Hi, Mum," I muttered.

"Oh, I exist again? How nice. I suppose you're phoning looking something?"

"No," I lied, "I was just checking in to find out the details about your birthday meal."

"That's weeks away, why do you want to talk about that? I thought it 'stressed' you out."

I knew she was rolling her eyes as she emphasized the word "stressed." The overuse of eye-rolling to illustrate our discontent was obviously a family trait.

"I was actually phoning to talk to dad about the surprise."

"What surprise?"

"It wouldn't be a surprise if I told you. Put dad on the phone."

There was no surprise of course. This was going to put him under pressure to organise something extra for her birthday but at least she'd be in a good mood with him for the rest of the day.

"For goodness sake, Amy. Your mother just gave me a kiss and said 'thank-you' what have you said to her about the class?"

"Nothing, but I will unless you suggest taking the kids for a sleepover on Friday night. Oh, and you need to have a surprise organised for her as well as the birthday meal."

"Are you blackmailing me?"

"Yes, pretty much. Consider this payback for having me see the mole on your left arse cheek in painful detail."

He agreed relatively easily enough and if the suggestion of babysitting comes from dad, mum can't lord it over me that I'm 'gallivanting' again. If you listened to her version of motherhood she didn't leave the house other than for mass or the school run in the 18 years I lived in the house.

Firstly: she was an atheist and secondly I walked to school, every day. Also, I had a dedicated babysitter for every Saturday night, who invited her low-life boyfriend to the house as soon as my parents were gone so they could put me to bed at 8.30pm and smoke in the garden. Despite me bringing this up when she got on my nerves about any time I wanted to go out for dinner with Ben, she would just look at me as if I'd lost my mind and deny all knowledge of said babysitter or aforementioned social life.

All I had to do was get through the next couple of days and by Friday I could do a musical montage makeover in the house. The ones from the movies where, by the key change of the upbeat ballad, I would look so unbelievably different he'd forget that we'd been living like relative strangers for months and we'd probably hump on the kitchen table.

Probably not, I mean do people actually do that? Isn't it horrendously unhygienic?

I heard Arthur starting to stir in his seat and I decide to rejoin the real world. This meant facing Elle at the coffee shop. There were still 301 things to sort out before the official opening party night and every day I wasn't there, Elle found more unnecessary things to add to the list.

Thirty seconds into consciousness Arthur was already demanding something to eat. By the time we reached Joseph's our stomachs were in a rumbling competition and I headed straight for the tray bakes. It was then a very smug looking Mrs Clunting appeared and blocked my way to the counter. My face must have looked a picture as she seemed satisfied with my reaction to her surprise visit.

"Amy isn't it?" She asked.

Swallowing hard I managed a faint 'yes' before she continued: "I remember you from your little visit to our parent and toddler group up the street. Tell me, were you interested in meeting friends and helping develop your child's social skills in a fun and friendly environment or were you just out to size up the competition for this place?"

She gestured around her, with a look of disgust at her surroundings. I could see Joseph pull Elle back into the kitchen; judging by her flaring nostrils it was the right decision.

We had been working hard on getting a nice, family-friendly vibe in the café and that was about five seconds away from being smashed, had Elle been let loose.

Mrs Clunting's eyebrow was raised as she awaited an answer to her loaded question. I offered nothing. My silence was beginning to grate her so instead she looked around at the customers who bought into the notion that this was the place for them and not her beloved Smug Club.

"I won't stay for tea, I just had to see for myself if this was for real. Unfortunately, it doesn't seem to be a case of tabloid fabrication," she scorned.

To have the local paper described as some sort of seedy red-top was laughable, but still, I said nothing. I knew she wanted some sort of reaction out of me but I didn't have the guts or a quick enough wit that could wound effectively. If I started working on it this evening perhaps my withering comeback would be ready in six months or so. I tend to have excellent arguments with those that have wronged me, all while I'm in the shower and mostly years later.

It's not all bad, if I ever get the chance to confront that horrible two-timing teenage boy who first broke my heart I'll know exactly what to say to him (albeit 16 years later).

Mrs Clunting left with her head held high and an aura of entitlement from around her. The woman was a tactless bully, but she still smelled heavenly.

Bitch

"What the fucking, fuck did that fucker want?" raged Elle, when she finally managed to get free from the kitchen.

"Swear jar," I said, as I pointed to the ever-increasing collection of pound coins in the huge vase on the counter. "At this rate, you'll be able to get that extension you spoke about Joseph."

"Fuck. Coming here is costing me a fortune, whose idea was this anyway?"

It had been a lightning bolt of inspiration after a particularly irate review appeared online. It raved about the food, the atmosphere and Joseph himself. They weren't, however, keen on the 'mouthy Australian, who cursed like a sailor'.

It took quite a bit of convincing Elle that she needed to tone down the language for the sake of business but when appealing to her business acumen didn't work I installed the swear jar (if she didn't fork out she was denied coffee – a fate worse than death for the 'mouthy Australian').

"I can't believe I'm being punished because some bloke with a stick up his arse can't stand a woman speaking her mind at any given time. For one thing I'm South African, and secondly how about: 'just fuck off, mate!'"

The concept of the swear jar was having little to no effect but at least we were seen to be making an effort.

"Anyway," she continued, "what did our bosom buddy from up the road want? What horrible names did she call me?"

"Believe it or not, you didn't come up," I replied with a forced air of easiness.

She looked shocked and a little offended at the lack of attention she had been shown by her nemesis.

"She wanted to know if I went that one time to be a spy for here."

"You? A spy?" she scoffed, "Don't make me laugh. You would never have the nerve to do something like that. That's not an insult, I don't think it is anyway."

I rolled my eyes and decided to leave the conversation there. I asked for a tea and perched myself at the counter waiting for Joseph to go back out into the kitchen so I could have a private word with Elle. This was always a dangerous notion as she had no volume control and was likely to repeat anything of a sensitive nature back to me while laughing and at least three times as loud as necessary for such a small place.

It didn't take long for Joseph to want to return to the kitchen and go back to shouting at Michael. Elle rested her elbow on the opposite side of the counter and asked: "Why so glum, chum?"

"I was having a think about what you said the other night," I said in a hushed voice.

"You're going to need to be a bit more specific, I say a lot of thought-provoking and deep things at any given time. Was it that thing about Neil Diamond? Or hamsters?"

"Wait, what? What thing about Neil Diamond? Is it something to do with Neil Diamond *and* hamsters or are these two things not connected? No, stop. You're going to get me sidetracked; I meant the thing after the art class."

"About making you sexy? Yeah, I remember. To answer your other question, I have this theory about Neil Diamond you see –"

"Stop! No more theories, I'm still not over the last one you came up with.

"What was that?" she asked.

"About using pumpkin pulp as a lubricant," I whispered, "So, I don't want to know about Neil Diamond."

I placed my hands over her mouth to physically stop any nonsense from coming out, therefore, preventing it from planting itself in my brain for eternity.

"Firstly, I just want to make a couple of things clear," I continued, "I don't remotely need your help on how to be sexy, I'm plenty sexy. I don't, for one second, think a quick fumble around in the sheets is going to sort my marital problems. While we're at it, I don't think it should be up to me to change anything. We're both grown adults and he has equal responsibility for the failing nature of this relationship."

I took a long, audible breath after my defensive argument and waited for Elle to laugh in my face. She didn't. Instead, she shifted her weight from one elbow to the other while a confused look was etched on her face.

"You're right," she conceded, after a prolonged silence.

"It shouldn't be up to you to fix things with some sort of sex bandage. There's obviously something deeper going on here. That was our problem, me and Keith I mean. Anytime we would argue we just tried to fuck it out but clearly, that didn't work. So, I'm all ears, princess; what's the plan to get the old marriage train back on track."

"I'm going to drink a bottle of wine and seduce him," I said.

"Right, of course, you are. That's a world of difference from what I suggested."

"Look, I wasn't expecting you to be quite so reasonable and I had already planned that speech out so I thought it was a waste if I didn't use it."

Her smug smile was unbearable, but I had to rethink my temper and reminded myself I needed her help.

"I need a favour." I continued, "I want to make an effort and I'm not sure where to start."

"I thought you were 'plenty sexy' and all that other stuff that I was definitely listening to as you waffled on?"

"I should have known better than to ask the help of a mouthy Australian." I pushed my stool away and went to walk towards the kids in the toy corner.

"Stop calling me a fucking Australian," she bellowed.

"Swear jar," I answered, without even turning around.

"I'll help, of course, I'll help. We can watch porn and…"

"No."

"I'm kidding, that would be weird. Besides the noises they all make are so off-putting, don't you think?" she asked with a wry smile.

I started to clean up the strewn toys and resisted the urge to join the conversation. I knew she was waiting for me to jump in with my usual argument about the misogamy and degrading nature of all porn. Instead, I waited for her next suggestion in the hope it could be something useful.

"We'll go shopping and get you some highly uncomfortable underwear that will make you look like a sex kitten and you'll get the ride. That better?"

"Yes. Although no floss-like underwear, that's just going to get swallowed up my arse crack and never come back."

We both giggled and simultaneously noticed the family sitting at the table beside us – complete with elderly granny. They had all stopped eating and were listening to every word we were saying.

My mortification subsided when granny piped up with: "*Primark* does a lovely underwear section now. Leopard print always got my Derek excited."

"MUM!" cried her horrified daughter.

"Leopard print it is," replied a stunned Elle.

Chapter 18

Elle picked me up, that evening, but didn't come inside.

When I got into the car it was obvious she had been crying and I was stuck in that difficult situation of wondering if I should mention it or pretend I didn't see her puffy eyes and tearstained cheeks. The socially awkward jerk within begged me to look out the window and talk about something else. The decent part of me prevailed and asked what was going on.

"Ah, nothing. Well, no, not nothing; I just don't want to talk about it," she said.

"Ok, we don't have to. How about we talk about Neil Diamond and his hamsters?"

"I just find it funny that you can marry someone and be with them for over a decade and then they turn out to be this complete and utter turd posing in man skin?"

I took a guess and assumed she wasn't finished with this particular rant, so I sat back and waited – it didn't take long for me to be proved right.

"How did he fool me for this long that he was a nice guy, who cared about me and the kids when really he was just a raging arsehole who only cares about himself?"

Am I meant to answer that? Best stay quiet.

"He was meant to come over tonight and put the kids to bed while I was out with you and instead he sent his mother over. His mother? I can't stand that shrew at the best of times and he sends her over because he 'was tired' from work and she let him go to bed while she offered to sit with the girls. What the actual fuck? Does he not think I'm tired? Does he not want to see his children?

Another silence, shit do I speak? Was she actually asking me this? Nope, this is dangerous ground. I'm saying nothing.

"I bet she's just loving this. She gets her precious son home and the grandchildren she wants without the hassle of being nice to me. She's never liked me – and the feeling is mutual. As for him? He is a joke of a man. Not even a man, or a father. A glorified sperm donor. Yes, that's exactly what he is."

For the remainder of the drive, she continued to mutter to herself about her family. I could only make out bits and pieces but I'm pretty sure I picked out 'no jury would blame me'. That was the point I thought it best to speak up.

"Elle, we can totally do this another time. Perhaps at a time when you're feeling a bit less murder-y?"

"What? No! You're fine, this is exactly what I need. What's the alternative? Sitting at home with my mother-in-law, both of us shooting daggers at each other across the room?"

We pulled up to the shopping centre and I automatically walked towards the giant discount clothing store until I felt a sharp tug on my arm.

"Looking for leopard print are we?" Elle teased, "If we're doing this, we're doing it right. It's time we took

you away from the cheap fanny pads and discount bras.
If you are seducing your husband with my help then I
will not be associated with anything that comes from that
lingerie section."

"I didn't realise you were such a snob for someone
whose skirt has a giant rip in it," I replied.

"I'll have you know my darling daughter ripped this
stylish hole in my skirt, on purpose, with safety scissors
and now I use it as a kind of pocket. Anyway, I'm not
out to impress anyone – you are."

I knew she was taking me to the one 'sexy' shop in
this town. The one that is always empty, because
everyone is far too embarrassed to be caught dead
coming out of it, but has always stayed in business. I
guess their loyal clientele knew when the best times to
get in and out without meeting their old primary school
teacher and causing (both of) them to die of
mortification.

There was no point in asking Elle if we could do a
casual drive-by to make sure there was no one around
that I knew before going in, suggesting that was as good
as guaranteeing that she would shout my full name and
address as we entered.

I played with the tassel on the end of my handbag and
looked at the ground as we headed inside the neon pink
shop and hoped that I wasn't walking head first into a
mannequin. Thankfully, I didn't. Instead, I banged into
my darling ex-colleague, Rita.

Fucking, Rita.

"AMY!" she squealed, wholly unnecessarily. Now,
my incognito entrance was completely gone. I did a
quick scan of the people staring at the sound of the
squealing woman.

God, was that my old principal: Sr. Patricia?

"Rita," I replied, without an ounce of reciprocal enthusiasm, "how are you?"

I resisted the urge to add: "Still stabbing people in the back?" I didn't want to sound bitter.

"Gosh, I'm so busy; like you've no idea," she said, "You were such a smart cookie to get off that career ladder when you had the chance! I'm totally snowed under and I can see a little promotion on the horizon, cha-ching! You'll never guess how much this bracelet cost, a small fortune I tell you. I hate talking about money, it's completely ghastly but this was a steal for £10,000 - thank you disposable income. Thought I would come out and spread the wealth in the local business scene this evening. Like to do my bit for the little people. Your face! I'm kidding... no really; it's so good to help out around here, I'm all about shopping locally."

"This isn't exactly a struggling independent retailer, Rita? This is a huge chain," I said, confused by the onslaught of information I was getting within ten seconds of seeing her. I dreaded to think what Elle was making of all this.

"Oh, I know that. I just meant like keeping local people in their job. If there are no customers then there's no need for them. Anyway, it's so hard to find something that really fits well with my figure; it's constantly changing – I can't stop losing weight and toning up – I'm such a gym bunny. You know my motto: eat clean, train dirty. This perfect ass doesn't sculpt itself.

"I've always admired the way you were so comfortable with eating whatever the heck you wanted and never exercised – unless you call that sprint you'd do to the canteen when someone told us there was cake, *amIright*?"

The last part was spoken in an unbearably obnoxious fake American accent.

God, was she always this annoying?

I didn't chance looking at Elle in case she was trying to see what vibrator she could impale this wretch with.

"Look, I have to go I just have *so* much to do and some of us still have a little career to get on with," she continued, "Ugh, I'm just so jealous of all your free time and you're looking just lovely. Really…'you', you know?

"We totally have to catch up and I mean it this time. I know you're free all the time. miss no-job, but I will have to check my diary and text. I'd better run before I spend another obscene amount of money in there. I keep telling myself: 'Rita I know you have all this money but stop dropping £249 on lingerie.' I'm just so crazy like that. So, so good to see you."

And just like that, she was gone leaving little miss no-job and her friend with the ripped skirt in her wake.

"What just happened?" asked Elle, as she came out of a type of trance, "That poor woman."

"I'm sorry, poor her? She managed to rip me to pieces in under a minute. How insulting could she have been about my life, whilst simultaneously bragging about her own? That was repulsive."

"Yeah, maybe; but how sad must she be about her own life if she feels the need to boast about it constantly and put you down? I feel sorry for her."

"You never react the way I think you're going to, Elle."

"Thanks, I think?"

We meandered through the rows and rows of sex toys and my novice nature was clearly etched on my face because a walking, talking, fetus with a name-tag approached me to ask if I needed help.

"I don't want to be incredibly condescending here but I have stretch marks that are older than you, I really don't want to take sex advice from a tiny child," I said.

She mumbled 'bitch' under her breath, and I didn't blame her. Nerves hadn't brought out the best in my character but I wasn't in the mood to be polite to a teenager who wanted to talk to me about my clitoris.

"Amy, over here," called Elle from the back of the shop.

She was pulling up black latex gloves that went right over her elbow and she was looking fierce. I was terrified.

"Imagine rocking up to Smug Club with these bad boys on, eh? Throw me the whip over, this is epic."

That was a sentence I wasn't expecting to hear this morning, but I obliged. The sound from the first crack of the whip made the grumpy fetus assistant come over and ask again if she could help us.

"You've got a challenge on your hands tonight. We're going to kit out that very nervous looking woman over there and make her feel like an empowered, sex goddess, you got it?" Elle asked.

"We're closing in a half hour," she replied, dryly.

"Then you'd better move quick, darling," replied Elle.

She looked me up and down, trying to figure my size – well, that's what I hoped she was doing – and walked off.

"Fucking hell, what's her problem?"

"I may have been one of those horrible customers who are mean to young people about three minutes ago?"

"Ah. Well, then we'll be lucky if she brings back anything other than one of those giant inflatable penis costumes. Will that work?"

"Not funny."

Despite my rudeness, the grumpy fetus (real name: Lucy) brought back a selection of rather nice – albeit flimsy – lingerie. I was pushed into a changing room and faced with a cornucopia of choice, I nervously tried on the first item my hands reached.

It was lilac. I hated lilac.

It reminded me of my granny's house. I dutifully pulled the satin material over my head and shimmied around to make sure it was covering all the lumps and bumps.

"I don't feel very sexy," I called out to Elle.

"I'll be the judge of that, come out so I can have a look."

I walked out and was greeted with a large belly-laugh from Elle and a look of confusion from Lucy.

"Christ, alive! Amy, you're still wearing a fucking sports bra underneath, of course, you don't feel sexy. There's more material in that sorry excuse of a bra than the rest of the outfit."

"I thought it was more hygienic to keep it on," I pleaded.

"It's yellow, and I can see stains on it. Is it meant to be white?" she asked.

"I don't remember, it's been in my possession for…a while."

The yellowing material squashed down my chest into one tube-like mound and wasn't doing the sweetheart neckline of the lilac baby-doll nightie any favours.

"I'll go get some bras while we're at it," offered Lucy.

When she left, Elle pushed me back into the changing room and ordered me to take off the "monstrosity" that was my bra and promise to burn it when I got home.

The rest of the exercise was slightly more successful. I stayed firm on my stance of anything that resembled floss was to be kept away from my nether regions and we eventually settled on a black frilly number that helped keep things up where they were meant to. It also sucked in some of the mum-tum I was sporting.

I had to admit that I was impressed when I looked at the woman in the mirror. With a bit of lippy, she could pass for an attractive specimen that may even get her husband interested in putting down his phone for the evening to look at her.

"Can I get you anything else?" Lucy asked, already hoping we'd leave so she could close up and get home.

"Yes, let's see some bondage stuff," said a gleeful, Elle.

"Bondage? Are you kidding me?" I was already out of my depth by purchasing the black frilly napkin that I was trying to pass off as underwear.

"Trust me, you're going to need this with the next part of 'Operation Sex Kitten'"

"This humiliation has an operational name now, great!"

Lucy brought over a selection of bizarre looking items, one of which was a ball gag.

"No, just no. Let me stop you there, Lucy."

"These are just suggestions. Have you ever done a lap dance?" she asked.

"Oh yeah, quite a few when I was an exotic dancer on my last maternity leave. It was just to help keep the finances afloat."

"Really?" asked the shocked looking assistant.

"No, Lucy. I was not an exotic dancer but was there really need for *that* much shock on your face?"

"I just thought with your thighs it was a pretty risky employment. Dancers need to have these strong thighs for the pole dancing bits and yours, well, they're kind of flabby."

The silence was deafening as Elle and I just stared at her. While I was trying to decide which thickness of leather restraint would be best to strangle her with, Elle stepped in and thanked her for her help.

After Lucy strutted back to the till to start cashing up, Elle said:

"She doesn't know what she's talking about, I think you could crush a man with those thighs."

I flopped down on the hard plastic seat and let the feeling of utter shame wash over me.

"What am I doing here?" I said, "If I show up in this stupid black thing Ben won't know whether to laugh or run for the hills. This isn't me."

"That's the point though, isn't it? Getting out of your usual routine and doing something new? Please remember this whole makeover nonsense, or whatever you want to call it, isn't about pleasing him. Think of it as a self-care session for you."

My look of complete disbelief was enough to spur her on.

"You are never going to get over this sex drought with Ben until you start looking in the mirror and liking what you see. When you feel sexy, you'll want him to see you that way. It's empowering, not degrading or like you're tarting yourself up just to keep him happy. It's a win /win. Don't you remember the feeling of being desired when you first started going out with him? With anyone? It's intoxicating. I used to get such a high from the thought of this person being so obsessed with wanting to sleep with me that I would glow. Screw that pregnancy glow crap, I'm all about the pre-shag one."

I laughed, despite myself, and I figured I'd got this far I might as well go fully down the rabbit hole.

"So, what's this stuff then?" I asked as I gestured to the array of straps, whips and what I think was some kind of clamp.

"Lucy may have been on to something you know."

"Yeah? Well, the world of erotica has nothing to fear because I don't have any immediate plans to take up a new career as a dominatrix."

"I'm talking about the lap dance."

"No."

"Hear me out," she pleaded.

"No, Elle."

"Look, I'm not talking about some choreographed Broadway number, I'm just saying that a little dance would definitely surprise him. You don't even need this overpriced crap anyway, he could definitely gnaw his way out of these restraints no bother."

"Gnaw his way out? What the actual fu-"

"Ssh, calm down, you're doing that bulgy, angry eye look. Just sit him down on a chair in the bedroom, whack a couple of candles around the place, throw on a tune and wiggle your arse in that black thing and you're sorted. He'll think all his birthdays have come at once."

I had a list as long as my arm about the reasons why I wouldn't be agreeing to this suggestion but I was tired and I wanted to get away from the judgmental gaze of Lucy, so I just said 'ok' in the hope that would be the end of the conversation.

It wasn't.

The whole way home it was a barrage of questions like what moves had I planned? What music did I have in mind? Did I want her to make a playlist for me?

Staring out the window and largely ignoring these questions didn't work so I decided to change the subject.

"Are you going home to sit with your mother-in-law now?"

"I'd forgotten about that."

I knew that would get the attention off me, yes it was a cheap tactic but it worked for now and that's all I needed. I waved her off to deal with her in-law and I managed to arrive back home in the middle of bedtime chaos.

"Arthur, for the last time: WHERE ARE YOUR PANTS?" demanded Ben.

Another joy of parenthood is the bedtime routine. You may not believe it but the noise and the general shouting match was monumentally better than the infant days of night-feeds and the 15 other times they used to wake up for no real reason. It was like surviving years of medieval torture methods and still loving those that put you through it.

"Hey, mum's back!" shouted Ben, "Tag, you're it."

He grabbed his phone and ran up the stairs to retreat into his sanctuary – the toilet.

The amount of time that man spends in the toilet could be an entry in the *Guinness Book of Records*. I knew he was just sitting there, scrolling through his phone until he could hear the shouting or the tantrums come to an end. I don't call after him, to be honest, it gave me a break from him too.

"Right, boys," I said in my best authoritative voice, "Time to go to bed and leave your parents alone for a whole ten hours."

All three of us laughed because we knew it would be at least half that before one, or both, of them, snuck into my bed for some made-up reason.

I tucked each of them in and said a silent prayer - to any deity that may have been passing by the house at that particular moment – asking that I get a night of uninterrupted sleep.

Just as I was about to close the door and run down the stairs to freedom, and be reunited with my neglected phone, Adam took the opportunity to ask: "Mummy?"

"Yes, sweety?"

"When are you going to die?"

Crap.

"Not anytime soon, my love."

"Like what age?"

"I'll be at least 100."

"That's not that far away."

Seriously? Kids are such jerks.

"It's a long, long, LONG time away actually. Go to sleep."

I closed the door and decided to start using the expensive night cream that promised to make me look ten years younger overnight, or something like that.

I settled down on the sofa and my husband miraculously appeared out of the bathroom. He was also ready for our evening of staring at our phones whilst simultaneously pretending to be interested in whatever was on the tv.

"Did you get anything nice when you were out," he asked.

I decided that I should start setting the groundwork for the sensual extravaganza I had planned for Friday night. I'm cringed even thinking about it.

"That would be telling, now wouldn't it?" I said in my best flirty voice.

"Are you getting the cold? What's wrong with your voice?"

Yeah, that reaction sounds about right.

I tried again, committed to humiliating myself as much as possible, "I just mean I have a sexy surprise arranged for you, this weekend. You eh…gorgeous, piece of ass."

Where the hell did that even come from? Please let the ground swallow me up.

To say that Ben looked disturbed was an understatement, it probably didn't help that we were both sporting matching looks of confusion and embarrassment.

"Did you have a bit of wine while you were out? Or receive a concussion of some description?"

"Jesus, Ben! I'm trying here, can you work with me please?"

He shifted uncomfortably in his chair and sat down his phone and said: "Sexy surprise sounds great, you also have a nice bum?"

A look of panic was etched on his face but I decided we were going to power through this horrendous attempt at dirty talk.

"Thank you, sexy. I sometimes do squats."

"I can tell?"

"Can you tell? Are you asking a question? Never mind, just say something else."

"Can we just kiss, Amy? I'm rubbish at this."

"No, this is all part of the seduction before Friday. Now, tell me what you want to do right now?"

"I want to watch that zombie show we like, it's coming on now."

"I forgot about that. Yeah, shove that on."

I reasoned there would be plenty of time after the show to pick up where we left off. Besides, we wouldn't want too much practice at it. It was meant to be natural and romantic not like a pre-scripted performance.

I fell asleep on the sofa before the end of the show and we went to bed, side by side, but barely touching as usual. We didn't even kiss good-night anymore. I was convinced one of these days he was going to ask for a 'fist-bump' to end the day.

As he snored beside me I picked up my phone and decided to call in reinforcements. I frantically texted my sex guru and awaited instruction on how I could turn this train around.

Amy: I tried to talk dirty to Ben. It didn't go well; I think I'm not as sexy as previously believed. Help.

It didn't take long for her to reply with her usual sensitivity to my personal life.

Elle: I would give anything to have heard that. Did you tell him to keep the lights on when you shagged?

Firstly, I would never have the lights on, that's just off-putting for everyone but her smugness about how bad I was at this was unnerving.

Amy: Just shut up and help me. Joseph's tomorrow. Operation Sex Kitten is a go-go.

There was no harm in getting a refresher course in what constitutes as sexy these days and even if was a waste of time I reasoned I could get some launch night work done.

Elle: Alright princess, we'll get that libido going and I will enjoy your painful expression as you try to say the word 'moist' without dying of embarrassment. Lulla, out x

Chapter 19

The next day, Elle and I sat in the pretty little yard area of the café. We were surrounded by compost, ceramic plant pots, brightly coloured flowers and enough solar lighting to give the Vegas Strip a run for its money. We had been working sporadically in this area over the last few weeks. It had been used for empty boxes and random equipment that no longer worked. Joseph was a hoarder and instead of clearing this space for something pretty, like a little summer terrace, he would rather it be the burial ground for all the old sinks and dismantled extractor fans that time forgot. He'd given up arguing with us when we had a new idea. As long as the customers kept walking through the door he didn't really interfere with our great vision.

I liked it out here, I wished my garden would look as pretty. Mine still looked like it belonged in a dystopian universe. I liked to think that this was some sort of mindfulness exercise, but it was hard to be present and 'in the moment' when Elle kept asking me uncomfortable questions like: "Does Ben enjoy getting his arse played with?"

I was hoping that 'Operation Sex Kitten' would be forgotten about. I was stupid to have even texted her about my failed attempt at dirty talk. I knew I was never going to live this down, but I was running out of time and soon I would have to face the music with Ben.

To be honest, it was more of a countdown to drinking wine so I could feel confident enough to wear very little clothing and hope that I'm not rejected by my husband. Last night was more than a knock to my confidence but I was just going to have to bull through and hope that everything would just fall into place.

"You're going to have to talk me through the whole dirty talk scenario," she asked.

"No, I really don't. It was just horrendous and I don't want to even think about it, let alone talk about it."

"Why don't you text him some smut now, I'll help you. It's been ages since I've had a good sexting session. Keith was always great at it; to be fair to him he was pretty great at all the sex stuff. He is just a useless husband and father."

"Ah, well you see we're always told we can't have it all." I really hoped the sarcasm wasn't lost on her, otherwise, I would just sound like an unfeeling bitch.

"Give me over your phone and I'll send him something that will let him know what he's in for later. By the time he gets home, he'll be hornier than a sailor who's been at sea for the last six months. That was a clumsy metaphor, wasn't it? If that's the best I can come up with, it means it's time for coffee."

She got up to her feet and went into the kitchen to help herself, and probably give Michael some 'helpful' advice about being more assertive when it came to Joseph and his bullying ways. He would never do anything about it, of course. He seemed happy enough in his misery. I hoped that his marriage was worth the daily abuse.

I sat back on my heels and rummaged my phone out of my bag. Arthur was already at my parents' house because I couldn't listen to an entire day of 'are we going to our sleepover yet?' I knew my dad wouldn't say 'no' to me when I landed at their door first thing this morning. He was still awkward around me after our bonding session over art, but I was too preoccupied with my own troubles to worry about how he was feeling.

There were no text messages from an irate grandmother, so he must be behaving himself. I decided to text Ben to see how his day was going, I was not going to be taking Elle's suggestion of 'sexting' anything. I even hated the word.

Elle returned with two cups of coffee and balancing a plate with a huge tray bake on top.

"My theory is that if we share one of these chocolatey things it doesn't count," she said.

"It's huge."

"I was hardly going to pick a small one to share, was I? Oh, the filth is on, I see. Hand it over Cole I will take over from this."

In the time it took her to put the cups down and snatch my phone out of my hands I still didn't have time to stop her. I always did have the reactions of a dead sloth.

"Let's see what you've started with... **'how's your day going?'** Ah, come off it, Amy. You've got to just jump right in there and state your intention from the get-go."

She furiously typed on my phone and looked very pleased with herself after she hit 'send' and handed it back to me.

I dreaded to think what I was going to find, but to my surprise, it wasn't that bad:

Amy: What are you wearing? Xxx

"I could have answered that for you, he's wearing a blue striped shirt and navy trousers. I know this because I ironed them and sat them out last night before I went to bed," I said matter-of-factly.

"It's not an actual question to find out what he's wearing. I promise he's going to read that and be so excited. He knows what you're up to, you know what you're up, it's on. Trust me."

We didn't have long to wait to find out who was right.

Ben: What? I'm wearing that stripy shirt and trousers you laid out for me. Is this a trick question, was I not meant to wear these?

"What did I tell you?" I said, smugly.

"What the fuck are you two like? This is ridiculous, I'm surprised it's only been six months – I mean have either of you actually *had* sex before? Give me that fucking phone."

She, once again, grabbed the phone and started to type, whilst muttering under her breath.

"Now, if this doesn't get his attention you're on your own."

I read with horror what she had sent:

Amy: No, big man, I want to know what I'll be ripping off you tonight. I can't wait to get my hands on you xxx

I fought the urge to vomit in my own mouth and decided to wait and see what he made of this. You never know, maybe I didn't know him as well as I thought I did. Maybe saucy texts were what we were missing all along.

My phone buzzed. I didn't want to read it but I knew If I didn't react quickly Elle would just take it from me and see what her handy-work had achieved.

Ben: Would you mind not ripping this particular shirt off? I quite like it.

I smiled to myself, happy that things weren't so bad between us that I couldn't predict that he would find this exercise as embarrassing as I did. I was about to show Elle my message of victory when the phone buzzed again.

Ben: I can't wait to get my hands on you either. I'm going to put my penis in you. A lot.

I couldn't hide the revulsion in my face and impatience got the better of Elle. She grabbed the phone and read both messages. Her face mirrored mine and I just looked at her completely at a loss as to what I was meant to say back to that.

"Are you happy now? I've just received the most unsexy text message in history," I raged.

"I'm sorry! I really didn't think you could go wrong with sexting. I mean who the fuck says 'penis' when they want to sound sexy. It's so…clinical."

"I feel ill."

"Oh, stop the amateur dramatics. He's trying and that's the main point. He obviously thinks this is what you want to hear so we should just keep on the same line of chat."

"Are you serious? You really think we should carry on with this charade? I want to be able to look him in the eye again."

"Look, just a couple more messages then he'll be happy and excited about his evening with you and you can drink enough wine that will blot this whole experience from your memory. You asked for my help, and believe it or not, I'm trying."

I handed her back my phone and gave my silent assent for her to continue to seduce my husband while I lay on the ground with my hands over my eyes and tried to pretend this wasn't happening.

Just think of the wine, just think of the wine, just think of the wine.

She typed away, barely looking up from the screen and every so often she would laugh at what she'd written or at Ben's response. I stopped myself from getting up to read the exchange over her shoulder. I thought it was better just to let them get on with it and I would catch the recap at the end.

Shouldn't I be jealous? I mean, technically, he is talking intimately with another woman. No, he thinks he's talking to me and besides, he would be mortified (and probably furious) if he knew it wasn't me at the end of the phone. Elle was right, I asked for her help this was just a part of that. I hope.

After ten minutes she looked up and said:

"Alright then, my work here is done. We got there in the end I think."

"What do you mean 'got there'? He wasn't like playing with himself or anything?"

"Fuck no, just read the messages. You guys have a long way to go before you get to that level of intimacy. You're both as bad as each other."

She handed me the phone and went to leave the empty cups back into the kitchen. I took a deep breath and decided to face reading what I was letting myself in.

Amy: Of course I won't rip it...unless you're bad.
Are you a bad boy Ben?

Ben: Well…I've been known to leave the toilet seat up on occasion and I don't pick up my socks from the living room. So yes, yes I am.

Amy: That is bad, Ben. I'm looking forward to running my nails down your back when you put your penis in me a lot.

Ben: I would like that. I'm full of lots of sperm and it's definitely going to you.

Ben: In you?

Ben: to you? Duck I don't know which one, you can pick whichever is the right one.

Ben: Ducking autocorrect.

Ben: I give up

Amy: I'll see you later Ben. I'm moist thinking about you now.

Ben: That sounds nice. Like a nice ham.

She didn't reply to his last message. I think her patience must have reached breaking point at that stage. I don't think I had ever read a less sexy conversation between two people. He was trying though and that made me feel better about putting the effort in this evening with dressing up. Maybe the dance and the candles weren't such bad ideas after all. I decided it was better just to take it one step at a time this evening and see where it took me. Besides, if I overthought this too much I was likely to scare myself and end up in a onesie with a 'keep away' sign around my neck.

"I added the word 'moist' in especially for you, it seems like a word that would make your skin crawl," said Elle as she appeared behind me.

I laughed and found myself relaxing. There was an unfamiliar feeling in my tummy; one that I'd forgotten even existed. I was actually excited about seeing my husband and it wasn't just because we had time to stare at our phones without the kids around.

"Right, time for the next stage in our plan," said Elle, "Road trip!"

Chapter 20

I wasn't that impressed with our road trip. The first stop was to pick up her girls from outside Keith's work. He'd taken the morning off to spend with them and she arranged to pick them up from the front of the building before he went in. It dawned on me that I hadn't actually met him before. Sure, I'd seen photos of him but that's never what a person really looks like.

He was taller than I thought, a stocky build, and had more hair on his face than on the top of his head. I couldn't really see the attraction, but he was grimacing so I don't think I had caught him on a good day. I could tell the conversation between the two adults was tense and formal. By the time she came back to the car with the kids, she had plastered a fake smile on her face as to not alert the girls to whatever her real feelings were towards her estranged husband.

She put on the radio louder than normal and spoke to me through her teeth.

"He's not taking them this weekend, again," she said, "Claims he has to work but that's such bullshit. I don't know why he's acting like this, but I'm not letting him away with it. If he wants to see these girls then he has to stick to a schedule and if he can't do that then he's not getting to see them. Unfit parent. End of. I haven't told them yet. I'll get chocolate first."

I hated not knowing what to say, and to my shame, all I kept thinking was how relieved I was that Ben and I hadn't got to the point where we were discussing custody schedules.

"This all sounds very definite," I said, "Is there no working things out."

"I don't know Amy, I really don't. I mean he hasn't mentioned anything about coming home and when I asked him about marriage counselling he changed the subject. I mean what am I meant to do with that? Has this break turned into a break-up but he just didn't bother to tell me? Either way, he's acting like a complete arsehole and I can't be bothered to try and talk him around. I'm concentrating on the girls because clearly, he's not."

The rest of the journey was done in silence and I didn't ask where we were headed, I didn't think it mattered at this stage. I needn't have worried, we pulled up at a huge chemist department store. I was familiar with this place at least.

"I'm going to take the girls over to that chipper and have a chat with them. You are to go get some makeup that will update your luxurious supermarket collection. We don't have time for au naturale beauty this evening, we want to knock his socks off."

She was gone before I could even respond, but I knew she was right. No point in half-assing things at this stage. I hated the make-up counters in these places. The women manning them were either too orange or too perfect. Either way, no one liked when I said I preferred looking pale. I'm pretty sure the name of my foundation colour was 'death'. I accepted I was pale a long time ago and I wish the rest of the world would catch up. This didn't do me any favours though. Even though I was pale the majority of the time, if I decided to skip a day without wearing foundation I still got asked if I was sick.

On numerous occasions in work I had to stop myself from saying:

"No, Rita I'm just not wearing any make-up, you bitch."

Fucking, Rita.

I browsed in a non-committal way and half-heartedly picked up a few mascaras. I didn't really know what I was looking for. What did a sex kitten paint her face with? The way Elle talked about it made me feel like I shouldn't be looking for anything less than full-blown war paint.

"May I help you?" asked a very pretty Oompa Loompa.

"No, I'm just really looking. Thanks anyway."

"No, don't worry it's my pleasure. So, are you looking for everyday wear or is this for a special occasion?"

Clearly, the Oompa Loompa wasn't taking no for an answer.

"A special occasion, I guess."

"Well, you are in luck. Our very talented make-up artist, Cheryl, is here today and she can do a makeover in store. That way you're all ready to paint the town red and if you like the look then you can buy exactly what she's used for you to replicate it at home. Lucky or what?"

I'm never getting out of here alive.

I was shepherded towards the counter and told to take a seat where I was greeted by the aforementioned Cheryl. Again very pretty, but was buried under a slightly radioactive-looking orange tinge. I was caught off guard by her Birmingham accent and I just let Oompa Loompa One speak for me.

"Now, this lovely lady has a very special occasion to get ready for and I told her you'd look after her," she said with a sickly sweet smile. I watched, helplessly, as she walked off to stalk her next prey.

"If that tangerine bitch thinks she's getting the commission for this sale after I do the actual work of doing the make-up she's another think coming," said Cheryl.

I wasn't entirely sure if she was talking to me, but I was too nervous to agree or disagree with her.

"First things first, we are taking this skin tone up a few hundred shades." If I wasn't nervous enough with this statement, the manic laughter afterwards was enough to keep me on edge.

Forty-five minutes later I was handed a mirror. I didn't recognise the person staring back at me. Gone was the deathly pale skin tone I wore with pride, replaced by a shade that brought the word 'cheese puff' to mind. She had assured me I was getting a subtle smoky eye look, however, I looked like a panda.

I was furious.

I was going to give her a piece of my mind when the original Oompa Loompa came back to praise the work.

"Oh, wow! What a transformation. You'll turn heads, tonight, Debs, come over here and see the great job Cheryl did.

"Oh, wow! What a transformation. You'll turn heads, tonight," she said.

"I've just said that," laughed Oompa Loompa One, "didn't I just say that? That means it's just double wow."

I turned round to face Cheryl, who was handing me a bag with all the products she'd used to complete this miracle makeover.

"That's £97.85," she said.

You've got to be fucking kidding me. I swear to God, Amy, if you pay this you're a lost cause. You should ask for a wipe immediately instead of paying for the 'privilege' of looking like Donald fucking Trump.

I dutifully handed over my credit card. I was never going to have the nerve to actually tell this woman she had turned me into a walking carrot. I would just buy the stuff and never return here again, that was the much easier option.

"Thank you," I said.

You're a fucking idiot.

I reached into my phone to call my chauffeur and see if I could grab her keys to hide out in the car in case anyone I remotely recognised saw me.

The phone rang out.

Where the hell was she?

Then I heard it:

"Amy? Amy Cole, is that you? Well, don't you look... different?"

"Hi Rita," I replied, as monotonously as possible.

Of course it was Rita, why else would the universe let any other person on the planet be standing in front of me right now, other than Rita?

"I can't talk long, you know how it is. Busy, busy. I just decided to go on a little splurge between meetings. We can't all be ladies of leisure like you! And where are the little excuses you used to leave your career?"

I knew this wasn't an actual question; she was taking a half second to catch her breath and carry on with her passive aggressive attack. My eye makeup was on so thick and the fake lashes, Cheryl had unceremoniously stuck on, were weighing down my eyes. I would have been quite happy to go for a little nap.

"I had run out of my favourite, must-have, eyeshadow. There are actual tiny grains of gold in the shadow, it really makes the green of my eyes pop. It even makes me less tired looking when I've had a late night with the girls at the latest rooftop bar. Maybe you should try it? Wind that clock back to when you didn't have those little rugrats keeping you up all hours and adding years to you! Ha! I'm kidding, no seriously you're looking fabulous as always. I'm loving this new look, really suits you. I'm so glad you decided to ditch that pale-girl-don't-care attitude. I mean it was fine when you were in your twenties but it really does you credit that you've decided to step up the beauty routine. Your husband will thank you for it, I mean he must wake up with a fright looking at that white pallor! Anyway, darling, I have to run. We must, must, *must* get that lunch. I will definitely text you next week and arrange. Love you!"

She was gone before I even had the chance to say 'good-bye' or 'drop dead'. I decided I had enough of people and was going to camp outside Elle's car and just wait for her to come back.

It didn't take long for the three of them to appear with ice creams and smiles. The girls didn't seem too bothered by the news their dad was letting them down. I'd assumed that was the work of the sugar in their system. Elle took one look at me and said:

"Only you could go into a chemist for some fucking mascara and come back looking like a glow stick. Get in the car you absolute bell-end."

Chapter 21

We drove back to her house and she told me to go have a shower to 'de-fuzz' and 'get that shit off my face'. It took longer than I thought and by the time I was downstairs again, Elle was already setting up her makeup collection on the kitchen table.

"That is a lot of makeup for someone who doesn't wear any," I said.

"That's a laugh, it takes a hell of a lot of makeup to make it look like I'm wearing fuck all, trust me."

I made her promise to keep me pale and not put enough slap on that Ben wouldn't be able to pick me out of a line-up. After a half hour, she handed me a mirror, I could have cried but it would have spoiled the mascara – I looked beautiful.

I was pale and beautiful with subtle smoky eyes and suspiciously fuller looking lips. I was so happy. Elle marvelled at her handy work and called the girls in to praise me too. I left her house with a glow and went home to try and make the house look a bit more romantic, as well as change into the dreaded black number.

But first: wine.

I didn't mind stopping at the off license this early in the day because I was so dolled up people would have to assume I was going to some party and not an alcoholic.

As I turned to leave, I caught my server give me a wink. Usually, I would have been disgusted by this but my new look was bringing out the unbearably shallow part of me that screamed: "he thinks I look pretty."

Eleanor Roosevelt is disgusted with you.

I decided on the fancy ready meals from the supermarket. That way, we could have something nice to eat without the hassle of me actually having to cook it and him running the risk of food poisoning.

Nothing kills romance dead like hearing your lover excrete the entire contents of their bowels over the course of a few hours.

I picked a white wine to go with the fish dish; I didn't give more thought to the drink choice than that. I just remembered being told that white wine went with fish. I don't know what kind of white goes with which kind of fish but I was pretty sure that the one that was on offer for 'three bottles for £12' would go down a treat. I wasn't exactly a sommelier.

I had my first glass of Dutch courage before I'd even taken my coat off. I decided to put some music on while I 'prepared' the food and cleaned about the kitchen. I dug out all the tea-light candles I could find, from under the sink, and started indiscriminately placing them all over the room.

I was pleased by my natural knack for romance and decided to head upstairs to find a suitable dress to wear to dinner. I didn't think the lingerie was a suitable choice for the meal.

Maybe it is? No - what if one of my nipples pop out as I cut into my food, that's just not pleasant for anyone.

I imagined when other people look through their wardrobe they decide on which colour would best suit

them for that particular occasion; when I look at mine
I'm greeted with a sea of black. Black for every occasion
just about works for me. My version of a 'summer
wardrobe' is the time of year I changed the black tights
and boots for black leggings and sandals. I hated
shopping at the best of times but now I wished I had
something remotely fancy for the evening. I settled for a
pair of jeans and a T-shirt, my defence being that the
lingerie will make up for the, seemingly, lack of effort I
had made.

I put the food in the oven and remembered to take the
plastic wrap off so we wouldn't have ingested something
a lot more dodgy than my normal cooking. I looked at
the clock and realised there was at least an hour before
Ben would be coming home. I poured myself another
glass of wine and settled down to the kitchen table. I was
too antsy to scroll through my usual social media sites,
so I decided to video call mum and see how she was
holding up with the boys.

She answered almost instantly, meaning she had the
phone in her hand.

Welcome to the lazy parenting club, mum

So far all I could see was the pink tinge of skin, no
doubt she had put the phone up to her ear to speak
without realising it was a video call.

"Mum put the camera down towards your face, I can't
see you," I shouted.

"Oh! Hang on. Right, there we go. Hello Amy."

"Hi, mum. How are the boys?"

"You could have warned me about the utter nonsense
that goes on at that school run, I thought your father was
going to have a heart attack with the stress of it all."

"Isn't video calling fun? This way you can give out to my face, as if I were really there."

"Stop the dramatics, Amy, you know I mean well," she snapped.

"How are the boys?" I asked, again.

"They're fine, they're helping their grandfather in the garden. They're digging, or something, I don't really know. I needed them out from under me while I typed a review."

About two years ago my mother discovered the internet and ever since she has managed to go international with her withering criticisms. She's not an internet troll per se; she just likes to leave overly harsh reviews for anywhere she's ever been. It keeps her happy and she finds it much more satisfying than snail mail. Gone are the days when she would write letters to places she was disappointed in and receive a politely worded reply (if any). Now she was given instant access to those that 'wronged' her.

"Have they had dinner?"

"We're getting chips from the takeaway place I like – although I did tell them they were on thin ice with our custom if they kept being so liberal with the salt."

"Send me pictures of them."

"Of the chips?"

"No, mum, of the boys."

"Why?"

"So I can see what they're doing. I miss them, the house is quiet."

"Well, you should have thought about that before you palmed them off on your elderly parents so you could laze around. Wouldn't get that in my day, that's for sure. My mother had spent her life raising her own children, she would never have agreed to start raising mine. You have it lucky."

"Good-bye, mum. I'll phone you in the morning."

Usually, my reply would have been quite snippy and I would have spent the evening re-running what I should have said. However, that wasn't going to happen tonight. Tonight, I was relaxed and happy to sip my wine while I waited for my husband to come home. We were going to have a nice dinner, free from forkful negotiations and the word 'poo'.

I could feel my whole body relax with every sip.

There were still 45 minutes on the clock and I was at a loss as to how to kill the time. I grabbed my phone and decided to put on some music. I was beginning to regret not taking Elle up on her offer to make a playlist for the evening, I had no idea what music goes with fish.

I decided to look up 'romantic songs'. The usual cheesy nonsense came up, ones that are played at every single wedding you've ever been to. I knew they would be fine for ambience over dinner, but it wouldn't really suit dessert.

By 'dessert' I meant: the awkward sexual encounter I was preparing for, by drinking my second glass of wine.

I changed tact and decided to try 'sexy songs'. I barely recognised any of the titles in this category, owing to the fact that I only listened to radio stations that played songs from the eighties.

I clicked on the first playlist I could find and tapped my feet along with the synthesized beat. It was quite catchy and it definitely went with my wine.

I could be a sommelier yet. There's a summery beat with a touch of autumnal grape. Maybe, I'm not ready for that change of career just yet.

I sat in my chair, listening to the next song and the next. They all sounded pretty similar and I had to keep checking my phone to make sure I hadn't just hit repeat on the very first one. The wine made my head feel a bit lighter and my legs were beginning to feel numb. My blissful state was interrupted by the timer on my phone alerting me to put on the remainder of the ready-meal containers. I had this romantic night in the bag. I loved feeling this smug about my abilities in the kitchen. It was easy when all I had to do was put things in the oven and pour myself another half glass of wine.

Just a half, I don't want to get too sloppy before he even gets home.

By the time I heard Ben's keys jingle in the door I had finished my sensible half glass and was concerned that there was barely a glass left in the bottle for Ben.

Clever me for buying three

He came in to find me half dancing, half swaying to the music. I couldn't tell if he was smiling, but he wasn't frowning, so I must not have looked too drunk.

He gave me a kiss on the forehead and I pulled his hips towards me to make him dance along to the music. Almost instantly he removed my hands and said he was going upstairs to get changed.

"Don't you mean 'get naked'?" I said, a little too eagerly.

"Eh, no. Just getting out of my work clothes."

What a spoilsport. This is going to be harder than I thought.

I was thankful for the wine in my bloodstream and found myself getting more into the music, with every passing second.

"Young people have it so lucky with this music," I called up to Ben, "I can definitely see myself in some hot new nite club gyrating to this with a toyboy."

He didn't answer.

My fantasy about the toyboy was getting a bit too graphic so I decided that maybe the wine was going to my head. I should go back to the romantic old tunes over dinner instead. I found a suitable selection of crooners while I dished out the food.

I was pleased to find that nothing was burnt – nor had any of the packaging melted onto the food.

I considered getting rid of the packaging to try and convince him that I had made it all from scratch but because he once thought my attempt at risotto was 'gruel' I didn't think I would get away with it.

I served up the food as delicately as I could and waited for him to come down the stairs. As I was about to sit down I realised that I hadn't lit the candles so I scurried around the room lighting them and burning my fingers with wax nearly every time I set one down. I had two large candles on the table and managed to light them without setting the tablecloth on fire, so again, things were going well.

I couldn't tell if Ben was blown away by the romantic setting he came into or if he was completely overwhelmed by the heat from the dozens of candles and the oven.

Did he just say 'wow' or 'phew'? Best not dwell on it.

"Come and sit down and enjoy this food and sit down," I announced.

"You said 'sit down' twice," he replied as he wiped his forehead, "Bit warm with all the candles, isn't it?"

"It's called setting the mood and I am here to tell you, Mr Cole, the mood is being set."

"Are you ok?"

"Yes, I'm more than great, I'm ok."

He spotted the empty bottle of wine and said:

"Started the party without me I see?"

"Oh stop with the judgy judgment eyes. It helped me create this magnificent feast I've put together. Besides, there's more wine in the fridge and I really think I've picked correctly because I've decided that I could be a Somali."

"What?"

"A wine expert, it's a legitimate career and I think I have the knack for it."

"A sommelier?"

"Yes, now stop yammering and we'll sit down and have a nice meal together and be nice to each other."

So far, I was confident that he hadn't picked up quite how tipsy I was, but I thought I should slow down my wine intake just in case. I handed him a glass and I sat down opposite him. I thought each of us sitting at either end of the table would make it feel like we were at a banquet. The problem was I couldn't actually see his face because the two giant candles were in the way. It was quite disconcerting having a romantic meal with a talking candle. I felt a bit like Moses and his burning bush.

"How was your day?" he asked.

"The usual, just chiselling the Ten Commandments and such."

"That sounds nice," he said absentmindedly, as he picked through the meal in front of him, in search of raw fish. I didn't mind that he wasn't listening to my reply, I barely listened to him when he droned on about work either, but that was the problem here: complacency.

"Ben, I know you're just a talking candle right now but I think we should be making the most of this evening and actually listen to each other. For God's sake, stop inspecting your food! If I wanted to kill you I would have smothered you in your sleep years ago."

"And they say romance is dead," he replied.

I moved the candles over to the sideboard and was instantly assured that I was, in fact, talking to a human.

After that, the rest of the meal went well. We spoke – and listened – to each other as the wine flowed. It was so relaxing to enjoy each other's company and it made me realise it had been a long time since we had made the effort to do so. We'd been so preoccupied with just functioning day-to-day we had forgotten to actually live as well.

When dinner was over, we left the dishes at the table and walked hand-in-hand into the living room. We were both a bit giddy and I had even convinced him to dance a little with me to the music on the television.

"This isn't that bad," he conceded.

"I know? I thought this young people music was all a bit naff but this is grand."

I gave him a kiss and it went on for longer than I expected. Things were definitely heading in the right direction so I asked him to wait on the sofa and enjoy the warbles of one of those miserable-looking teenagers while I slipped into something else.

I tried to wink at him, but the weight of the fake eyelashes and the wine just made me do a prolonged blink. By the time I opened my eyes again Ben was looking at me and trying to figure out if I had, actually, just fallen asleep on my feet.

I ran up the stairs two at a time and by the time I got to the top I needed to dry heave.

I really need to exercise more.

I stood at the top, leaning up against the bannister and holding my side which had sprung a painful stitch. The recovery was taking a worryingly long time.

Why didn't I just walk up the bloody stairs?

I pulled out my secret purchase from the bottom of my wardrobe and laid it out on the bed.

Along with the black 'thing', Elle had also convinced me to buy a suspender belt and stockings. She assured me these extra details would make him 'blow his mind and his load.'

I felt ill when she said that.

Setting my nausea aside, I started to get ready and pulled the labels off with my teeth. I laughed at the thought of him seeing me now – hopping on one foot trying to get the damned thing on – it wasn't exactly gracious or sexy. I was thankful he would only see the finished article: a sweaty, out of breath, finished article.

I was trying my very best to rub the stockings up my legs. I had a terrible habit of ripping at least one pair of tights before even getting out the door and I didn't have a spare pair of these. Something told me my thermal navy woolly tights wouldn't really go with the rest of the ensemble.

After ten minutes of struggling with this contraption, I was tired, hot and not feeling in the least bit sexy. I decided to lie down on the bed to get my composure and when I closed my eyes I could feel the room spinning. I wasn't sure if I was *that* unfit or if I was drunk. Either way, I had to stand up in case I vomited or fell asleep. I took one last look in the mirror and decided that 'Operation Sex Kitten' was a success.

I looked like a new woman – this may have had something to do with the fact that my eyesight was a bit blurry and I wasn't entirely sure that it was me in the mirror. The wine had given me the false bravado I needed, but also made it difficult to see two feet in front of me.

At the last minute I grabbed a pair of stupidly high heels and popped them on. As I tottered down the stairs I heard that Ben had decided he was no longer impressed with the 'new chart releases' and had switched something a bit more mellow. I think that was Neil Diamond.

Fuck, please don't be Neil Diamond I can't bear to think about him and what he may or may not do with hamsters. That's not sexy. Think sexy thoughts, think sexy thoughts...

New stationery

Organised Tupperware cupboards with no lids missing

Brand new bed sheets

Yeah, that's the stuff, now we're back on track.

I shouted to Ben to change the music and strip down to his underwear while I wobbled my way into the kitchen to get a glass of water. Now was my time to shine and I didn't want to ruin it by falling head first into the fireplace.

Can you imagine the absolute mortification of going to A&E on a Friday night for stitches on your forehead because you were trying to be sexy? It doesn't bear thinking about.

I found the remains of my last glass of wine from dinner and decided that a final shot of courage would help things go smoother rather than water.

Once I let that settle in my stomach I had a flash of inspiration. If I was really going to score, tonight, I was going to have to really sell this new, sexy persona of mine.

I grabbed one of the giant candles from the sideboard and dragged one of the kitchen chairs behind me into the living room. With each step, I dropped another blob of wax onto my wooden floor and I remained thankful that I hadn't relented and put carpet everywhere like my mother suggested. She was convinced the house would be perpetually cold with wood and tiles everywhere – 'sterile' I believe she called it.

Stop thinking about your mother, you weirdo. Sexy thoughts, come on!

Parallel parking in one go

That time you had no make-up on and got carded for wine

Remembering every word to that Missy Elliot song you like and not messing it up

Ok, we're back in business.

I made my grand entrance and awaited my husband's gasp of disbelief at the sex goddess that lay before him.

He was asleep.

"BEN!" I screamed.

There wasn't a hope that this was the way the night was ending. He jumped out of his skin and rubbed his eyes.

He looked more terrified than aroused. In his defence, he had been woken up by a flushed looking dominatrix wielding a candle.

"I'm awake," he said, drowsily, "Well don't you look...cute."

Cute? What am I, a puppy?

"I'll show you cute," I replied, sounding a little more menacing than sexy, "Come over here and sit on this chair."

He looked rather uneasy, moving his gaze from me to the candle and back again.

I beckoned him over with my finger and tried to set the candle down on the mantelpiece to make him more at ease. As I stretched over to my destination, I realised too late that I had overextended. I began to topple over to the side as Ben jumped up and grabbed the edge of the lingerie. With my trip to A&E averted, I composed myself once more and sat the candle down squarely on the wood. I asked him to sit down on the chair once again.

He nervously did as he was told and took the seat. The wine and the power trip had well and truly gone to my head, so, I decided to throw caution to the wind.

How hard can a lap dance be anyway? I've seen many a dance floor with gyrating drunk people on them, I could do that. I gave birth – twice! What the fuck is a little dancing compared to that?

I took off his shoes and used his socks as make-do restraints. I clumsily pulled off his trousers and left him sitting on the chair in his superhero underwear. With his hands tied behind his back he was at my complete mercy. The look of nervousness hadn't completely gone but he did manage a half smile at this change in the proceedings.

I changed the channel back to the new releases which had a predictably synthesized beat on, and I started my 'routine'.

It wasn't a routine, as such. It was mostly me shaking my hips from side-to-side as I tried to keep my balance on the stupid heels. As it progressed, I decided to ditch the heels.

I walked towards the window and seductively ran my hand down one leg to take off the first shoe. It popped off into my hands and I threw it over his head so it landed on the sofa.

I repeated the process on the other leg but this time decided to be playful. I threw the second one over my shoulder like a bride with her bouquet.

"JESUS FUCKING CHRIST, AMY!" He wailed.

It took me a second for the reality to sink in.

I heard the shout and turned around to find his nose streaming with blood as my shoe lay at his feet.

"What were you thinking? You know you can't throw?!"

"Oh yeah because I'm a woman, is this really the time to be sexist?" I countered.

"No, Amy, because you're a fucking health hazard not because you have two 'X' chromosomes."

I ran into the kitchen to get a tea towel to soak up the blood and decided to pour him – and me - another glass of wine, for medicinal purposes.

I came in with the towel and his wine.

"Can you untie me?"

"What? Why?"

"I've just been hit in the face with a shoe, Amy."

"Yes, that's what the towel is for. Now here, drink some wine while I soak up the blood."

"There's blood?"

"I thought you realised that. It's fine, just a little."

"Please untie me."

"No! This is going to go much better from now on, trust me."

"You just hit me in the face with your shoe. Actual shoe in my actual face."

I shoved the wine glass into his mouth and smiled. The blood was practically all gone but his nose was pretty red so I decided that we needed to kick this up a gear before the mood was finally lost to all.

I took a sneaky gulp from his glass and left it beside the candle on the mantelpiece. There was no time for sexy thoughts to get me in the mood, I just had to power through and get it done.

I turned up the volume on the tv to drown out Ben's confused shouts of: "Amy? What are you doing? Untie me, I'm bleeding!"

Thanks to the years of being able to drown out my husband's voice, I was easily able to concentrate on the bass line of the music, once more. I tried to make the dance routine impressive enough to make him a happier hostage but it wasn't working.

Just as I was about to attempt a twirl, the music abruptly ended and was followed by a decidedly less upbeat song.

It was a love song about a heartbroken girl and it was not the stuff of lap dances. I half-heartedly gave a bit of a shake but I could tell that Ben was getting more and more pissed off by the second. It didn't help that the bleeding had started again.

He glared at me and I knew I should have given up, but instead I grabbed the remote and gave one last attempt to rescue the disaster of an evening.

I flicked through the channels to find the first video I could see not featuring a sad woman, looking out a window into the rain.

I settled for death metal.

It was a panic move but it was, at least, up-tempo and I needed to really get a move on before he lost more blood.

I jumped up and down with my hands in the air like I was in a mosh pit.

Jiggly boobs are bound to look sexy, aren't they?

I jumped until the stitch at my side reappeared and I felt the underboob sweat gathering. I caught a glimpse of an amused Ben and decided I was onto a winner. I started to head bang and walk slowly towards him, being careful not to head-butt him in the process.

When I reached the chair I got him to open his legs so I could run my hair over his thighs.

This was another mistake.

Ben was notoriously ticklish so his knee-jerk reaction was to kick out, shoving his knee squarely into my chin. The force made me fall back on my ass.

"Ah! I'm so sorry! It was just an instinct to being tickled," he said. He pulled at the restraints more and made the knots tighter with every pull.

I put one hand up to let him know I was 'totally fine' and used the other to rub my chin.

On your feet champ, we've got one more trick up our sleeves. Fuck, I think I've bitten my tongue.

I returned to my mosh pit moves, albeit slightly less enthusiastically than before, but I kept going as I turned to the mantelpiece.

"Yuff been a wery bad boy, Ben," I tried to sound sexy but I just sounded ridiculous.

"I'm so sorry. Seriously? Still with this?"

I picked up the candle and walked back towards him.

"It's a well-known fact that a little pain heightens the thenses."

"What are 'thenses?' What are you doing with the candle?" There was definitely a panicked edge to his voice now.

"Twust me," I said, as I poured the melting wax down his thigh and I waited for the sound of his pleasure.

It was a strange feeling - knowing I was on the cusp of a new age in our relationship. We'd been together for so long that we just assumed we'd done it all, in terms of sex. However, tonight, heralded a whole new era for us as lovers.

I wonder what he'd want to try next? I mean the world really is our oyster.

By the time I tuned back into my surroundings I realised that I was kneeling too close to Ben the whole time and had let all the pooling wax pour completely over his leg. It was cooling quickly, dripping down and entrapping a lot of leg hair. In my hurry to get away I managed to singe a large portion of the remaining wax-free hair on his thigh. That didn't help with the screaming situation.

There was a lot of screaming.

He screamed.

I screamed.

I blew out the candle and lay back on the mat, in the middle of the room.

I told myself to get up and fetch some scissors, or a knife, to undo the impenetrable knots he'd caused by pulling at his sock restraints.

I just need to rest my eyes until the room stops spinning.

Is there someone shouting my name in the distance?

This mat really is so comfy and my eyes are so heavy.

I've had a very busy day, what harm would a little nap do?

Isn't there something I'm forgetting?

I'll probably remember in the morning.

Chapter 22

"So, what you're telling me is: you set your husband on fire?" asked, Elle.

It was a few days after the debacle that was my night of debauchery with Ben. My head was still pounding – again, the joys of hangovers in your thirties. He still wasn't speaking to me, I didn't blame him. I did leave him tied up, bleeding and singed. When I thought about it like that, it sounded a lot more sinister.

When I woke up on the mat, the next morning, I saw the carnage that was left. The kitchen chair was toppled on its side, the socks were ripped to shreds and there was a trail of dried wax and droplets of blood, leading from the living room right up to our bedroom. He was passed out, face down on the bed, sound asleep, or concussed, I couldn't tell.

I crawled in beside him, still dressed in my ridiculous outfit, stinking of wine and tried to piece together the evening. I could remember a surprising amount of it for once and I had no idea how I was going to fix my relationship now. By the time he woke up and realised I was beside him my hangover had fully set in and I ran to the bathroom to get sick. I spent most of the day curled up on the tiles on the bathroom floor because it was cool on my skin. My parents left the children home and I just about managed to wave from the top of the stairs. My unsympathetic mother shouted about the dangers of food poisoning up to me but I was too busy making my way back to my spot on the floor to care.

The days that followed had been miserable. I tried to explain how sorry I was, but anytime I walked into a room he would limp out to a different one. I imagined he wasn't feeling very receptive to my apologies after suffering third-degree burns, all in the name of romance.

Today I managed to venture back into the outside world but had to keep my sunglasses on inside because my head was still pounding and I couldn't figure out if it was the remains of a hangover or the anxiety of the situation at home.

"I mean, you actually assaulted him. What part of your brain thought this was going to be sexy?" she continued.

"Please stop talking and get me water, I can't stomach coffee yet and I think I'm still dangerously dehydrated."

We were sitting at the counter at Joseph's and I was trying to get my head around the fact that I may have permanently scarred my husband.

"We can fix this, all you have to do is…"

"No," I said firmly, "No more advice, or suggestions or plans. I've royally screwed this up.I know Ben, and right now he needs time to calm down before we can have a proper conversation about what the hell is going on in our relationship."

She fell quiet for a whole three seconds before she started humming to fill the silence.

"Are you ever quiet?"

"The girls were with their father last night, I've had enough quiet thank you very much. I'm used to noise and shouting and mess. Without it, I feel uneasy or something. Shall we get on with this launch night list? Or have you forgotten about how much we have left to do."

Like I could forget.

The menu was finalised, all the regulars and the community groups that were using here as their base had all RSVP'd and I managed to get quite a decent band for the music. A band was a bit of a stretch, it was two brothers I met on the high street while they were busking. It was going to be a black-tie event, much to the horror of Joseph but he didn't have a choice (it's not like he was the owner or anything). I rested my head on the countertop and let Elle talk about fairy light placements for the inside. I wasn't particularly listening when she stopped midsentence.

"Fuck me," she uttered.

"Swear Jar," I replied without lifting my head.

"Excuse me, I'm looking for the manager," said a very stern looking man with a clipboard.

"Yeah, no worries, mate," replied Elle.

She disappeared into the kitchen to locate Joseph while I tried to pretend I wasn't a hungover mess. It didn't take long for Elle to push Joseph out from the kitchen. He reached out his hand to greet the stranger in the suit.

"Mr Blanco?" he asked.

"Yes, sir…how can I help you?" his usual friendly tone was there but it seemed guarded.

"We've had several phone calls from concerned citizens detailing some serious allegations regarding health code violations," he said.

"Violations? Like what?" I demanded.

"What citizens?" said Elle, mirroring my outrage.

"Mr Blanco, can we continue this conversation in private and then I will be conducting a spot investigation throughout the premises as well as checking all paperwork is present and up-to-date."

The colour was draining from Joseph and he silently ushered the inspector down the hallway towards his tiny office.

"This is all we need," said Elle, "What violations? Joseph runs a tight ship and it's not like Michael would ever dare slack off hygiene wise, he'd be terrified."

I ran through the possibilities of what or who would do this. If the claims were unfounded – and I was certain they were – then it was completely obvious who was behind it.

"You know this was the work of that witch down the road, don't you?" said Elle.

"I'm beginning to think that, yes."

"I think we should go down the street and kick her arse," she suggested.

I wasn't entirely confident that she was kidding. I peered over my glasses to check.

Nope, she isn't joking

I watched her take off her apron and come to my side of the counter.

"What do you think that would achieve?" I asked.

"Why does it have to 'achieve' anything? Why can't it just be about releasing some anger at someone who completely deserves it? Actually, screw this, I'm not debating this with you. I'm going down there to give her a piece of my mind and an imprint of my fist in her face."

She took off with a purposeful stride and I called to Michael to man the front of the café, while Joseph was busy.

It didn't take long for me to catch up with her, she was angry but not exactly fast.

"So, what's the plan here? Go assault this woman in front of a room full of children and get arrested? I'm sure Keith would love to lord that over you."

She stopped dead in her tracks.

"Don't you dare try that on me," she said, her voice barely above a whisper, "I will do as I please and my darling husband can go to hell."

Although the determination in her stride was still there as she began to walk again, I knew I had given her something to think on and help hold some of her anger back.

"For God's sake, Amy!" she said, "I'm not letting her get away with this, she's trying to ruin his shop and for what? Because we don't want to hang out in her poxy club? She needs to be taken down a peg or two and if you're not going to let me punch her in her smug bloody face then you better have a better idea."

I didn't.

We kept walking as I tried to think of something that would get our point across but also not leave us facing criminal charges.

Put her car wing mirrors in? Too small

Kick off the wing mirrors? Too big

Find a rabid badger and realise it into the group? Definitely too big

We stopped at the gate outside the car park, it was full – as usual.

"What's her fucking problem? It's hardly like she's starved of business? There's plenty to go round," said Elle, "So, brains, what's the plan of action? Am I peeing in a bottle and lobbing it at the window?"

"No, Elle!"

"Keep your knickers on, I was kidding."

I knew she wasn't.

"Which one is her car?" I asked as I peered through the bars of the railings.

"That big minivan thing."

I stayed hunched over and snuck up to the car.

"Now, we're talking," whispered Elle.

I kept my crawl technique going until I arrived at the front of her car and reached up to the windscreen wipers. I pulled both of them up, did the same at the back and pushed in her wing mirrors.

Take that minor inconvenience to your next trip!

I staggered back to the safe side of the railings awaiting a high five for my mischief.

"You've got to kidding me?" said Elle.

"What? I'm not here to cause criminal damage and I'm not exactly imaginative when it comes to this sort of stuff."

"Wait here, I'll sort this."

I watched as she crawled up to the first tyre, taking something small out of her pocket.

Is that a pen knife? I'm going to jail.

She made her way round to the second one, then the far side to enact more damage. I should have rugby tackled her to the ground to stop this but I was just frozen to the spot.

It felt like an eternity before she was at my side again, with a look of complete satisfaction on her face.

"I can't believe you did that," I said, "You went so far beyond the line of acceptable pranking."

"Pranking? She put a bogus call into the health inspector and is literally trying to get Joseph's business shut down and you think the acceptable retribution was a childish prank? We sent a message."

"Give me that knife, now!" I used my 'angry mummy' voice and was about to dish out the 'I'm not mad, just disappointed speech'. To my surprise, she handed over a teaspoon. I looked back at her completely confused – and impressed that she could do so much damage with something so innocuous.

"Why on earth would I have a knife?" she asked.

"To…to..to slash the tyres."

She covered her mouth to stifle the laughter, knowing her natural volume would be heard miles away.

"I didn't slash them, you nutter, I just let the air out of them – I needed the spoon to push in the button thing under the valve," she continued, "I've met a lot of dickheads, in my time so this really is a handy skill to perfect."

She then stood up and started walking back towards the café to find out how Joseph was getting on.

I cantered up beside her and hugged her shoulders.

"What's that for?" she asked.

"You're a good egg."

"Too rights I am," she smiled and hugged me back.

Chapter 23

The inspection seemed to go ok but it had left, a normally effervescent, Joseph pretty shaken.

"I didn't want to get involved in this gang war you two have," he said, "I just want to sell coffee."

I felt guilt wash over me about stooping to Mrs Clunting's juvenile level. He was right, he was a business owner and the last thing he needed was to get involved in a petty vendetta.

"She started it," said a petulant Elle.

"I don't care who started it, it ends here. No more trouble is to come through those doors or I will hold you both personally responsible."

We watched him silently as he went back into the kitchen to torture Michael before the lunchtime rush.

The bell announced more customers coming in and as I turned to welcome them I was faced with our nemesis and her cronies.

"Well, hello Mrs Cunting what can we do for you on this fine morning?" said Elle in a sickly sweet tone.

A bolder of dread hit my stomach, I was not physically or mentally capable for a showdown with this woman and her band of harpies. I sat up and was thankful that I hadn't taken off my sunglasses yet so they could hide my darting, nervous eyes.

"Hello Elle, I'm sorry to disturb you, clearly you're holding court in your den of disappointing mothers," said Mrs Clunting in her usual condescending tone.

I know she was talking about me, my hangover was still evident and I looked a state even with my telltale eyes hiding behind glasses. I straightened up to pretend I was a functioning adult.

"Where are your feral children, Elle? Off running the roads?" she continued.

"I suggest you state your business here *Cunting* before I put your abnormally large head through that glass for even mentioning my children."

"We're here for some coffee, obviously. Be a dear and fetch us three cappuccinos, we'll sit over there on that lumpy leather thing passing for a sofa."

She turned and walked away, with her followers close behind. All three of them shot us matching dirty looks.

"It's like they don't know I can easily spit in all of their cups?" said Elle.

I called for Joseph in order to be some sort of voice of reason. It wouldn't do if Elle jumped the counter and made good on her threat to shove her through the window.

"Joseph, can you take care of those women on the sofas? I think if Elle is left unsupervised with their order it could result in legal action," I pleaded.

Joseph agreed and set to work on the drinks order while muttering something about 'gangs'. He was an expert barista. There was a world of difference between his coffees and Elle's. In fact, I wasn't entirely sure why Elle spent so much time actually serving customers. I'd lost count of the number of unofficial jobs she had in order to make some extra money. I assumed Joseph was giving her a few sneaky pounds for her help around the place, or at least I hoped so – especially with Keith gone from the house.

For the next half hour, I couldn't get a word out of Elle that wasn't about Mrs Clunting - none of which were complimentary.

"Just don't even look over there, Elle," I said.

"I'm not backing down, she's the one that came into *our* territory and is pissing everywhere. She's looking for a fight."

"Oh, for goodness sake! If you can't be an adult about this then you're as bad as her. One of us has to be the cooler head and just get on with things, we're not in a bloody playground this is a business. A business that we've been working very hard to bolster and I'm not about it let that be ruined by childish rivalry. She runs a playgroup for pity sake, she's not the bloody mafia."

I decided to clean up some of the tables and pretend to look busy in order for the unwelcome visitors to get bored of the staring contest. It didn't go as planned.

"You missed a spot there, Alice," said Mrs Clunting.

There was something so demeaning about her purposeful misremembering of my name. It grated something in my subconscious. I could feel my face flush and I picked up the tray of empty cups and left it over on the counter with Elle. I pushed my sunglasses off my face onto my head, pulled my shoulders back and walked over to the sofas. Mrs Clunting looked me up and down with a perplexed expression on her face.

"May we help you, Alice?" she smirked.

"Yes, actually you can," I said as calmly as possible, "It's Amy, by the way, but you know that already because you were here recently lurking around to see

228

what you're doing wrong at your place. Obviously, because you've nothing better to do with your life - I can help you with that if you like?"

I motioned to one of her cronies in order for them to budge over on the sofa. I sat down to face a shocked looking Mrs Clunting.

"This coffee shop isn't a personal slight against you or your playgroup, Margaret. You don't have to see it that way. This is a place where parents can come and relax for a bit while their kids play in the toy area, over there. We're not reinventing the wheel here, we just wanted somewhere to relax."

"Don't you mean somewhere to slack off and sit on your phone? Lazy parenting dressed up as a coffee shop," she spat.

"What does that matter to you?" I continued, "Why is it so important to you, to come here and try to make us feel bad? I don't understand what you're getting out of it? We tried things your way and Elle didn't last ten minutes. Then I felt so uncomfortable I couldn't wait to get out of there. Maybe that's on us, maybe we're the problem but so what? What does it matter that we tried your place, didn't like it, and now we have here? Does this really need to turn into a turf war? Which of us are the *Sharks* and which are the *Jets*?"

I smiled hoping that my poor attempt at a joke would be enough to make her see sense about how ridiculous this situation had become. She didn't match my smile. Instead, she sighed and said:

"You see *Amy*, this isn't about my way or your way. This is about *the* way to properly parent children and you two peddling this 'haven' for parents - or whatever you're marketing it as - is the reason the whole of society is going to the dogs. The point of the S.M.U.G organisation isn't to make mothers feel bad, it's to hold us all up to a higher standard of parenting. I'm sick to death of all these lazy, gross, and frankly, unworthy mothers being catapulted to stardom for writing on the internet about how happy they are about being inept at the most important job in the world. It's tough enough without me having to deal with you two, your crass café and this 'come one, come all' attitude. It has to stop somewhere and I've decided it stops with me, on this street and with you two. By all means, sell the coffee but I'll be damned if I see this place promoted as a mum club of any description."

I was stunned; the woman was insane.

She was declaring war on a coffee shop because she thought we were the embodiment of a crumbling society.

I just wanted to drink coffee while it was hot, that was the main motivation for me – well, that and the tray bakes.

"Margaret, I think you're being a bit dramatic about this." I tried to sound reasonable but I came across as if I was talking to an unpredictable horse that was ready to buck at any moment.

"Well, I think you're being naïve. I suppose that's to be expected judging by the company you keep and the state your child was in when I saw him. I shudder to think what the home life is."

I had often read about this phenomenon that makes seemingly average people lift cars off their children or stop trains with their minds (ok, I made up the last one) and I wondered if there would ever be an occasion for this to happen. I don't know if that was what I experienced at that moment, but I did know that a red mist had descended. The implication that I was doing a shitty job with my children crossed a line and she wasn't getting away with.

I didn't care that my children had chips for dinner two days in a row because I was too hungover to cook, or that my husband had questionable bald patches on the bottom half of his body. She didn't know this and all that mattered was: I was trying.

"Were you not hugged enough as a child?" I asked, "Is this where the incessant need to have some sort of fake accolade as the perfect parent comes from? Whatever it is, just stop. Stop judging every single person that walks through the door of your stupid club by an unrealistic standard of parenting. I was willing to be reasonable here, I was trying to be adult but if you can't even manage that *Cunting* then you and I are going to have a problem.

"Let's break down the Holy Grail that is Special Mothers United in Growth, shall we?

"Firstly, to their child, every parent is 'special' and unique and awesome - even if they don't match your checklist of parenting perfection.

"Next: Mothers. How about remembering dads exist too? I mean family units come in a whole range of shapes and sizes. The whole ethos of your damn club is concentrating on those solely with ovaries.

"Thirdly: United? What a joke. You mean only if you follow your ridiculous example as a parent.

"Finally, Growth implies you're ready to evolve and change as the situation demands. Clearly, that's another lie. S.M.U.G is utter bullshit and you lot are a bunch of judgmental asses.

"Don't worry though, if you want to change and embrace every facet of the parenting community you're more than welcome to come here anytime you like. If not, then I do hope you have a wonderful day, but get the fuck out and make room for decent people, you pathetic, and downright embarrassing, excuse for a human."

She was stunned.

It took a few seconds for her to compose herself once more.

"I know it was you two that let my tyres down," she snarled.

"Prove it," I said, with a steely determination I wasn't aware I had.

She stood up and left without saying another word, with her lackeys in close pursuit.

I cleared the table and tried to hide the fact my hands were shaking.

"So, was that you 'being an adult' about it then?" said Elle.

Without looking up, I could hear the smile in her voice.

"Shut up, Elle."

"You're a legend, princess."

Yes, at that particular moment, I think I might be

Chapter 24

On a high from my run in with Mrs Clunting, I picked up Adam from school and took the boys to the beach. It was a bit of a stretch to call it a 'beach'. It was better described as a rocky patch with a smattering of sand in between.

We skimmed stones on the water until their noses turned red from the cold, and then we headed home for hot chocolate and marshmallows.

I had earned brownie parenting points for my afternoon with them and, for the first time in days, I felt at ease in my own home.

When I heard Ben come in and do his normal boisterous 'hello' routine with the kids I had settled myself at the table ready to confront him about the ongoing silent treatment. He walked in and said 'hello' but I didn't answer. He was about to walk out the door when I kicked the legs of the chair in front of me pushing it out into his way.

"Sit down, please," I said.

"Haven't you caused enough injuries without bruising my shins as well?"

"We need to talk about Friday night."

"I'd rather not," he said, monotonously.

"I know, but that's how we got into this mess. We haven't been talking properly. We've been happy to get through every day without any hassle instead of working on us."

"No, we got into this particular mess because my wife burnt the hairs off my thighs and I've been cutting wax out of my remaining leg hair for a few days now."

"I meant the bigger picture."

He sighed, his signal for giving into my way, and sat down on the chair.

"What do you think is going wrong with us? Are we just out of sync or something?"

"I don't know, Amy. All I know is I can't have an honest conversation with you without wondering if what I say will upset you and you'll go running off to a lake."

And there it was. The big black elephant in the room.

I was never going to escape my actions of that day and now my husband is afraid to even speak to me properly.

"I'm not suicidal, Ben."

The shame was overwhelming and it choked at my throat to even have to say those words out loud. I felt myself shrinking inwards, to the point where I was physically trying to make myself smaller by curling my legs in under me.

"I know, I don't know why I said that - it isn't true. I'm just tired and pissed off about Friday, I shouldn't have said anything."

I knew he was still panicked about the precariousness of my mental health, but it was upsetting to learn that he was this nervous, still.

I'd spent the last six months trying to find a way back to being me, without realising what it was changing Ben into. He was afraid of me, or at least what I was capable of doing. The shame was growing and it felt like the walls in the kitchen were starting to move in.

"I'm sorry," I said, quietly, "Not just for Friday, for everything. I don't know how else to convince you I'm trying to get better. I'm doing all this stuff to figure out how to stay healthy. I'm taking the tablets, I'm keeping busy and I just don't know what else you want me to do."

"Therapy."

"It doesn't work, I can do this myself."

"Can you? Because all I've seen so far is you running around with a new friend, trying every which way to distract yourself from your skewed way of thinking and how you process things. You're filling your life up with all this nonsense so you don't have to face the fact you tried to kill yourself."

"I went to therapy and I didn't like it."

"You didn't give it a proper chance. Cognitive Behavioural Therapy has a real chance of helping you actually deal with depressive episodes, instead of you ignoring that nagging voice in your head. I know it's still there because I know you. I've been watching you and I can tell when 'she's' talking. I just want to help and this is the best way I know how."

"Shame?"

"I was going for nagging, but I'll take whatever abuse you want to send my way if it makes you go see someone and get advice. I'm not saying all this stuff with Elle isn't helping, you seem to enjoy yourself with her, but I think it's going to take a culmination of things to fight this."

I wondered how long he had been preparing this speech for me. Weeks? Months? I hated the thought of going back to therapy. I held the firm belief that it was nonsense. My belief was based on zero scientific fact or experience and more to do with my sheer pig-headedness. I had survived ok, so far, by basically avoiding anything uncomfortable.

"Is this because I poured wax on you? There's a whole community dedicated to S&M out there, and I bet they're not told they need therapy."

"Burning me doesn't really help your case, no; but that's not the reason.

"I just thought we could confront the easy stuff first like: why you bullied yourself into thinking you needed to take your own life rather than talk about your grief with me. When you figure that out, then we can build up to S&M," he said, smiling. He reached out and gave my hand a reassuring squeeze. It was the first time he'd come close to me since our disastrous evening.

"Fine, I'll try therapy - but I'm buying nipple clamps for you," I replied.

"That sounds fair, but please let my leg hair grow back before we bring pyromania into our lives on a full-time basis."

The horrible dark cloud that had plagued the house had started to shift. It allowed me to enjoy the evening with Ben and the kids. It was much nicer to sit in a room together and not feel stifled by an awkward atmosphere.

I kept my phone to one side and enjoyed their company for a whole half an hour until Arthur wouldn't stop singing *'yummy, yummy, yummy I've got poo in my tummy and I'll give you a punch in the gob'*.

Even a spell on the naughty step, for repeated use of the word 'poo', did not stop him from singing it over and over again.

Instead, I decided to look towards the summer holidays and researched the possibility of our first foreign holiday as a family. I thought it would prove as great incentive to lose weight.

I could put pictures up all over the house like those 'fitspo' posts I keep seeing online. Or I could also try chopping off a limb; that's about as appealing as clean eating is to me.

I quickly became addicted to looking at all the wonderful holiday destinations we couldn't afford. I loved imagining Ben and me in luxurious destinations (without those horrible humans we brought into the world).

We never had a honeymoon. Ben's business was just starting up when we got married and we said we'd go later on in the year, once things were up and running. As time went on it never seemed like a good idea to take the time off, for either of us, and then the kids came along. Of course we'd had nights away, here and there. The thought of going away for longer than a night without the kids just didn't seem right. Although I was starting to come around to the idea more frequently the cheekier my children got.

I knew holidaying together, so we could all be miserable, as a family was the only way I was going to see some sun. I suspected that holidaying with children was just shouting at them in a new location.

I hoped I was mistaken and the warm weather, perhaps, wouldn't turn them into heat-activated gremlins, but I suspected my initial hunch was more likely to be correct.

As bedtime approached, I watched the three of them build things with blocks. I loved to lie on the sofa and think about how happy I was, in moments like these - mostly, because they were ignoring me and weren't demanding snacks.

I felt very lucky and it made me think of Elle.

I knew she wasn't telling me everything that was going on with her and Keith and I know if I pressed harder I could find out the information. Although she was ridiculously bossy when it came to changes in my life, I felt I could do with prying into hers a bit more to make sure she wasn't feeling isolated without him.

I hated the thought of her being on her own - without her children - on an evening like this.

I wondered if she used to lie on her sofa, as I did, and think about how lucky she was? She had been so patient with my marital woes, from day one, and hadn't asked for much in return.

I had done little to help her, other than distracting her with my nonsense. I decided to send a text and see if she wanted to meet up tomorrow, not for launch night preparations or for some problem I needed fixing, just for a chat.

Amy: Lunch at mine tomorrow? X
Elle: Sure, I'll bring the restraints I hear socks are nowhere near as durable these days.
Amy: Bitch. See you then.

I felt better already, like a decent friend.

I'll make something. No, wait, I am trying to be nice so I probably shouldn't subject her to my cooking. I'll buy lunch in and we will sit in my kitchen and I'll try to help her like she's been helping me.

Geez first therapy and now being a better friend, I certainly am on the road to becoming the perfect person today.

I felt smug as I packed the kids off to bed and decided to return to the book I'd been trying to read, for the last year, while taking a bath.

I barely remembered the plot but I'd made it this far and I wasn't starting again. I had just settled into my bubbles when I heard a knock at the door. I predicted that it was Adam wanting to talk about the existential meaning of life.

"Yes, sweety," I called.

"It's me, can I come in?" said Ben.

"Of course," I replied, trying not to sound too surprised by his visit.

"I was just thinking about your effort to try and get things back on track here and because you're so receptive to the therapy idea I thought I should put some effort in too," he said. He was sheepishly standing in the doorway, edging his way in and then locking the door behind him.

"What did you have in mind?" I asked.

"Nothing quite as exciting as you had on Friday, I thought I could keep you company in the bath, I mean I do remember you wanting this particular one because it was big enough for two?"

"Oh really? Then afterwards we could try this thing called the 'rusty trombone' that Elle was talking about today." I added, excitedly.

"Do you know what that is, Amy?"

"Not really, she said Keith loved it though and I thought we could look it up."

"It involves putting your tongue in my bum."

"Oh. Right. Maybe just the bath then."

"Yeah, maybe, just the bath."

The water level nearly spilled onto the ground when he came in, but the crisis was averted when he accidentally sat on the plug, popping it up and letting a portion of it out.

We settled into the water and although he complained about the temperature being too hot, he sat on with me. We talked about the kids, about the prospect of a holiday and about the start of our relationship, when we couldn't keep our hands off each other. I would never have guessed that we'd be faced with a sex drought back then. Then again, I didn't think I would be married with kids either.

When the water started to get cold and our fingers wrinkled, he got out of the bath and got the towels that were heating on the radiator. We wrapped ourselves up and continued to talk nonsense. We faced each other on the bed, not really drying off, just enjoying the conversation

When I eventually got up to dry my hair he pulled me back to the bed.

"Where do you think you're going?" he asked.

He drew me in closer and I enjoyed the smell that was distinctly his.

I'd come home.

Chapter 25

Reader, I banged him.

That's as close to *Jane Eyre* as my story gets.

The drought was over.

I wished that I could have woken up the next day completely cured, without the need for therapy and all our marital problems sorted, but I didn't. It was a nice evening though.

Ben certainly had a spring in his step, and he brought me toast and tea in bed - unheard of on a school morning.

He was happy; I loved that something so simple could do that for him.

With one aspect of my life finally getting back to where it should be I decided today would be about cultivating my friendship with Elle and seeing what I could do to be a decent person.

I went to the shop and got lots of little tubs from the deli counter so we could stuff our faces with buffet-type nibbles and chat. I bypassed the alcohol section and decided if I were to add wine into the occasion I would end up getting pissed, talking nonsense – probably about myself – and not find out any information about Elle.

She arrived around 1 pm and while Arthur had his nap, we sat down at the table in the kitchen to eat.

"Well, what's the special occasion here?" she asked.

"It has come to my attention that we have been very busy distracting me from my problems. As much as I appreciate that, I wanted to be a decent friend and see what I could do for you. Not distract you, of course, just talk about things properly."

I sat and waited for the free flow of information to spring forth. I prepared myself to listen, and not pass any advice or judgments, until the end. I knew it would take a while for her to get it all out, after all, she'd been bottling it all up for weeks and now was her time to vent. I would sit with her, dry her tears and just be that sister she never had.

"No thanks, arsehole, I much prefer solving your life drama than mine – what's for lunch?"

Is that it?

I tried again: "I know you might be a bit reluctant to open up, but I really think it will be good for you."

"Nah, is that couscous?"

"Elle, a problem shared is a problem halved." I continued, in my best calm voice. A voice reserved for when my children are pushing my buttons in public.

"I've never understood that phrase; I've always found a problem shared is a problem doubled. You tend to bum out the other person too and I'm in a good mood today, so I don't want to think about it. Did I tell you I got a dress for the launch? I look pretty rocking in it, and it makes it look like my tits are defying gravity."

This is getting ridiculous.

"No, you get a sense of camaraderie with sharing your feelings with others."

She didn't look convinced as she plopped the egg salad onto her plate.

"Since when have you become so 'zen' are you high? *Are* you? Is that why you called me here? Were you just pretending to do this boring lunch? Are we going to blaze up and lie out in the garden, this afternoon? I knew you were a legend," she squealed.

"No! You're not here to get high, you raving lunatic. I just wanted it to be about you for a change instead of me, I was trying to be a decent person with my 'boring lunch'."

We sat facing each other at my table, both of us picking at our food lost in our own thoughts.

"I can't believe you thought I wanted to get high with you," I said.

"Well, I don't know! You're not exactly all about the sharing; it's like pulling teeth with you most of the time so I thought it was a trick to get me around here."

"Says you? I'm trying to get you to talk about something other than me, for a change, and you're just insulting my delicious food."

"Did you make this?"

"That's not the point!"

We let ten minutes pass before either of us dared to look up from our plates.

"Do you want to go through the final checklist for the party?" she offered.

"Fine," I replied, tersely.

"I got the fairy lights and I'm just going to put them everywhere that's free, oh and an artist friend of mine is making a few fake cherry blossom trees for the entrances front and back, I think it will be beautiful."

"I haven't even thought of a dress yet, I'm sure there's something in the wardrobe. A couple of the local papers are sending photographers and that student photographer guy, Marcus, said he would be there to take a few shots of people milling about for the social media side of things," I added.

"Why don't we bunk off, this evening? I've got a voucher for this new leisure club we could just float about in the pool and lie in the steam room – we have to get our ageing, decrepit skin picture-ready for the launch," she suggested excitedly.

It had been years since I'd been in a steam room. I hated the heat, but I remembered reading about the benefit of steam for your pores. The breakout of adult acne on my chin resembled a blotchy goatee, so I agreed to go.

"It's a date," I said.

We ate the rest of the meal in silence and I felt like I'd failed, but at least in a steam room she'd have nowhere to hide and maybe she'd feel brave enough to talk in person.

*****

That evening, I was waved off by the menfolk and drove down to meet Elle at the leisure club. It was very plush and I was already unnerved by the ridiculously attractive woman at the reception desk.

"You look like you're about to shit yourself," said Elle, as we walked up to the changing rooms, "Just get your kit off and let's relax."

Despite all the hang-ups I had about my body, I didn't mind getting into a swimming suit. I didn't love it, either, but I wasn't at a point where I refused to put one on and not go to the pool. I did spend the majority of my time in the changing room, pleading with the universe that I didn't meet anyone I knew.

I was confident that I wouldn't meet anyone in this place, it had only been open a week and it usually took the people in town a year to try anything new.

We dove into the dimly-lit pool and I did a few half-hearted lengths while Elle rested her head on her arms at the side of the water, kicking out her legs.

"Are you not swimming?" I gasped, as I tried to catch my breath.

"Nah, can't swim. I'm just here for the lying around parts."

We stayed in the water for ten minutes before I started to feel bad about Elle being bored. I suggested we went into the steam room first and lie there for a while.

She can open up her pores and her heart. God, I'm a genius.

As the name suggested, it was very steamed when we entered. We assumed we were the only two there, so we spread out and lay on opposite benches.

"Elle?"

"Hmmm?"

"Tell me what's going on with you and Keith please, I want to help."

"For fuck's sake, can't a girl just get her steam on without this touchy-feeling shite? Next, you'll be wanting to hug," she snapped.

I didn't reply, I was happy that the steam was hiding my scarlet face. I clearly wasn't helping the situation. After about a minute she said: "I'm sorry, I really didn't mean that and if you want to hug that's fine too. I like hugs.

"It's shit, Amy. I brought up the topic of counselling again and he was completely shocked that I would suggest it, as far as he knew 'we' were completely over."

"Is he seeing someone else?"

"I don't know, maybe. I didn't ask and to be honest I don't want to know. By the end of the conversation, we agreed that we should only have contact with each other when it was directly to do with the girls and not be one of those couples who trade horrible text messages and wind up hating each other.

"I don't know if he's staying with his parents indefinitely or finding somewhere new; I don't know if this is a trial separation or this is a divorce; I'm too afraid to ask him in case he says something I really don't want to hear. I mean I know things were a bit shitty but I didn't know it was splitsville, shitty."

"If I could find you I'd give you a hug," I offered, "I'm sorry this is happening to you and the girls, is there anything I can do to help?"

I couldn't manage to think of anything less trite than that.

"No thanks, princess." It was all she managed to say before the emotion in her voice betrayed her.

The heat was making me sleepy so I closed my eyes and let myself relax while I tried to think of something more helpful to say, I needed to think of something practical that would make her life easier.

I felt a breeze come in and assumed that someone had walked into the room. I let out a cough to make sure they knew other people were here.

I could have her over for dinner on nights she feels lonely? Maybe take up a new hobby or even come here once a week. It was so relaxing here.

I felt my subconscious dropping deeper and I knew sleep wouldn't be far off. I had a feeling it wouldn't be particularly safe to fall asleep here so I decided to open my eyes and sit up. I lifted my head slightly and found that it made contact with a rather large, rather sweaty arse that was just about to put its full weight on top of me.

I tried to scream in surprise but as I opened my mouth it was filled with a section of the owner's pink, hairy skin. Thankfully they must have noticed something awry because they jumped up into a standing position.

"Oh my God, what do you think you're doing?" asked, the bum's owner.

I was too busy coughing and picking out one of his hairs from the tip of my tongue to reply. Instead, I struggled towards the door and hoped I wouldn't encounter anymore foreign body parts en route.

I got outside and started to breathe deep, free from ass invasions.

"I asked you a question!" the man, shouted.

The owner of the ass had followed me outside, a towel now wrapped around his lower half.

"I'm sorry?" I was confused as to why me, the victim, was being shouted at by him, the owner of the offending ass cheeks.

A member of staff came walking over to check who was disturbing the lovely serene atmosphere.

"Excuse me, sir, what seems to be the problem?"

"I'll tell you what the problem is: there's been an assault," he fumed.

"I would hardly call it an assault, it was an accident and I'm not likely to press charges," I laughed, nervously.

"I don't think this is a laughing matter here, miss, it is *I* who has been assaulted by *you!*"

What fresh hell is this?

At this point, Elle came out to see what the commotion was about and realised I was in the centre of it.

"What's going on?" she asked.

"I'll tell you what's going on here, I went into enjoy a steam and I have been grossly assaulted by this woman who took it upon herself to bite me on my bottom," he roared.

There wasn't a single person pretending not to be listening to every single word. His face was practically puce in colour, as he shouted about his traumatic experience. All I could do was just stand there, humiliated, and wondered how this had happened.

He, along with Elle and the bemused-looking member of staff were all looking at me expectedly for some sort of explanation as to why I thought this kind of behaviour was appropriate.

"I obviously didn't mean to do it!" I said, exasperated.

"I was lying down with my eyes closed and he backed his hairy arse into my face. If anything I'm the traumatized party here, if anything I should be given some water and a crash course in dealing with PTSD instead of being accused of assaulting someone. Why weren't you wearing any swimwear, I'm going to be picking hair out of my teeth for a week!"

By the time I finished my tirade, I had gone bright pink and wanted the ground to swallow me up.

"Settle, petal," soothed Elle, "Clearly this was a misunderstanding, my friend and I were just here

relaxing the gentleman didn't see us with the steam –
these things happen."

The member of staff seemed relieved to be talking to
someone with a cooler head – physically and
emotionally – and offered all of us a free spa treatment
as compensation.

"I won't be paid off with a free manicure," said my
victim, "I want to talk to the manager."

He strode off in his towel with the staff member and
headed towards the office.

"Can we go before I'm arrested, please," I said to
Elle, "Or at least get dressed so I'm not dragged away in
handcuffs in my swimwear. I know you're giggling
behind me."

I went into the changing rooms to scrape back some
dignity from my 'relaxing' experience when I heard:

"Amy Cole as I live in breathe! Here we are again!"
Fuck my fucking life

"Hi Rita," I replied, with my usual level of
enthusiasm.

"Are you a member here? You are such a dark horse!
This place is soo expensive but with all the new business
I'm bringing into the company I just thought to myself
'go on, Rita, splurge!' so I did and here I am. Surprised
to see you here. Delighted, of course, but just thought it
would be a teensy bit out of your price range with the
kids and the no job thing.

"Have you met Milo yet? He's an angel with the
hands of a god. I swear, the man can work miracles. I'm
so stressed out with climbing the career ladder, the move
to the bigger apartment and out every night, wining and
dining clients. Ugh, just exhausting! I make sure to see
him once a week to work out the old kinks and get me

back up to 110%. Well, not 'old' kinks, I'm not *you*! Ha! JKJK darling. Such a pleasure to see you, I love our little catch-ups. I will definitely text you during the week and we will have brunch or I'll even call to your house, I'm sure you'd prefer to be indoors instead of out with rowdy kids in a restaurant. Love ya!"

After another run-in with Rita, I thought that being arrested for assault wouldn't be the worst part of my day. Elle gave me a sympathetic nudge and said: "Let's get dressed and see if your teeth have left a mark on that poor man's bum, you kinky weirdo."

By the time we got to the reception, the member of staff who had been dealing with us outside the steam room was waiting for me. I braced myself for what new humiliation I was to be faced with.

"Hi ladies, as promised here's your voucher for the free spa treatment and I wanted to apologise for the scene earlier. I hope your time here was enjoyable otherwise?"

"Oh, you mean before I was accused of assaulting the man that sat on my face?"

"Eh, well, yes. He is now satisfied that the whole situation was an unfortunate accident. The client seemed to calm down after he had a free massage with Milo." He explained, "We hope to see you both here again soon. Have an excellent night."

Never again

As we walked back to the car park I handed Elle my voucher and told her to give it to someone she hated.

"I have had enough humiliation at the hands of this place, so I'll pass. Time for home."

"Don't be completely put off, let's give it a while and we'll try again. Besides at least it got you out of the house and away from the awkwardness with Ben."

"Things are sorted with Ben, actually. Like, *everything* is sorted, if you know what I mean."

I feel like a creepy teenage boy that lies about his hundreds of conquests to impress his mates.

"Oh really? Well, aren't you a dark horse."

Her tone was a bit off. She sounded happy but there was a sad edge to her voice.

"You'll have no need for me then now you're on the straight and narrow," she added.

"Yes, that's you done with. You've served your purpose and I have bigger fish to fry," I said it in an American-mob-boss voice, in an attempt to make her laugh.

She looked like someone had punched her in the chest.

"Elle, I'm kidding! Nothing changes here, in fact, I'll probably need more visits to that shop for lingerie and random sex toys I can hurt Ben with."

She gave a half smile in return. I decided on a change of subject to cheer her up.

"Why don't we go to one of those pop-up gin places that serve drinks in candlesticks or something else completely nonsensical?"

"Nah, I'll pass. I've some painting I want to get done before the next class and I don't want a hangover when I'm bouncing on that fucking trampoline in the morning, you know?"

"Fair enough, I'll see you at Joseph's afterwards though, yeah?"

"Yeah, see ya."

I couldn't help but worry as she walked away. Her natural effervescent self, was being extinguished with her marital woes and all I could do was offer sarcasm and a bit of company once in a while.

There has to be something more I can do, but what?

Chapter 26

"I need your help," said Elle, as she stood in my doorway.

"You're soaked through, get in here," I said, as I rushed her into the house.

She hadn't been returning my calls since our hellish night at the steam room and I was just relieved she was in front of me, despite her leaving sizeable wet patches everywhere she stood. She had obviously walked from her house in the pouring rain. That was at least two miles away and she still couldn't sit still long enough for me to make sense out of her. I finally gave up trying to get her to sit on a towel, while she was dripping water on the fabric sofa and thought that listening to her was probably the best thing I could do, right now.

If I could just get the tea-towel underneath her feet then that would be a start

"He's cheating on me," she said, "I know he is. I logged into his *Facebook* account, the stupid man hadn't changed his password and – Amy? Why are you on the ground?"

"You're dripping everywhere, I was just trying to sort out… drippage."

"Get off the floor, I'll take off my shoes so we can concentrate on the fact my husband IS CHEATING ON ME."

"Yes, you're right. I no longer care about the dripping."

Even as I said it, out loud, I knew it wasn't convincing.

"If I take off my clothes and sit in my underwear on a paper towel will you please be a normal human being and help me?" she asked.

"Yes, I'll put them in the tumble drier and you can have some pyjamas and I swear I will be a good listener."

"Fine," she huffed.

I ran up the stairs to try and dig out semi-matching pyjamas – a more difficult task than it sounded.

Every year, Ben would get me lovely new pyjamas for Christmas and by Boxing Day one part (usually the top) went missing into the ether along with all my favourite socks.

I took a wild guess and assumed that Elle wouldn't care what she was wearing whilst having an emotional breakdown, so I grabbed the first thing I saw from the drawer and headed back down the stairs.

I found her studying her phone intensely, as she sat cross-legged on my sofa. I threw the ancient t-shirt and shorts in her direction and picked up her soaking clothes to get them in the tumble drier. I resisted the urge to mop around her and decided to sit down to find out exactly what Keith was up to.

"He's cheating on me, Amy," she repeated, "I know we said we were taking a timeout, or whatever crap thing people say to each other, but I didn't give his dick permission to go on a little vay-cay, you know?"

"Are you sure?"

She pulled out her phone and read aloud: "'***Yeah, we can go to dinner if you like but we're having dessert back at your place straight after***' he's even put one of those creepy horny devil Gifs. What is he, 16? He can't deny it now. I've read the lot. I should confront him at this romantic dinner he's got planned. You know he was meant to have the girls tonight? He cancelled, yesterday, and that's when I just got fed up with these nonsense excuses so I checked the account and there he was, making plans with her."

I felt like I should say something horrible about the woman she was showing me on her phone, but I really didn't want to get into a session of slut-shaming a complete stranger.

"Will you come with me?" she asked, with a look of complete desperation that I had never seen on her. She really was looking like she was at the end of her tether and I couldn't blame her. By the sounds of things, Keith was being a complete and unmitigated arse and it was time someone held him accountable – I just really wished that person didn't have to be me, or that it involved causing a scene at a restaurant.

At that moment I heard Ben's keys in the door, followed by the usual explosion of noise that comes from my family entering any building. Elle quickly wiped her eyes and turned to face the door to greet the three of them.

"Oh! Hello, Elle, when Amy said she got a babysitter for the evening I wasn't expecting you. Are the girls with Keith?"

Neither of us was expecting the mere mention of her estranged husband's name to cause her to burst into tears. There was a look of sheer panic on Ben's face. He grabbed a boy under each wing and they all backed out of the room, into the kitchen.

I hugged her as best I could and let her cry it out.

"You're really bad at hugging," she said after thirty seconds of awkward holding had passed.

"I know, I'm better at alcohol and sarcasm."

"Go check and see if I've emotionally damaged your children by subjecting them to that pathetic display," she added, as she used the sleeve of the top to wipe her nose.

I joined the males in the kitchen where I found Ben trying to convince the boys to stay quiet.

"It's too late," I said, "You can't hide out in here, we know you're in the house."

"I'm sorry, love. What did I say?" He was ashen-faced after his unintentional upset.

"She thinks Keith is cheating on her and she wants to catch him in the act, tonight."

"When you said you had organised a fun date night, this isn't what I was expecting," he replied.

Fuck

It was meant to be our first date night in months. I had organised the neighbour's teenage daughter to sit with the boys (for an extortionate hourly rate) and we had dinner reservations. I had even shaved - in Winter. This was a big effort for me.

"I'm sorry, I don't think I'll be able to leave her like this. She's pretty fragile."

At that second I heard a smash coming from the living room.

Ben and I ran in to see what carnage our visitor had caused and found her standing on the sofa, phone in hand, and face red with fury.

"He's only taking her to *our* restaurant!" she roared.

"The café?" I asked, confused by the very liberal use of the word 'restaurant'.

"No, you daft bint, Keith and I go to the same place for every special occasion and the unoriginal turd is taking her to it."

I was picking up the broken shards of the vase she had knocked over when she jumped.

"What are you doing down there? Do you obsessively clean around all your visitors?" she asked.

"Just the erratic ones," I replied, with flippancy.

"I think we should tail him," said Ben.

Elle and I both looked at him, shocked. Firstly, because, both of us had forgotten he was even there and, secondly, Ben was meant to be the voice of reason. A wide grin spread across Elle's face and she started doing a little bounce on the sofa as if she was on one of her trampolines.

"I knew you were a legend, Benny," she said with unmistakable glee.

"Can I talk to you for a second, Ben?" the tension in my voice was poorly disguised as I dragged him back to the kitchen by the arm in order to talk some sort sense into him.

"Are you mad?" I hissed.

"What? I'm being supportive. We have the babysitter, we want to spend some time together and you don't want to leave your upset friend. I thought this would be the perfect solution."

"If we go through with this we will have lots of time together in the back of a police car when we are arrested as accessories to murder."

"I couldn't help but overhear," interrupted Elle, "mostly because I was standing outside the door trying to hear, but if you guys come with me tonight I swear to Lucifer I won't get us arrested. I just want him to know that I know, you know?"

I sunk my shoulders in defeat and traipsed upstairs to find my best sleuthing outfit.

I could hear the groan of my sofa springs as Elle encouraged the boys to try some boogie bounce moves while Ben and I tried to find something black to wear on our stakeout.

"How is it that I have so many black clothes but none of them are matching blacks?" he asked.

"Because I'm a terrible wife who doesn't separate the fabrics or colours, so it's anyone's guess what shape our clothes come out like when they come out of the machine."

"Fair enough, I'll not admonish you this time Cole, but sort it out."

I glared at him from across the bed and threw a blackish top in his direction.

"Cheer up, Amy this is going to be fun. Date night with added danger," he smiled.

"I'll remind you of this mirth when you're getting carted away by police or punched in the face by Keith – and his date."

I could see him mentally run through the possibility of this actually happening and he must have decided that the chance of either of those scenarios occurring were slim, so he continued to get dressed.

The doorbell heralded the arrival of the babysitter and after a brief conversation about bedtimes she asked for the Wi-Fi code. This interaction didn't fill me full of confidence about her dedication to her charges but she was a regular babysitter throughout the area and hadn't killed any of the other kids so far. I accepted that this was a pretty low standard to set for letting people look after my children.

"Good-bye boys, possibly forever, because I may be going to get arrested," I said, as I kissed each of them. Judging by their complete lack of worry at the thought of never seeing me again, I knew it was fine to leave. I decided their unemotional states were because I was successfully raising two self-sufficient, independent children and not because they didn't like me.

"I'll drive," shouted Elle, as she ran out towards her car.

"Chauffeured on our date, this is getting off to a good start," Ben joked.

"Yes, I can't wait to sit in a freezing cold car to stake out a restaurant for a few hours." I knew I sounded sulky and I knew it would probably be better in the long run that we supervised this run-in with Keith and his new lady friend instead of letting Elle go by herself, but I wasn't relishing the prospect of what the night had in store.

"Cold? Don't worry that pretty little head of yours, I've got it covered," he said with a mischievous smirk.

I was beginning to worry that Ben was getting far too into this private investigator fantasy and I just hoped that he wasn't concealing night-vision goggles under his coat.

As we drove towards the restaurant, which I'd never heard of, on the other side of town, I tried to regulate my breathing. It had begun to get laboured with anxiety. When we pulled up, I could see that this whole situation had started to get to Elle.

The neon sign above the doorway said 'Mike's Meat Boutique' and that alone, made my stomach feel a bit queasy.

"Are you sure this is the place?" I asked, tentatively.

"It looks like a shit hole but they do the best steak I've ever eaten and they've always been our secret little place away from the hipsters."

"A 'yes' would have covered it," I said, looking out the passenger side window.

I pretended not to see the glare from Elle and spotted small newsagents open across the street.

"I'm going for supplies, unless we're going to all hide in a booth and stare at them during dinner?" I asked.

"What is your problem here, Amy?" said Elle, "Ben is being much more supportive over this plan and I have enough to deal with without you acting like a teenager who didn't get to go out with their friends and had to hang out with mum and dad."

I wasn't entirely surprised she was directing her frustration towards me and I knew my attitude wasn't helpful. I silently got out of the car, after my telling off, and decided to come back with chocolate and a better approach.

In the grand scheme of things I was missing one date – yes, we really needed it – but she was about to watch her husband go out to dinner with another woman and I was being a jerk. I had been vowing to be a better friend, this was my chance.

By the time I got back to the car, Ben and Elle were talking animatedly about a television show they both loved. I handed out the goodies from the bag, as well as offering a sincere 'sorry' for my grumpy behaviour.

My good intentions of a better mood didn't last long, due to the rapidly dropping temperature outside.

"It's freezing," I said, as I blew on my fingers to get some feeling back into them.

"I told you, I've got you covered," said Ben, from the backseat. He reached into his pocket and pulled out a hip flask.

"I knew this would come in handy one day. People are always getting me these bloody drink sets at Christmas and we have a cupboard at home full of random drinking vessels that come with them. Now, I finally get to use one."

His enthusiasm for using this flask was bordering on sad but I took it from him all the same. I took a slug without even asking what it was, but the familiar burn of whiskey in my throat was not hard to mistake.

"Christ, Ben," I said, as I tried to stop myself heaving it all back up again, "I haven't drunk whiskey in years. What were you thinking?"

"What was *I* thinking? What did you think would be in a hip flask? Tea?"

"I was kinda hoping for that, yes."

"When do you ever see a private investigator sipping tea while on a stakeout? They're always hardened alcoholics so we have to look the part."

"For who exactly? Keith? I don't think he'll care what we're drinking, he'll probably be more concerned about the three people, stinking of booze, standing over his table giving him grief for being such a shitty husband."

Elle held out her hand for the flask but I refused.

"You're driving," I said.

"Give me the flask, princess, I need some Dutch courage and if I get pissed I'll pay for the taxi back."

I reluctantly handed her the whiskey, in keeping with my new attitude of being a more supportive co-conspirator.

The three of us sat in the freezing car, passing around the horrible whiskey, talking about all our worst hangover stories in order to find out who was the most pathetic. It came as no surprise to me that I won the title.

It was for the time I showed up to my after-school job carrying a plastic bag full of my own vomit. It was the worst hangover of my life but I was worried I'd get fired if I called in sick. The manager took one look at me, along with my pathetic – and frankly disgusting – bag of puke and sent me home.

"We're out of whiskey," said Ben, "Do you want me to go find an off license?"

"No need, they're here," said Elle.

Chapter 27

My stomach instinctively contracted into a ball of panic. I desperately looked around to see if this had all been some horrible misunderstanding and Keith was alone – he wasn't.

His date didn't look a million miles away from Elle (albeit younger looking), something I thought would be better kept to myself in case that really sent her over the edge.

"She looks like a younger version of you, Elle," said Ben.

Elle and I stopped our snooping long enough to glare at him.

I married a moron

"She looks nothing like you, Ben isn't wearing his glasses. He's not even sure which one is her and which one is Keith," I explained.

"I don't wear glasses," he piped up, sounding confused and completely unaware of the damage he had done. If he was close enough I would have kicked him.

They were about to walk right past the car so the three most conspicuous private eyes in the world slumped down in our seats.

"Won't he recognise the car?" I asked, poorly hiding the panic in my voice.

"Are you kidding," said Elle, "He hasn't taken his eyes off that woman's chest since they got out of the car. He used to look at me that way."

"Like a piece of meat?" asked Ben.

"If you aren't going to say anything helpful, please stay quiet!" I said in my best shouty whisper.

"I thought I *was* being helpful?"

"No, Ben, no you are not."

"Elle, am I being helpful?"

"Will the two of you please shut up! I'm trying to find out if my husband is going to have sex with that woman and I can't concentrate with you two bickering like children – and no, Ben, telling me that the father of my children is on a date with a 'younger version of me' is not helpful."

We both said 'sorry' and went back to trying to see over the dashboard and into the restaurant.

"This is useless, I can't see a thing," she huffed.

"We could go in – Amy and I – he doesn't know what we look like," offered Ben, "I really need to pee and we could sit at the table next to them with you on the other end of the phone the whole time."

I didn't hate the idea.

Keith had only seen me the once, when I was sitting in the car outside his work. I was confident that he wouldn't recognise me. My willingness to go inside was also driven by the fact Elle wouldn't be within knife-throwing distance. I looked at her in order to see what she thought of this new plan and she seemed to be mulling it over.

"Fine," she said, "but as soon as I hear something I don't like or you two mess this up then I'm coming in and I'm smacking him across the head with my shoe."

I slipped off my seatbelt, which I realised I could have taken off some time ago, and crept out of the car. It had been raining so I crouched down on my honkers, trying to find a graceful way to creep around the back of the car and pretend to be getting out from another vehicle, whilst trying to avoid slipping into a puddle of mud. I shimmied around the car, like a crab, and tried not to laugh at how ridiculous this was. I looked up to see Ben simply step out of the car, like a normal person, and look upon his crab-like wife with curiosity.

"I've been in this relationship this long that I don't even really find this particularly weird," he said, "but if you're planning on impersonating a crab for the rest of our evening can you at least get the pincher hands right, you're not committing to the character at all."

"Shut it and help me up," I said, as I threw a hand in the air for him to help me off the ground.

"I feel like I'm getting told to 'shut up' quite a lot on a romantic evening out."

"I feel like it's a stretch to call stalking someone else's husband while he's on a date a 'romantic evening out'."

"Beggers can't be choosers," he shrugged.

I couldn't tell if he was genuinely enjoying himself or if he was drunk. Either way, I couldn't help but smile at the enormous goof that was my husband.

I tried to look completely casual as we entered the restaurant, but the place was empty and I knew it was going to look ridiculous to sit at the table next to Keith and his date. I tried to pull at Ben's top to stop him walking in their direction, but he was out of my reach and headed straight for our target.

Keith and his lady-friend were understandably concerned-looking as we took our seats at the table right next to them. I offered a type of sympathetic smile to her but then remembered that she was the enemy and my face contorted into a bizarre grimace.

She probably thinks I'm deranged.

They returned to looking at their menus while we grabbed ours from the holder in the centre of the table. Ben decided to hold his up, so it blocked Keith's view of the window and gave Elle a wave.

She shook her head at our less-than-incognito entrance and when I snuck another look at her, she was banging her head on the steering wheel.

The waitress came over and shot us a strange look, presumably about our seating choice.

"Hi folks, the specials tonight are the chicken feast, chilli bomb or the BBQ meat platter," she said without any real enthusiasm.

"Can we have a couple of minutes to take a look at the menu," I said.

"Sure, I'm not exactly run off my feet."

"I'm dying for a slash," said Ben, "back in a minute"

"You really are a poet."

I tried to sneak a look at Elle's love rival. I wondered what she knew about Keith's situation. Perhaps this was their first date and he was going to talk about his crazy ex-wife who forced him from his home and his children.

That bastard.

The bored waitress appeared beside them to take their order.

"I'll have the meat platter," said Keith, "why don't you get the bacon salad and we can split it?"

God, he's one of those plonkers who order for the two of them. What did she see in him?

"That sounds great," agreed his date.

God, she's one of those plonkers who agree to get food ordered for her. What does he see in her?

I felt a sharp kick to my shin from Ben, who was attempting to stop me glowering in their direction.

My knee shot up, banged the table and made everyone jump. The waitress gave us another suspicious look, then went back to the kitchen to put in the order.

"When did you get back? I didn't even hear you," I said.

Ben made a barrier with our menus and ushered me behind them to have a less-than-subtle confab.

"You are being so obvious," he whispered, "If looks could kill they'd already be dead."

"Because this is the epitome of subtlety?" I asked as a gestured to our menu fort.

"Yes, we are shy kissers."

I was mid eye-roll when our waitress announced herself with a cough.

We both bolted upright once we realised we weren't alone.

"I'm sorry, we are shy kissers and this is our second date," said Ben, a little too loudly than necessary.

He did a fake laugh and looked at Keith but he wasn't remotely interested in the peculiar behaviour of the people beside him.

"Sure you are," she replied, "What can I get you?"

"I liked the sound of what they're having," he said, gesturing towards Keith's table, "We'll take that."

"No, we won't actually," I interrupted, "I think it's a bit presumptuous to assume I would want whatever you order like a mindless lemming without even asking me - no offence," I added for the date's benefit.

She blushed and then I instantly felt bad for inferring that she was a lemming.

She's the enemy, go back to giving her the stink eye

I tried to control my shame blush and decided to look back at the menu.

"So, what do you want then?" asked the irritated waitress.

"I'll have the chilli special you spoke about, it sounded delicious." I tried to keep the sarcasm out of my voice but deep down I knew there was going to be spit in my food.

My phone started to buzz as a message from Elle came through.

Elle: What the fucking, fuck is going on?

Amy: We just ordered some food, do you want something?

Elle: I meant with my husband not what you're eating.

Elle: Order me a bacon salad, to-go.

Elle: Call me and set the phone on the table so I can hear.

I sat the phone on my lap as it dialled, then placed it at the furthest part of the table – and as close to Keith as I could manage. Ben was giddy at the espionage that was going on at the table.

I really need to make sure he gets a healthier hobby when this is all over.

We both remained quiet while trying to overhear the conversation going on beside us. It wasn't that hard - or interesting.

She was mostly talking about her new job at an art gallery and how it really inspired her to get back into her own painting; she was even considering teaching a class at the local community centre in her free time. I could just imagine Elle's face screwed up in anger at hearing the shared interests between her and 'the other woman'.

I could hear a tiny voice shout something indistinguishable from the direction of my phone so I looked towards the car. Elle was clearly having an argument with an invisible person, she hit the horn as she gestured wildly to make a point. All four of us looked out the window to find out who was behind the noise and she ducked down as quickly as she could. Keith's gaze stayed on the vehicle for a bit longer than the rest of us but he must have decided he was imagining things and his attention went back to the woman sitting across from him.

"I know you said you didn't want anything too serious too quickly, I just feel like we have a definite connection already," she gushed, "Do you feel it?"

She's eager.

"Yeah, I absolutely do," said Keith.

He absolutely did not.

"We've been talking for so long now, I feel like this is our fifteenth date," she continued, "I just wanted to tell you I really appreciate you sharing this special place with me. I know it meant so much to you and Eleanor."

"Actually her name was Elle," he said.

Was? I don't like where this is going.

"Goodness, I'm sorry! It must have been such a tough year raising those girls on your own without your wife. I'm just so glad that you felt well enough to reach out

269

and 'like' my picture. The internet really is a matchmaker."

I looked at Ben, his face mirroring my look of shock and disgust at what we were listening to. So far we had found out that he'd killed Elle off, was dad-of-the-year and was perving over other women's photos on the internet. It really wasn't the stuff of romance novels.

I couldn't bring myself to look outside again in case I saw her crying - or worse - see her get out of the car wielding an axe.

"It's been tough, but right now, being here with you, I feel like a completely new man. Elle would want me to move on and I'm glad it's with you."

They stared at each other over the tea-light candle and I could feel the verbal diarrhoea forming in my stomach. I couldn't just sit here and listen to this drivel while my best friend sat outside watching her letch of a husband pretend to be a widower in order to get into this woman's knickers.

The speech of hate was on the tip of my tongue when Ben beat me to it.

"Actually, I don't think she would like it," he said, "I think she would be pretty damn annoyed, wherever she is watching you from, right now."

"Excuse me?"

"I mean if my wife was dead I wouldn't be creeping at younger versions of her on the internet."

"You don't know what you're talking about, mate."

"I think I do, *mate*."

They were squaring up to each other from their perspective tables and I didn't know what to do. Do we excuse ourselves or come clean about what we are doing in order to ruin his night?

"You clearly don't know what you're talking about, you don't know what this poor man has been through and I want you to apologise right now," demanded his new soul mate.

"I'd like to apologise on behalf of my companion, he has boundary issues," I offered, "We don't know you, or your story and I'm sure you've been in mourning for a long time."

He seemed to be placated by this and stopped staring at us.

"What did your wife die of?" asked Ben.

I put my head in my hands and wanted the ground to swallow me up.

"What the fuck is your problem?" replied Keith, "I'm trying to have a nice evening and you keep butting your nose into our conversation. I don't even know you."

"You're right. Sorry, buddy. By the way isn't that your dead wife at the window?"

We all turned to the glass and found Elle standing very still with her chest heaving in fury.

His date screamed in shock, while Keith went deathly white.

"Oh my God, is that really her? I've heard of this happening - visions of loved ones appearing to give their consent to a new union," she said, as tears of emotion pooled in her eyes.

She started to shout towards the direction of the window: "MY NAME IS CLAIRE. I WILL LOOK AFTER YOUR CHILDREN."

She turned to a sick-looking Keith and added: "This is truly remarkable, Keith, say something before she disappears."

"Oh for fuck's sake, Claire! HE'S LYING TO YOU, SHE'S NOT DEAD," I said, exasperated.

"What?" she seemed utterly confused.

I beckoned Elle to come in.

Keith sat where he was and waited to face his very much alive wife.

"Keith, is this really your wife?" she asked.

"Yes."

"You are a complete and utter ball-sack. Was anything you told me true?" she demanded.

"Claire, these two need to talk, why don't we go outside," I said.

It was then the waitress appeared with the food. She wasn't sure what to do with the tray so Ben asked her to leave it all at a booth across the room. We led Claire towards the new table and joined her at the seat, in order to give Keith and Elle some space to talk.

"I can't believe this," she fumed, "I mean you think you've met a nice bloke who liked all your bikini pictures in the space of ten minutes and he turns out to be a complete sleaze ball."

Seriously?

"Yes, I'm sure all this must be a shock," I said, as I patted her shoulder and tried to catch a glimpse of the scene that was unfolding across the room.

From what I could tell they hadn't spoken yet, they were still staring at each other.

"We've been talking for months and he told me this big sob story about how he had been nursing his wife for years before she finally kicked the bucket a year ago. Since then, he's taken time off work to look after his children. Does he even have children?"

"Yes, they have twins," said Ben.

"Well, at least that's something. Not a complete sociopath."

"Yeah, he just killed off the mother of his children in order to start a relationship with someone else. Definitely seems like a catch," I replied.

She shrugged in reluctant agreement.

"Ben, are you seriously eating while this is going on?" I said.

"I'm hungry and I want to soak up the whiskey," he replied, defensively.

Claire picked up a fork and started to dig into the platter. The bacon 'salad' was more a case of melted cheese and bacon on one salad leaf with a ridiculous amount of coleslaw. It looked delicious.

Elle and Keith began to speak to one another, their demeanours as cold as ever. I don't know how she remained calm. As usual, she completely surprised me. I could never predict what way she was going to react.

"I think I'm going to be a vegan," said Claire, to no one in particular. She seemed to be over the heartbreak and the ghostly apparition. Perhaps internet dating disasters weren't uncommon for her.

She took a heaped forkful of bacon and cheese as she pondered her new life choice.

I can't stand this woman.

"This isn't even the worst date I've been on," she continued, "One guy brought along his 'twin' brother along. Every so often he would go to the toilet and the other one would come back and take his place. They swapped about four times,"

"Were they twins?" asked Ben.

"No, I don't even know if they were actually related. The only similarity was that they both had blonde hair."

"Did you not confront either of them?"

"Nah, I liked the restaurant so I stayed until dessert, then I climbed out the bathroom window."

The more she spoke, the more I felt relieved not to be single.

"I guess I'll be going. I'll let Keith pick up the cheque in lieu of being a lying scumbag."

She picked up her coat and bag, offered a limp wave and walked out.

We sat in our booth picking at the food waiting for Elle to join us.

"Should we go?" Ben asked.

"She's our ride," I said as I nibbled on a chicken wing, "I can understand why they come here, it's nice."

After we polished off ours – as well as Keith and Claire's order - we were joined by Elle. She looked defeated.

We didn't see Keith leave and we all sat in an uncomfortable silence waiting for her to break the tension.

"I don't know why I didn't rip his face off," she finally said, "I don't know what to do. I never thought he could be so callous."

We said nothing, we just waited for her to continue talking it out.

"He said they had just been talking and this was their first date. I don't know if I believe him or not, it's probably another lie."

"It's ok, it's bound to be hard to take this all in but just know we are going to be here with you every step of the way. Just because your marriage is over, doesn't mean you're on your own," I said.

Elle's face snapped round to mine: "Who said it's over?"

"Are you serious?" Ben said.

"You don't have to be scared, Elle. This is tough but you've got us," I added.

"What the fuck would you know about it? How many marriages have you walked away from just because things got a little rocky?"

"A little rocky? He killed you off so he could screw some random woman he met online!" Ben roared.

The waitress popped her head out from the kitchen to see what the raised voices were about.

"He didn't screw her," she replied.

"Yeah, because we gatecrashed the date. If we weren't here they'd be heading back for dessert - you know, like in the message you read?" I said.

Why is she defending him? Was she seriously considering taking him back?

I took a breath and continued: "I'm sorry, we just assumed…"

"Yeah, well, no one is as perfect as you two like to make out you are. He made a mistake, he's been found out, everything that happens now is still in flux."

We went back to sitting in silence until the waitress came down with the bill.

"I'll sort this," said Ben, awkwardly. He headed up to the counter to leave me with Elle.

"I'm sorry, Elle," I said, "Whatever you decide we will support you, no matter what. What can we do?"

"You can start with ordering some more bacon salad."

Chapter 28

"Mummy, this is Una," said an ecstatic looking Adam as he shoved a decrepit looking horse into my face.

"That's a lovely looking horse, sweety, but can you get it out of my face please?" I asked.

"It's not a horse, it's a unicorn – look at her horn!"

The flaccid looking horn looked more depressed than majestic, and the smell of the damned thing reminded me of a port-a-loo on the second day of a music festival.

"She's staying with us tonight and we get to do lots of fun things with her and take pictures and send them to my teacher and then do a talk about our adventures with her tomorrow. Isn't that great?" he beamed.

For the love of all that is holy, why does his teacher hate me?

"That's just fantastic news, love."

"I thought we could bring her to the beach, then the funfair and the cinema, I think she would like all that."

Not half a demanding cow is she? Sorry, unicorn.

"Eh, I don't think we'll be able to fit that all in. How about the park and some ice cream after?"

He weighed up the compromise and decided that sugar would suffice.

"Una isn't allowed ice cream."

"Oh, I know she's just a teddy."

"No, she's real – it's just Mrs Carroll said she was lactose intolerant."

But of course.

Before we even got out of the car at the park I had already turned into the horrible cross-sounding mummy, because my children were wailing in the backseat over who Una would sit beside. I explained that unicorns only liked the front seat and both of them had been sobbing since.

Tears were wiped away when I threatened to 'turn the car around and go straight back home' – I had gone full Irish mammy at this stage of the tantrums.

Una was dispatched with her two protectors while I spotted a coffee cart with an enthusiastic woman serving customers. I felt like I was cheating on Joseph, so I opted for water and sat down on the bench beside the slides to watch the children 'show' Una the joys of the park.

Their version of showing Una a good time was throwing her down slides and up in the air (and never catching her).

No wonder the poor girl was looking so rough

I took my phone out of my handbag to check in with my huge circle of friends – or one – there was nothing waiting for me.

Elle had fallen off the radar again since she left us home from Mike's, a week ago. I had phoned and texted several times, each day, since then. I was trying not to take the radio silence to heart but my anxiety on the situation was increasing by the day.

I just wanted to know she was ok or if she was avoiding me because she had let Keith move back home.

That pang of disappointment at the blank screen reminded me of teenage years waiting for my crush to text me.

Never happened, of course. I never had the nerve to even talk to him in school so why on earth did I think that an awkward teenage boy – who didn't know I existed – would take it upon himself to get my number and text me out of the blue?

Teenagers have it easy now. They get to find out all this juicy information about their prospective partners without even having to resort to following them around the school like a lovesick puppy-dog.

Amy: Hey quiet, are you all set for the launch night? Looking forward to seeing you in your finery. Gimme a call later x

I started to feel panicked that I was too late and maybe she'd given up on our friendship as quickly as she cemented herself into my life. Now that Ben and I were in a happier place, I worried that she would feel like I didn't need her anymore.

If that was the case, then she couldn't have been more wrong.

I depended on her because she understood me, she didn't judge, she didn't care that I was a little bit damaged – if anything we were both as damaged as each other.

I could feel a lump in my throat along with the panic in my chest.

I knew, at this age, it was common that you lose touch with people when kids come along.

I made that transition a lot easier by having a breakdown and cutting off anyone I had a sliver of a connection with – apart from my family.

It wasn't hard, people had their own lives and, to be honest, I wasn't that bothered. There was no one I missed but clearly, I hadn't experienced a friendship like this before. We had very little in common on the face of things – in terms of actual interests – but we worked and I was damned if I was going to lose it now.

I took my phone out and there was no reply to my message. I wondered if I should phone again, but I can't stand talking to people on the phone.

No, keep it safe. Text messages all the way.

Amy: I'm sure you're busy but I've missed talking to you the last while, so if you're not too busy and Keith has the kids, why don't you come stay at mine tonight? Ben is away and kids will be sleeping early. Wine and trashy tv? Let me know x

I hoped that would entice her out of her shell and I would love the company. I hated when Ben had to travel for work. The novelty of having the house to myself wore off after the first hundred times he'd been away.

As much as I liked to complain and kick him in his sleep when he snored too loudly I could never fall into a deep sleep until I could feel him in the bed next to me.

Even when things were bad, or we were going to bed after an argument, we would always sleep in the same bed. Both of us seething at each other from our perspective sides of the mattress, but I wouldn't want him debunking to anywhere else in the house.

I eventually rounded up the troops, after I could feel the first drops of rain. I tried to talk them out of the ice cream due to the monsoon-type rain outside but they couldn't be swayed. I stopped at the shop for the sugar on a stick and let them devour it on the drive home. I knew there was no chance I was going to win the dinner negotiations tonight.

"Did you take lots of pictures, mummy?" asked Adam

Fuck.

"My phone was dead sweety,"I lied.

"No, it wasn't! I saw you on it," piped up an unhelpfully accurate Arthur.

"No, that's when I was just checking it. It was definitely dead."

I could see my eldest son's eyes filled with tears and I felt like the worst parent on the planet, right now.

"It's ok, petal," I soothed, "We are going to get home and charge up my phone and take some really clever photos that will make it look like they were taken in the park. Besides, Una knows she was there and she'll definitely be able to tell Mrs Carroll."

He seemed satisfied with this and the crisis was averted – for now.

When we got home I ran up the stairs to 'charge my phone' and check to see if Elle had replied. There was still nothing from her; resulting in another pang of rejection.

I came down the stairs to try and be a halfway decent mother at least.

We positioned Una on the grass in the back garden with a little cocktail umbrella I found in the drinks cupboard.

"Now, it looks like it was such a sunny day she was protecting herself from the sun – like all sensible unicorns do," I explained.

"But she's not on the swings or the slides," wailed Adam.

"Yes, but you can tell the class that she was. You didn't get a picture because she was going so super quick on everything."

Work with me here, kid!

The photo shoot continued like this, eventually, I managed to get enough 'park' pictures that even kept Adam happy. I also had her help me make the dinner and we gave her a bubble bath in the sink and a spin in the tumble drier (which didn't hurt her because unicorns can't feel pain).

Just to make sure she was safe the two boys sat cross-legged in front of the machine waiting for the cycle to finish. This meant I got to clear up and do the dishes completely uninterrupted. I began to wish Una would stay on a more permanent basis.

By the time bedtime came, Una was dry and the boys were happy with the selection of photographs I showed them.

"You have to send them to Mrs Carroll tonight," said Adam for the 327th time since dinner.

"Yes, I know. I have the email address downstairs and Una's adventure will be sent as soon as you're asleep."

"Is daddy coming home tonight?" asked Arthur.

"Not tonight, but he'll be back tomorrow."

"You can have Una in your bed if you like? That way you don't have to stay by yourself," offered Adam.

My heart swelled because of my thoughtful little boy. Before I could tell him it was 'ok' and I didn't need her, he was already pushing her towards me.

"I'll get her back off you in the morning."

He smiled and turned over to go to sleep. I held Una up to my chest and felt very privileged to be given her for the evening. This must have been exactly how Adam felt when Mrs Carroll gave Una to him this afternoon.

I sat outside their bedroom for a while, listening to them both snore. Admittedly, I spent a lot of my day wishing the kids were quiet, or there wasn't mess around the house, or I had a minute to myself but I really couldn't imagine my life without them.

This last year had been a mess, but they were the one constant. I wanted, so much, to be better for them. I didn't want them to find me broken and afraid of living my life.

"I love you both," I whispered, at the doorway.

Arthur began to waken, so I turned and ran down the stairs as quickly as I could in case either of them properly woke up and I would have to parent again.

"Well, there's that nice moment ruined. Una? What do you fancy doing now?"

We both collapsed the sofa for the evening; there was still no word from Elle. I decided this was the final proof that I was definitely in the bad books.

Self-sabotage Amy would be hitting the bottle of wine in the fridge, phoning Elle and crying about how much she meant to me. Instead, I opted for some orange juice and television.

I really am a responsible adult these days

Things with Ben were getting better, kids were happy and healthy and I had reached a point where I didn't need alcohol to enjoy myself.

I've got this adulting, shit, covered.

I propped Una up on the pillow beside me to watch some awful soap opera. It made perfect sense to me that I needed to explain who the characters were, on screen, to a stuffed unicorn. I knew it made less sense to have a full conversation about the show with her. It didn't stop me though.

"That's a good question, Una," I said, "Tristan *was* kissing Abigail in the last scene and now he's trying to get into Caroline's pants. I don't know what the dating scene is like for unicorns but this type of man is what we humans refer to as a 'complete shit'."

She seemed to appreciate my keen insight into the male psyche. When that particular trash was over I decided I'd better get my laptop out. I dutifully wrote my email to Mrs Carroll with all the pictures and a bit of an over-zealous narrative for each one; I'm not sure she cared that Una 'slipped into a Zen-like state in her bubble bath in order to reflect on the day and her lost youth' but I sent it anyway.

With that done I decided to do some old-school networking. That was my polite way of saying I was looking up all my old boyfriends on the internet and pouring through their pictures in order to see if they're:

Miserable, having dumped me decades ago or

Fat, bald AND miserable.

I had successfully hunted them all down. In truth, there was only two that I was ever interested in checking in with: Ciaran and Declan.

I found that neither of them looked particularly sad without me.

How dare they get on with their lives 15 years after we parted ways? Calm down, they're hardly going to put up a miserable picture in their profile, are they?

I made a good point and decided to dig further.

I was engrossed in my snooping for 90 minutes and thought it was time to step away from the computer.

I had found out what they graduated university with, their first few jobs after and managed to get a fairly deep insight into a few of their ex-girlfriends lives too.

I was about to flick through Ciaran's 2003 Ibiza holiday photographs when the computer froze.

My technical know-how was poor at the best of times, but this time I decided just to keep bashing the mouse pad until it finally came back to life.

Thankfully, it did so quickly enough and just in time for me to share Ciaran's photo album publicly to my profile.

"HOLY MOTHER OF FUCK, WHAT HAVE I DONE?" I screamed, as I jumped up from the sofa and dropped the laptop.

The screen went black and I threw myself to the floor in order to undo my mistake before he was notified of my snooping.

It was the worst ex too. He was such a pretentious ass and really got off on how upset I was by being dumped.

Over the phone.

Two days before Christmas.

Bastard

If he saw this it would completely blow up his, already massive, ego and probably make him think I'm still obsessively checking in on him.

Just because I like to check in from time-to-time, doesn't mean I was still hung up on him. I was just nosey and bored.

God, I know I don't believe in you, but if you're up there please let this laptop switch on and let me scrape my dignity back. PLEASE.

I decided the Almighty's intervention was taking too long so I scrambled around the house to find my phone and go on the app in the hope I wasn't too late.

By the time I found it there was already a message waiting:

Ciaran: Hey doll, looooooong time. Can I ask you to take down that photo album you just shared? It's of a holiday – one with me and my ex – and honestly, I think it's a bit weird that you shared it. Hope you're keeping ok?

I stood, rooted to the spot, re-reading the message and thinking of a reply that didn't make me sound completely pathetic. A few minutes later, he sent another one:

Hey, listen, if this is your way to reach out to an old flame I don't think it's a great idea.

I'm sorry if you're not happy, but I am. I think it's best to leave the past where it belongs. You were always a nice girl and I hope you don't have to wonder about the 'what if' scenario any longer because now you know I'm definitely not interested. Like, ever.

Anyway, if you could delete the album that would be great and I hope you find the closure that you need soon.

Kind regards

Ciaran

I sat staring at the screen for a few minutes. My emotions flew from rage to mortification and back to rage again.

I swiftly deleted the album and promptly blocked Ciaran from my profile permanently. He would, no doubt, take this as the actions of a lover scorned but really I was saving him from the drunken abuse, I knew I would send after a bottle of wine, in the very near future.

I decided to text Elle and tell her all about my evening from hell. Surprisingly, she decided to reply to this message – perhaps the humiliation of my evening made her feel slightly perkier.

I was so happy to see her name on the screen but my elation was short lived when I read the message.

Elle: No way. Mortified for you.

Short and sweet

"At least I have you, Una, you're here for me – until tomorrow. Never mind, you're a bitch too."

Chapter 29

Today, was the day.

It was Joseph's official launch and if it went well it would cement the cafe into the community, as a haven for us undesirable parents.

I half expected to find protesters outside, fronted by Mrs Clunting. I was relieved to find none when I arrived to check how the final preparations were going.

She had spent the last few days leaving bogus reviews about the business online and trying to get a petition against us off the ground. It claimed that Elle was dealing drugs under the counter while I was an 'erratic drunk'. It didn't attract much attention so I decided it was best to just ignore her desperate attempts to derail us and take the high road, this time. More importantly, it didn't stop people coming through the door.

Things still weren't sorted with Elle, I felt like she was avoiding me. She came in and worked on her fairy lights and other little touches at times when I'd be at home with the kids and this morning was no different. When I arrived, the cherry blossom trees at the entrance were already in place, she was right: they were beautiful.

I took out my phone and quickly typed her a message:

Amy: the trees are amazing, you've such an eye for this. Do you want to get ready at mine tonight and we can come together? Xx

Elle: Yeah I was pleased with how they turned out. I'll see you there later

I hated her blunt replies. It was so frustrating but I didn't want to push her in case I caused an explosion and she didn't show up to celebrate our success. I could hear Joseph and Michael fighting in the back but I heard a female voice as well - one I didn't recognise.

"Ah, Amy, you're here," said Joseph, "Can you please tell my imbecile son-in-law that there is no need to start setting out the canapés now? They will be inedible by the time the first guest takes a bite."

A smartly dressed woman appeared behind him and introduced herself as Joseph's daughter, Maria.

"Amy," she said, "can you tell my father that he has no need to call my husband an imbecile? He meant that he wanted to start preparing the ingredients for the canapés so there's no rush later on but my imbecile father shouted at him before he could finish his sentence. Is this what it's always like? Does he bully my husband every day like this or are you just stressed about the party and taking it out on Michael?"

I didn't know how to answer her without putting my foot in it, so, as usual, I stayed quiet and hoped for the problem to go away.

"No!" he replied, "Of course I don't shout at him, he's my family. Do you think if I disrespected a man day-after-day he would show up to work for me? Don't be silly, my darling."

She seemed satisfied with this answer and went back into the kitchen to help her husband.

Joseph took me to one side and whispered: "I love my daughter but she will believe any old rubbish I tell her, including that her husband is a genius. If that man is a genius, I'm the Queen of Sheba." He roared with laughter at his terrible joke and went to greet customers at the door.

I made sure the fridge was full of sparkling wine for later and we were stocked up with plastic champagne glasses. There were no plates for sit down food. People would have to use napkins, if needed, for their canapés so we could cut down on the clean-up time.

Besides, this was still a café. We weren't looking to change that, we just wanted an excuse to get dressed up and have a little fun after all the work we'd put into the place – it was an added bonus that should the pictures make the paper, Mrs Clunting would be spitting venom for weeks.

I knew I was being petty but I couldn't stand the woman, and I could enjoy this little victory without descending into more criminal damage.

Five of Joseph's nephews were coming in to be waiters for the night. I left their uniforms and hoped that they'd fit – if they didn't it was too late to change them now.

Without Elle here there was no real reason to hang about, I could go home and get ready in my own time and meet her here later, like she said.

I'm not going to overthink this anymore, she's just busy.

I waved 'good-bye' to Joseph through the window as I left and headed back home to start the grooming process. My attempt to not overthink Elle's avoidance failed instantly. I abandoned plans to head home and instead readjusted the course and went to her house.

I'll just check in. It's not stalking. I'll make up some fairy light emergency

When I pulled up to her house I found her front door already open and three bin bags haphazardly left outside. I knocked the door to announce myself but I knew she wouldn't be able to hear me over the loud music, coming from inside the house.

I walked down the hallway and dodged falling clothes, coming from across the bannister. I called out for Elle again but there was still no answer.

I climbed the stairs towards the sound of the music and found her surrounded by men's clothing and boxes.

"Elle?" I shouted.

She turned around and turned off the stereo so I didn't have to roar a conversation at her.

"Spring cleaning?" I asked, tentatively.

"Kinda, yeah. I mean I'm cleaning Keith out of my life for good, nothing serious," she called over her shoulder.

"I'm sorry, Elle."

"No need to be sorry, it's not like you didn't see it coming. He was already done with me the second he walked out the door. 'Take a break' my arse. He's been playing the single man for months now. Painting the town red with his underwhelming penis, I'm sure Claire was just the tip of the iceberg."

"I take it you didn't talk to him about the counselling suggestion again then?" I asked.

"No, I didn't ask. It's bad enough I was going to look past that bullshit date night, never mind be pathetic enough to ask him to work through it. He quit on us already so I'm not asking him to stick around when he clearly doesn't want to."

"If you still want to salvage something with him then don't let pride stop you. Ask him, all he can say is 'no' and at least you know you gave it your all."

"I hate that phrase: 'gave it your all'. I mean why do I have to pour every ounce of myself into a relationship that he's already given up on? I gave it my all every day; he's the coward, not me."

"I didn't mean it like that, I'm sorry. I know you were 100% committed to the relationship. I just thought –

"Well, don't. I don't need anyone's advice, I can navigate my own life. I'm my own person and I'm certainly not as pathetically lost as you claim to be."

The words struck a chord in my heart. I didn't realise that's how she viewed me. Some lost soul who needed someone to tell me what to do at any given moment.

"I know you're hurting right now but I don't think I deserved that," I replied.

"Oh, you don't? Well, I don't think I should have been spending my time helping to sort out your life and helping in that café while I could have been home trying to save my own marriage, but here we are.

"I'm alone and you're hunky dory, so why don't you just leave. I need to keep throwing out the last decade of my life. I want a fresh start with the dead weight gone."

I wasn't sure if she was referring to me as the dead weight or Keith but I didn't want to stay and find out. I know she had put so much energy into me and the café but she did so willingly.

She said she welcomed the distraction, didn't she? I'm sure she was just upset and will calm down by tonight. I'll be gracious and accept her apology then and I'm sure, by tomorrow, we'll be laughing about it all.

"I'll see you later, Elle," I called.

She didn't reply or stop her packing to watch me go.

I hated that she was hurt and I couldn't make it better, I hated Keith and everything he was putting her through and I hated that she was pulling away and setting off down a dark path on her own. I felt useless and I didn't know how to help.

I spent the afternoon trying to look at makeup tutorials online, until I realised I could hear Ben coming in from work. I'd lost over two hours looking at them and hadn't even started getting ready.

"You are a vision," said Ben, "Although why do I have to wear a monkey suit while you get to wear jeans?"

"I'm obviously not wearing these. I lost track of time."

"I thought you wanted to be early to make sure everything is sitting right?"

"I do, I won't be long. I'm sure I have the know-how to get this makeup malarkey perfect, just give me a half hour and I'm all yours."

"I'm just saying, if you could shave three minutes off that total time we could start the evening off with a bit of fun?" he said hopefully.

"Three minutes? At least make it worth my while. If you behave, you might be entitled to a quick fumble next week."

"I'll take it!"

I loved when he was hyper. It was infectious and my mood was made instantly better by being around him. I couldn't shake the feeling of hurt by my interaction with Elle but I was going to force myself into a jovial mood - even if I had to plaster enough lipstick on me to rival a clown.

Tonight was months in the making and I wasn't about to let a silly misunderstanding, like her ripping out my heart, spoil that.

My parents came over to sit with the boys for the evening. They loved it when they babysat. It usually meant a later bedtime and a 'secret' sugary treat given, after we left.

When I was finished getting ready, I braced myself for the passive-aggressive comments on my dress from mother, as I tried to tame my hair. I hated wearing my hair up, I was always convinced I looked more like a man with it brushed back from my face but I hoped the sweetheart neckline on my green gown would be enough to prevent people mistaking me for one.

"You look beautiful," said my dad from behind me. He kissed my cheek as I pinned the last tendril of a curl in place.

"You really do," added my mother.

"Thank you!" I couldn't hide the shock from my voice at her disarming compliment. Perhaps retirement was mellowing her out, or perhaps I was high on the fumes from the hairspray.

"Don't sound so shocked, Amy, I am your mother. I am capable of giving compliments when they're deserved. I just don't want you to become one of those Americans who think that everything is 'amazing'."

I'd waited decades for a compliment from her, and it didn't disappoint. Now I was ready to take on the crowds of people and ignore the building tension caused by my social anxiety.

I can do this

We didn't arrive as early as I'd hoped and the place was already busy with members of Joseph's extensive family. Members of the community groups, that used the space on a weekly basis, and regular customers were all pilling in to celebrate with us.

I wondered if Mrs Clunting would show up, and make a scene, but I was more concerned that Elle wouldn't be there at all.

Joseph was delighted with the turnout and said he was going to do his speech soon before people 'got too fat and drunk on his free food'.

I hadn't planned on saying anything, public speaking was something best left to much more confident people. I was happy enough to clap and help bolster his confidence if he was nervous.

"Have you seen Elle?" I asked.

"No, she is probably late. That girl is always late." He waved off my concerns and went back to mingling with people I didn't know.

Ben appeared, beside me, holding two glasses of fizzy wine. "No booze tonight for me," I said, "I tend to get over-excited and set people on fire."

"One glass won't hurt, and I hid the matches around the house days ago. Have you found Elle?" he asked.

"No, I'm sure she'll show up. It's not a big deal," I lied.

"Then why have you not stopped searching through the crowd since we've got here?"

"I'm sorry, I'm just nervous. I want to make sure she's ok."

"She'll be fine, just relax and enjoy the achievement here. You've done what you set out to do: you've 'freed the fuck ups' and given the middle finger to Smug Club. I'm proud of you," he added.

"You are? You don't think I'm completely ridiculous for declaring war on a parent and toddler group?"

"Maybe a little, but look how happy you've made everyone here. Besides, they started it."

I scanned the room and saw what he meant; everyone was looking very dapper in their finery. I knew, at one stage, Joseph hated the idea of hosting a night like this - without charging everyone – but I noticed that he was smiling and even had an arm around Michael's shoulders.

Miracles do happen.

Joseph took to the stage and recalled how I'd first fallen into his coffee shop and into his life. He talked about how he'd spent the last few months being bullied into almost every business decision since that day. I blushed as he sung my praises and tried to hide behind Ben when he asked me to come on the stage to receive a present.

"You coming into this shop was predestined by God. I know this to be true, Amy Cole. I am thankful every day for that, as are my family and so is every person that walks through this door knowing they have a home away from home even for thirty minutes. You and Elle did that.

"Speaking of Elle, where is she?" he called out into the crowd, but no one came forward.

"That girl is always late," he laughed, "She is a tornado and I love her like a daughter – a horrible daughter that I never wanted!"

The crowd chuckled and I could make out one particularly shrill laugh coming from the back of the room.

It was Elle.

She was still dressed in the sweatpants and T-shirt from earlier, but now, she was drunk. She downed the last of the bubbly from her glass and dropped it on the floor.

"Whoops, sorry dad," she called from the back.

The crowd started to part as she walked up to the stage. She gave mock waves to people she didn't know and did a 'what's your problem?' face when they didn't wave back. The atmosphere became uncomfortable with every step she took.

This can't be good

"Eh DAD you're not meant to have favourites, where's my present and pat on the back? Especially as I did most of the work," she said, in a sing-song voice.

"Of course, Elle, I have your present here. Like I was saying, I am so thankful for these two women walking through the doors and turning my business around.

"We are all a family now and I can never thank them both enough," his voice was broke with emotion so I squeezed his hand to reassure him that I felt the same.

"Ah now isn't that an awesome sight?" said Elle, "We're all such a happy family. I'm so glad to hear it because DAD I'm moving home. You see, my husband is a dick and has left me up shit creek," she laughed.

"Elle?" I asked, "Let's just go sit down and get some coffee."

"Is that you Amy? I can't see you over that push-up bra you're sporting. I know you've pushed them out so no one thinks you're a bloke with your hair up," she said, too loudly, as usual.

Speaking directly to the crowd she added: "She thinks she has a big moon face but I don't think she looks like a bloke, a pig with lipstick more like it. Ah come on, I'm clearly joking. I'm simply here to make a lovely toast on this very special occasion."

Please don't do this

She grabbed the glass out of Joseph's hand and raised it towards me.

"To my best friend, Amy. To the woman who is so totally clueless and repressed she almost ruined her life - but instead, she ruined mine.

"To the woman who takes her husband and children for granted so much, she's more than happy to run out the door any evening so she can talk shit to me about how crap things are.

"To the woman who wouldn't know a genuine problem if it hit her in the face and to the woman who keeps talking about how bad she's got it when she has a life most people would kill for.

"Spoiler alert, princess, you're full of shit. Get your act together and fuck off."

She finished off Joseph's drink and handed the empty glass back to him.

"Later, losers."

She pushed through the crowd and went out the door. I stayed where I was in a stunned silence and tears streamed down my cheeks.

Somewhere close-by, Joseph was shouting for the music to start. I could feel Ben put his arms around me and take me over to the side of the room. He began wiping away my tears and I pushed his hands away.

"I'm fine, stop fussing," I said.

"You're not fine, no one would be fine after that shit. That was completely uncalled for and I should have given her a piece of my mind."

"For telling the truth?"

"That wasn't the truth, Amy. You are not any of those things. You have depression, it has made things difficult for this last year but we are getting through it.

"You have not been the cause of her marriage ending so don't, for one second, believe that.

"Keith was already trying to hump strangers, from the internet, while still married to her. That's what ended it.

"I love you, I'm going to get you something to eat and you're going to enjoy the rest of your evening because you deserve it. Just because she's said that, when she's bitter and drunk, doesn't make any of it true."

He left to corner one of the waiters for tiny canapés but it was too late for me.

I was already soaking up every word Elle said and feeding the inner bitch with fundamental proof that I was, in fact, everything that she accused me of.

I could feel the fog getting thicker and I wanted to get out of there and never see any of these people again.

Chapter 30

It had been a week since the launch night. Elle's outburst aside, we had some nice pictures on the website and there was another write-up in the paper which made the place sound like a hotspot for young families.

I resisted the urge to text Elle, to be honest, I just didn't feel up to receiving more abuse. She hadn't shown up at Joseph's since that night and I managed to avoid any locations that she would be likely to appear. It was very stressful avoiding someone - someone who is probably actively avoiding you at the same time.

A ball of anxiety was sat in the pit of my stomach ever since and it hadn't gone away. I was doing my very best impression of someone who wasn't bothered about their public humiliation from a loved one, but I was in turmoil on the inside.

It was the perfect breeding ground for the bitch. She was bigger than ever. I tried to ignore her as much as I could during the day but it was at night when she really did the damage. I tried sleeping tablets to knock her out but, a week on, I was still unable to sleep.

It was a losing battle and by day eight I gave up.

I couldn't get out of bed. I was aware that Ben was talking to me about eating but I couldn't comprehend what he was saying. I was lost to him, I was lost to everyone.

I didn't bother looking for my phone, there was nothing on it to interest me and I couldn't face the thought of drinking water, never mind any type of food.

I don't know how long I lay there but the curtains remained pulled and all I managed to do was blink. My eyes were burning with tiredness but I couldn't rest my brain long enough to sleep. My stomach was sick from the abuse I was saying to myself but I couldn't stop it. The record was on repeat and I hadn't the strength to turn it off long enough to rest.

Ben had tried to guilt me into getting up to see the children because 'they missed me'.

It didn't work.

He tried the softly, softly husband routine and on one occasion he even attempted tough love but all tactics were met with the same blank look on my face.

I wanted to scream and shout and shake myself, but I couldn't physically move. I couldn't even lift my head to apologise to Ben; I just continued to stare into the darkness.

The pity party was in full swing and I was the guest of honour. I lost track of time, soon I couldn't even tell if it was day or night.

"Amy?" a familiar voice called from the darkness.

"Mum? I'm not really up for visitors," I said, as I gathered the duvet around myself like a cocoon.

What was he thinking letting her, of all people, in to see me?

"Amy it's time to get out of bed," she said.

"I can't."

"My fearless daughter can do anything, she's just a little lost right now but that's why I'm here."

I started to cry.

The floodgates opened and I was not sure how to stop them. I was already dangerously dehydrated to begin with, never mind adding this unprecedented emotion to the mix.

"We are going to get you better and the help you need. I'm not going to leave your side until you've at least had a wash. The smell in here is revolting."

I knew it was my mother's attempt at a joke. I appreciated it internally even if I didn't vocalise it then and there.

After a few moments, she took a deep breath and said:

"I don't know if you realised this before, but I'm not a natural mother. When they handed you over to me I wasn't filled with that instant feeling of love everyone talks about. I was terrified. I don't think I ever stopped being terrified from that day. No matter what I did I always thought I was doing the wrong thing. That's why I thought it was easier if I just pushed you closer to your dad. I think that's why you are, the way you are. It's my fault."

"What way am I, mum?" I couldn't hide the hurt sound in my voice. I knew I was far from 'normal' but I didn't expect to hear it from her, now.

Talk about kicking a woman when she's down

"You're just sensitive, Amy," she said, tentatively.

"I rejected you and kept you at arm's length and you spent your whole life trying to fill the void of love you didn't get from me. It's made you think you're not good enough, all this time – but you are, Amy. You are so enough.

"I'm just so sorry."

She put her head in her hands and started to cry.

I looked at my mother and wondered was everyone as broken as I was but they just hid it better. Did everyone carry around pointless and unnecessary guilt? My susceptibility to depressive episodes weren't caused by my mother's imagined rejection. I loved her, I had a lovely childhood, I just wanted the woman to compliment my hairdo once in a while.

I reached up, took her hand in mine and waited until she stopped crying.

"This isn't your fault," I said, "This *isn't* your fault."

She lay down on the bed beside me in the darkness. It didn't take long for either of us to fall asleep. It was the best sleep I'd had in a long time.

I felt nothing but complete comfort being close to her and it was probably what she needed to forgive herself too. I hoped this conversation would help her to let go of the guilt that she'd been plagued with, all these years.

I've always felt that sleep was a healing force when I was at my lowest ebb and I think that's why my subconscious made me stay awake; just another way to torture myself.

When I woke up my mother was still asleep. I wrapped the throw from the bottom of my bed, around my shoulders and decided to venture downstairs.

The house was quiet; I assumed Ben had taken the kids out so they wouldn't get wind of the breakdown, going on upstairs. A fresh wave of guilt hit me, at the thought of me letting down my children, once again.

My stomach started to rumble but I wasn't confident enough to try food after one good nap. If this was me coming out the other side of this episode I was taking baby steps.

Water first, a bath maybe?

My hair was matted and greasy, my breath was toxic and I could feel a crust on my teeth as I ran my tongue across them.

A bath first, food after.

I ran the water and waited for it to be full enough to get in. There was a knock on the door and my mother popped her head in.

"It smells lovely in here," she said, "Do you want some help?"

"I think I can manage to get in the bath on my own."

"Amy, you're skin and bones and you're gripping onto the sink to hold yourself up."

In truth, my head was light from my short jaunt down the stairs and the heat in the room wasn't helping.

I got undressed and she held my hand as I stepped in. Self-consciously, I tucked my knees under my chin and let my head rest on them.

She picked up the little jug from the sideboard and I started to relax as she poured some water on my head.

I closed my eyes and left my head where it was. She repeated the process over and over until my hair smelled like the lavender from the water.

She massaged the shampoo into my scalp, then the conditioner, and I wanted to fall asleep there. It was so comforting and with every pour of the water over my head, I felt a little bit more human.

I tried not to think of my anxiety or what had happened to get me there, but the ball of dread was still sitting like lead in the pit of my stomach.

When she finished with my hair, she gathered it up and clipped it to the top of my head.

"You just relax there for a while and shout when you want a hand out," she said.

Her eyes were still puffy from the tears, earlier, but she gave me a smile as she closed the door behind her.

I lay back and rested my head on the side of the bath.

That's another fine mess you've gone us into, Amy.

One thing for certain was: there was no getting out of therapy this time. The medication wasn't enough to stop this and I don't think I stood a chance talking my way out of it with Ben. He would be delighted to see me out of bed but not even a fresh pair of pyjamas would convince him I was better.

Is there a cure for depression? Or will I just be coping with this for the rest of my life?

I couldn't think of the rest of my life, all I could concentrate on was the next half hour.

If I could manage that much then maybe I can pull myself out of this

By the time Ben and the boys came into the house, mum had wrapped me up in a huge woolly blanket on the sofa. The kids jumped on top of me, instantly. They started talking animatedly about their day and what I'd missed when I was in bed with the 'flu' for the last while.

I liked that I didn't really have to speak, I couldn't get a word in edgeways even if I wanted to. Ben hovered in the background, unsure if he should just give us privacy or join in the conversation. I offered a weak smile and it was all the invitation he needed to sit beside me. Mum didn't say anything before she left, she just made herself scarce while I reconnected with my family.

I didn't know if my afternoon with her was a turning point in our relationship or if she would put her wall up again, as soon as I was feeling better.

I'll worry about that later

I watched the kids play while Ben offered every food he could think of in order to tempt me to eat. I finally relented and took some toast to curb the hunger that was growing in my belly.

I tried not to drink too much water, too quickly, but as soon as the first drop hit my stomach I was overcome by an overwhelming thirst. After three pints of water, the sloshing in my stomach couldn't be ignored.

I tried to read for a while but my eyes were hurting from overuse, this afternoon. I didn't attempt to switch on my phone - that was too much visual stimulation for my attention span.

Ben looked relieved that I was downstairs and I know he would want to have a talk when the kids were in bed, but I wasn't ready. He would have to be patient a little while longer.

When I thought of Elle my heart panged a bit.

I didn't know how to resolve the situation. She obviously didn't want to hear from me - she made that painfully clear - but I still wanted to make amends. I wanted my friend back but I didn't know how I could help her heal when I was a mess myself.

A problem for another day. Just rest now.

It was the kindest sentiment I'd said to myself in a long time. It was soothing to be nice to myself, and not something I'd ever been good at.

I was once given a book of '101 ways to love yourself' and it was never even opened. I wasn't convinced of my recovery enough to dig it out. I was still fixating on half-hour slots at a time.

I lay my head on the cushion and closed my eyes. I assumed there would be no way I could sleep, because of the noise with the children in the room. I knew I could have gone upstairs to rest but it was comforting to be around the chaos of my everyday life.

I stayed where I was and drifted off to sleep within minutes.

Chapter 31

I wasn't asleep long before I was woken by voices I couldn't place. Ben was one, for sure, but there was another female in the hallway.

Elle? No, too quiet to ever be her

Ben came in with a blonde woman, I had never met before. She had a huge trolley and wheeled it into the centre of my living room.

"This is Olive," said Ben, "She's here to help you with your hair."

"My hair? What's wrong with my hair?" I panicked and I couldn't think of anything else but finding a mirror.

"It's fine, it's fine, Amy," he soothed, "Your mum thought it would be a good idea to get a professional to come in and try to work on it. It's badly matted still and she thinks you may need some of it cut."

Tears burnt my eyes and I experienced a mix of feelings. I was thankful to my mother for the lovely gesture but sad because my hair was about the only thing I liked about myself and now depression would take that away too.

In the grand scheme of things, I knew it seemed trivial, but it didn't matter.

"Don't you worry yourself my darling," said Olive, "You just let me work my magic and we will see what we can do."

I nodded through the tears and took the clip from the top of my head to let my, still-damp, hair fall to my shoulders.

Olive started digging through her trolley and brought out several spray bottles, all different colours and sizes. She generously started spraying my hair, all over, with a large pink bottle – it smelled heavenly. I wasn't sure how many different types of sprays or hair masks she was putting on my matted nest but the combing was the hardest part.

Hours passed as she took each tiny section and carefully started to work her comb through it. It was painful and boring but I didn't speak a word of annoyance. This woman was trying every trick in the book to save my hair and I could put up with the pain if it meant I wasn't sporting a bob for the next year.

Some may see it as a 'fresh start' with a new hairstyle but I would see it as a constant reminder of a particularly painful time in my life. Physical evidence of failure in a never-ending battle against depression.

Ben would pop his head in every so often offering tea and clearing away the cold ones that lay, untouched, on the coffee table. He would give me a wink every time he came in and I tried to smile to reassure him I was doing ok, but I could tell he didn't buy it.

I liked Olive, especially because she wasn't a talker. Other than sheer laziness, I spent my life avoiding hairdressers out of fear of having to make small talk with them.

After every strand she managed to get through, without using her scissors, she would take a little break to stretch out her arms, de-cramp her hand and walk around the room for a break.

"I'm good friends with your mother," she finally said, "She told me you had a case of the blues and you needed a pick-me-up."

The blues was such an innocent way of putting things; clearly Olive was of the same school of thought as my mother. I don't think Eloise had ever said the word 'depression' out loud before.

"I have depression," I said, "When things get bad I call them episodes but really it's starting to feel that depression is my real life. It's when I'm out there pretending to be fine, that's the real episode. I don't want this to be my family's life. Looking after me and hiding the knives."

Olive stopped her combing regime.

"My sister had your sickness," she said, "She had it her whole life, it took her away from everyone and everything she loved until she had no one else but her and the sickness. Finally, she must have had enough and one day decided that she didn't want to live this way anymore. So...she killed herself."

"I'm sorry," I said, quietly.

"Thank you," she replied, "I read something once after my sister died, it said: 'suicide is a permanent solution to a temporary problem'. It struck a chord with me. You won't always feel like this, but you won't find that out unless you stick around. I was angry at my sister for a very long time, but I know it wasn't her fault."

She went back to combing the next tangled strand and I continued to keep quiet and look at the wall ahead.

I had no idea where I was going or what I was meant to do next, but I knew I didn't want to end up back at the lake.

I needed help and I needed it now.

***

It took two weeks before I had the confidence to venture out the door again. The noise of the cars on the street was already making me nervous but I had to get outside or I would start climbing the walls. Ben had returned to work five days ago and I was struggling to keep the kids entertained inside all the time.

I decided on a local park to ease myself back in. It was bitterly cold so I assumed more sensible parents would be inside on a day like this. I was right – we had the place to ourselves. I couldn't feel my fingers after ten minutes and I tried to coax the boys into the idea of a hot chocolate at Joseph's instead of staying there a minute longer. I had to throw in a scone to get them moving, but it was worth it so I could feel my fingers again.

I was nervous about seeing him, it would be the first from the party but I told myself I had nothing to be embarrassed about.

When I came in through the door, the café was quieter than I expected for this close to lunchtime, so I scanned the room to see if I could see any familiar faces. I tried not to look for Elle but it was second nature at this point.

She wasn't there.

Joseph came out of the kitchen with a bright smile on his face, one that told me he was genuinely happy to see me. It did my heart good.

"Ah, Amy! My boys! You look frozen and you need fattening up, all of you. Sit, sit. I'll bring over all you need."

We were jostled over to my usual spot and waited to see what Joseph would provide.

It didn't take long for a woman I didn't recognise to come over with two hot chocolates, a coffee and four oversized scones - with a ludicrous amount of butter and jam on them.

"We really don't need all this," I said.

"I'm just doing as I'm told, I don't like to get on the wrong side of him in case I get shouted at – I'm new," she smiled.

"Don't worry about Joseph, his bark is worse than his bite."

"Not Joseph, he's a lovely man I'm talking about the head chef, Michael, he is a hard taskmaster."

She walked off with the tray and I tried to process what I'd just heard.

In the short time I was gone, Michael had found his voice – by the sounds of it he was now a bit too vocal – Elle was no longer working here and business is slow.

I need answers

When the boys had demolished everything in front of them and decided to go find out what new toys were on offer, I beckoned Joseph over in order to find out everything.

"A lot of changes around here then?" I said.

"Not really. Business is slow today, but good all around. Don't be worrying."

"New faces, too."

Come on, Joseph don't make me ask

"Natasha? Yes, she's been here a few weeks; but I don't think you are asking about her."

"No," I said, "Have you seen her?"

"She came in two days after her little scene. I think she was hoping to see you here but she was too proud to say. She said she wouldn't be coming back around anymore; I gave her the wages she was owed and we parted ways."

"Did she say anything about me?"

"No, I'm sorry, Amy. She's hurting but you know she didn't mean those things. The mind can get a little twisted when it comes to matters of the heart. A broken one can be deadly."

I didn't know if I was relieved that she didn't leave more abuse at Joseph's feet to relay back to me.

Perhaps she did and he was being kind by not telling me.

When I eventually turned my phone back on, after my sabbatical from sanity, I expected something. A text message, a voicemail, anything; but there was nothing. I typed out a few messages to send, ranging from righteous indignation at her outburst to sniveling apology that she was feeling this let down. I couldn't find the balance between the two so I thought it best to stay quiet. That was my answer to everything. Perhaps if I hadn't stayed quiet all those times she was trying to tell me how crap she was feeling than maybe she wouldn't think I was the cause of her perceived ruination.

The boys and I stopped at the library on the way home so I could browse through the self-help sections and see if I could find something on depression or mindfulness in order to get Ben off my back.

I was right about my therapy prediction. Each evening he would present me with the professional profile of a new therapist and each evening I would find some arbitrary reason why I didn't like them. The excuses were wearing thin – the most recent one was: "He's got ginger hair, I've ginger hair, that's a recipe for disaster"

Ben wasn't fussed on pressing that bizarre reason any further because he seemed to drop it.

I never made it to the self-help section, I got sidetracked by celebrity biographies. As I perused the section it was obvious that they were celebrities in the loosest sense of the word. I became engrossed in an ex-reality star's book simply because there was glitter on the cover. I literally judged a book by its cover and took it home with me.

By the time Ben came in, I was reading about her second divorce in the space of three years and I was hooked.

"What are you reading?" he asked.

"Self-help book," I lied, "I'm just getting to the point where she's hitting rock bottom."

"Oh, really? That's great, Amy – very proactive of you."

I put the book in my bedside drawer and decided to change the subject for fear of follow-up questions.

"So, what do you fancy for dinner?"

"What do you mean?"

"I don't think that's a very misleading question, Mr Cole?"

"Normally it's not but I want to see the menu first."

Fuck. Mum's birthday dinner, I'd completely forgotten.

"By the look on your face, I'm going to assume you forgot about tonight, even though we were talking about it at breakfast.

"You were to head out and get the present with the boys, remember?"

"It may have slipped my mind. Can I play the 'I'm still depressed' card?"

"Meh, maybe, she's not my mother. Look, it's fine we'll get this dinner over us and say the present is 'on its way'."

"I like that, that way I'm not committing to anything it's just 'on its way'. Could be a new top, could be a llama, who knows?"

"Please don't get her a llama."

Chapter 32

We were the last to arrive at the Italian restaurant. We were meeting my parents with their closest friends, the McDonnells, and they all resented the fact we had to go for dinner this early to accommodate the kids.

That level of resentment is always nice to start the evening off with. My mother hadn't completely put her wall back up since I managed to get out of bed again and rejoin the real world, but she wasn't suddenly a cuddly person either.

"Where have you been? What *are* you wearing? You could have got Olive to do your hair" she asked.

"Happy birthday, mother," I replied, as I kissed her on the cheek, "I'm absolutely famished, what looks good?"

"Nothing, we're stuck with the early bird menu like a group of pensioners," huffed Dad.

"You *are* a group of pensioners, dad, now suck it up and pick something that won't irritate your dentures."

"You cheeky mare, these are all still my real teeth!"

"Now that my daughter has finally graced us with her presence, how about the presents," suggested mum, gleefully.

For all her gruffness she really was still a child at heart. When it came to her birthday she still wanted to be the centre of attention and God help my father if he didn't make her feel as if she was the most important woman in the world for the entire day.

I remember, one year, he suggested we do a 'low key' affair so she didn't speak to him for a week. I believe that was the year he bought her an eternity ring after day six of the silent treatment.

The McDonnell's were first:

"Oh, Deirdre! How thoughtful! A spa day is just what I need. I'm an unpaid child-minder these days with Amy taking liberties so this will be just perfect for 'me time'."

Bloody, Deirdre

She looked expectantly towards me, so I invited the boys to hand over the cards they both made for her before we left. She did the obligatory proud granny routine and made a fuss of what 'talented' grandsons she had, but she was still expecting her 'real' gift.

"And what did my daughter bring?" she asked.

"Well, mum, I wanted to get you something really special. Like really special and I think I've finally got it," I said.

"By all means, don't keep me in suspense, Amy?"

"It's on the way."

"On the way?"

"Yep, it should be here any minute, actually."

Ben looked at me completely flabbergasted at the fact I could mess up a simple lie like this.

"What Amy means is that it's not on the way this evening, but it should definitely arrive by tomorrow, sorry for the delay, Eloise."

"Well, Amy? Which is it? Is it arriving any second or is it coming tomorrow?"

When I looked into her sad eyes I knew I couldn't let her down; after all, she'd been so nice and I did owe her one for giving birth to me.

"It's arriving at any minute, mum," I lied, "I'm just going to go check and see where it is. Excuse me, I just need to make a call."

I left the table and went outside, scanning the deep recesses of my mind to find some sort of miracle.

What does Eloise Galbraith like?
Italian food
Opera
Leaving passive aggressive reviews on the internet
Painting? No, that's dad.
Fuck.
Well, we're eating in an Italian restaurant so that's out. That leaves me with opera. What in the hell am I going to do with that?

As a car drove by, the passenger sang out the window towards me. It was a rubbish novelty song and when that didn't change my expression he shouted: "Smile, love!"

I responded in kind by giving him the finger.

It was in that second I had a flash of inspiration. I just needed a singer. They could show up and do one of those impromptu serenades, like the fake waiters you see at weddings.

How can I possibly get someone here to sort this?

I scrolled through my address book, in the hope that I had some random part-time opera singer's number I had forgotten about. By the time I got to 'M', without being any closer to my goal, I could feel sweat dripping down my back. I decided that I should just phone the next person I got to and see what they can come up with, they couldn't be any more clueless than I was.

It rang four times but there was no answer. I was about to give up when they eventually picked up.

"Hello?"

"Michael! Thank goodness you picked up!"

"Amy? What's wrong? Is the café on fire?"

Perhaps I should have started with a less melodramatic opening

"Nothing like that, I need your help," I said.

"Of course, what can I do?"

I explained my predicament and instead of being completely outraged at my poor organisational skills as a daughter, he said he may be able to help.

"I knew I could count on you. You have such a huge family, I figured there was bound to be an authentic Italian opera singer in your hive somewhere."

"Amy, you know I'm not Italian, right? Have you thought that this whole time? That's very racist."

Fuck, abort! Abort!

"No, I haven't always thought that. Sometimes I think you're from the Middle East or Cork."

*What part of your brain thought that would sound **less** racist?*

"I am Columbian, Amy. Joseph and his family are also Columbian.

"I'm sorry, Michael. Really I am, I just need some help."

"I have a cousin called Pablo, he's a performer... of sorts."

"Of sorts?"

"Well he doesn't do opera but he puts on a show and he can do that to some opera music if you like?"

"Like a mime?"

"He mimes in parts. Look, do you want me to phone him or not?"

I was desperate, and if a Columbian mime artist was all I could manage at this stage, a Columbian mime artist was what my mother was getting.

"Yes! He's got an hour to get to the Italian restaurant on Leslie Square, and tell him to look a little Italian."

"Again, racist."

I hung up the phone and turned to find Ben running out the door towards me.

"I came to find out the progress on the present that doesn't exist?"

"I have it all in hand. I have an authentic Columbian mime artist coming to perform an interpretive routine for my very cultured mother. Trust me, she'll love it and definitely won't be expecting it."

We rejoined our table and ordered the food. I received a text from Michael letting me know my performer was en route. The waitress had arrived to take our dessert order when I looked round to see my present.

I walked over to find him speaking with the manager and handing him an iPod.

"Amy?"

"Pablo?"

"Yep, that's me. Just sorting out my signal for my music. I got some real classical shit on this that I know you're gonna like."

"Out of curiosity, do you get a good reception to the routine? I never realised that it was still as popular."

"Oh yeah, I mean I'm out most weekends doing this. First time here though – you cool with this, man?"

The manager was beginning to look a bit concerned with this artist and his iPod.

"I'm just going to do a quick change and then I'll give you the thumbs up to start the music," he said, to the reluctant-looking Italian.

Just as he was about to leave I managed to remember one important deal breaker: "No clown makeup, she's terrified of clowns."

Dodged a bullet there, that could have been a complete disaster.

I reassured the manager that it would be a quick routine and wouldn't disrupt the other diners.

How disruptive could mime be anyway?

I rejoined the table and cleared my throat.

"So, mum. The time has arrived for your very special birthday gift," I smiled. The next part would need to take some creative embellishment and a hope that her memory was faltering in her old age.

"I decided this gift would be appropriate because of the days we would spend, walking on the pier together, and seeing acts like this.

"I remember feeling so happy because it was graceful, artistic and rather poetic. All these qualities I see in you. With that in mind, I've invited this performer to express just how much you mean to me.

"I love you."

It worked. There were definite tears in her eyes and I was confident that I had trumped Deirdre and her stupid, spa day.

I saw Pablo give the thumbs up to the manager and settled on my seat to watch his performance.

Alarm bells started to ring when I realised that Pablo's definition of 'classical music' was, in fact, New Order's, *Blue Monday*. I closed my eyes and hoped that when I opened them again I wasn't faced with the horrifying realisation that I had, in fact, hired my mother a stripper.

I opened my eyes to be greeted by a leather-clad Columbian gyrating in front of a very shocked looking Deirdre.

"Now, let's really get this party started," he purred, "Which one of you fine women is the birthday girl."

With a dead-pan expression, my mother raised her hand and waited for the horror to continue.

In his defence, he did mime - unfortunately, it was a sex act.

We all sat there, stunned, as he mimed cunnilingus on my 70-year-old mother, at the table, in front of a room of strangers and my two small children.

It was the longest three minutes of my life but Pablo seemed to be getting into it. He was really working the crowd trying to get them to clap their hands to the beat and chant 'take them off'.

He was one large tug away from completely naked when the manager had the sense to intervene.

There was a collective moan of disappointment from a table at the back. Pablo was handed the clothes he'd already discarded and pushed into the bathroom.

I didn't know who to look at first.

The McDonnells' were in a state of shock, Ben looked purple with embarrassment and the children were in kinks of laughter.

My father had his head in his hands, hoping that he was going to wake up from this nightmare at any second, and lastly: my mother. She glared at me. I don't think I'd ever seen a woman look madder. I didn't know what to do, so I just smiled.

"Do you think that was *funny*?" she raged.

"I thought he was rather good," offered Deirdre.

"Thank you, Deirdre; so did I," I replied.

That seemed to anger her more.

The fury was, momentarily, paused as the waitress brought down the birthday cake to the table.

We then all had to sing a very miserable rendition of 'Happy Birthday'.

There was no conversation over the subsequent dessert and cake eating.

We all ate our chocolate sponge in silence and in an attempt to fix the situation I said: "We haven't seen dad's present yet."

"That's right, James. Hand it over."

"It's at home," he murmured.

"No it's not, it's right there, granddad," said Adam, who looked very pleased with himself.

"I'd rather do this in private," he pleaded.

"Nonsense, if you thought that then why on earth did you bring it with you?"

"That was before Amy's 'gift'."

It took a second for the penny to drop.

The fool had gone and had the painting completed.

If she opened it now her reputation as a sex-mad pensioner would be solidified.

"I think dad is right, maybe you should leave it for home," I said.

"I think you've done enough, Amy," she growled.

Sorry, dad, you're on your own.

We all watched helplessly as my parents started to wrestle with each other, both attempting to grapple the present out of each other's hands.

"For goodness sake, James what has got into you?"

She finally managed to wriggle it out of his grip and tore at the paper greedily. Her change of expression was instantaneous. It evolved from delight at winning her prize to sheer shock when she realised she was faced with my father, in all his naked glory, in watercolour form.

"What?" was all she could manage.

"To explain: I decided to get something a bit unique this year and I thought getting something real classy, like this, would be a great idea.

"I'm sorry, love. I didn't realise Amy would be turning your birthday into some sort of sex party and now my present seems a bit…seedy."

Deirdre was rummaging through her handbag for her glasses to see what she was missing but was thwarted by her husband who just gave her a firm 'no' through gritted teeth.

"I don't know what to say," she eventually said, "I love it."

No one was expecting that reaction, but the relief around the table was palpable.

"It's a real work of art," she beamed.

She proudly passed it around the table for everyone to have a look.

I decided to bypass my turn, as I'd seen the live act, far too recently for my liking. Ben nudged me to look but I refused.

"Not the picture, the signature at the bottom," he said.

It was Elle's. She'd done the painting for my father and it was beautiful. The gesture – even if it meant nothing to her - meant a lot to me.

She had made my parents, and I, very happy.

I never thought a naked painting of my father would have the potential to do that.

That may be something I should bring up in therapy

The dinner finished up without any more drama. Mum was so happy with her painting she even managed to stop glaring at me long enough to give me a hug.

As we were leaving, I caught a glimpse of the manager sitting at the bar with Pablo. He was talking animatedly and gesturing as he spoke. I assumed he was regaling him with tales of his wilder nights as a 'mime'.

I wasn't going to disturb them and decided I would get in touch with Michael in order to arrange payment for the worst birthday present ever.

I was lost in my own thoughts on the way home when Ben interrupted my stream.

"Are you going to call her?" he asked.

"Who?"

"You know who - Elle. Maybe it's time you reached out, she might need you."

I knew he was right, but I still wasn't sure if my pride had healed enough to face her.

"Perhaps. I'll see how I feel tomorrow."

"Have you given any more thought to the therapist I showed you?"

"The one that looks like a member of the Weasley family?"

"Yes, he comes very highly recommended and I think that if I don't press you on this, you're never going to decide on anyone."

"Ok, I'll meet him."

The look of shock on Ben's face was a picture and I couldn't help but laugh.

"Sometimes, dearest, I've been known to be rather reasonable. I may even let you spoon me tonight."

"Hear that, boys? Daddy's on a promise."

"Really not appropriate."

"What? I'm not the one who paid a man to pretend to hump my mother at the dinner table."

"Neither did I!" I protested, "I haven't paid him yet."

Chapter 33

I waited in the hallway for Ben to arrive and take me to my first therapy session with Dr Jeremy Kelly.

It has been a week since the birthday dinner and I had run out of excuses not to go and meet with him.

I knew he was going to force me to confront my demons in some horrific, sadistic way like...talking.

The horror.

The kids were with my parents, who had finally relented and decided to laugh at the stripper incident. However, I suspected, my mother would be expecting a cruise as next year's present from me.

I saw a silhouette approaching the door and decided to grab the Batman mask sitting at the door to surprise Ben. I squeezed my face into the tiny mask and opened the door, jumping out from behind it as I did.

It wasn't Ben standing there with a look of shock, it was Elle.

I pulled the mask off my face and looked at her completely agape. I couldn't believe she was really here and smiling nervously on my doorstep. I pulled her into the biggest bear hug I could manage and refused to let her go, even though I could hear a moan as the oxygen was pressed out of her.

"What are you doing here?" I asked.

"Let...go...Amy," she wheezed.

"Oh, sorry. There, breathe. Now, what are you doing here?" I asked again.

"Ben called, said you might need a lift and some moral support for your first therapy session. Thought I could ask you about getting my job back as your sarcastic chauffeur. "

My smile was so big it hurt my cheeks, "Of course you can, I'm just so happy to see you."

"Can we sit a minute, I think we should have a chat," she said, as she sat down on the doorstep and patted the space beside her for me to join her.

"I like the new hair," she began

I self-consciously touched my shorter hair and smiled. Olive avoided giving in and cutting it into a bob, but it was still noticeably shorter.

"I have a lot of apologising to do, to a lot of people, but I needed to start with you."

She took a big breath before she continued: "I had no idea how bad you'd gotten again, after that night at the party. To think that I caused you so much pain just kills me inside. I'm so sorry for all of the nasty things I said. It wasn't true, I was just out of my mind with bitterness over Keith. You had absolutely nothing to do with the breakdown of my marriage, it was dead before you and I even met. We'd both stayed much longer than the use-by date. "Everything I did with you, I wanted to – not because I was forced.

"All I ever wanted to do was help you find yourself, and I loved every second of it.

"When Keith finally left and I knew he wasn't coming back, I lashed out. Then when you told me things were on the mend with Ben, instead of being a decent friend and being happy for you, I was jealous. I'm sorry.

"I pushed you away and I've regretted it every day since. I just want to know if there's still room for me in your life? I would love if we could be friends again.

"Just because I'm a pathetic mess sitting on your doorstep shouldn't guilt you into saying 'yes'"

"Looking put together is overrated anyway," I said, "I know I'm meant to say we should work through these feelings and address underlying issues but how about I say we both let each other down in the friendship and we should just wipe the slate clean?"

"That's very self-helpy, have you been reading grown-up books?"

"Celebrity biographies and trashy magazines, exclusively," I said, with a solemn face.

"Thatta girl," she laughed.

I was comforted that we could fall back into our nonsense repertoire without missing a beat. I didn't want to pull apart everything that had been going on since we last spoke but I didn't want to gloss over the awkward conversations like I had done in the past. I wanted to be there.

"How are you, really?" I asked.

"Pretty shite. All his stuff has gone and I'm pretty sure I've lost a lot of my clients because I've been cancelling classes left, right and centre."

"You can get new people, you needed time to heal after the breakup. Now, have you posted at least ten inspirational quotes about 'new beginnings' with a few 'I hate men' ones in between on social media AND considered getting a 'live, laugh, love' tattoo somewhere on your body? These are all legitimate stages of the break-up process."

"You're a bitch, princess," she laughed, "Shouldn't you leave the sarcasm until we get through this awkward first meeting? You're meant to be helping me; I'm officially your next project."

"You're right, what are you going to do?"

"I don't know," she answered, honestly.

"Well, I do. You're going to pick yourself up – or let me help you do that - and you're going to find your inner badass."

"You sound like me."

"No better person to sound like."

"We'll get your class numbers through the roof if that's what you want or help you start a whole new career if that's what will ignite the fire in your belly again."

"I could be a writer?" she mused.

"What would you write about?"

"I don't know, a blog about single girl sex in your thirties – or true crime investigations, I could ask Benny to come on board as a PI partner to help sniff out stories. He could use his hip flask and everything."

"Let's maybe just put a pin in that idea for now and we can brainstorm later…"

I stood up and pulled her to her feet.

"We can start with a pity party tonight at mine if you like? Tomorrow, the real work begins. I can't be seen about town with a wretch like you."

I gave her another hug and took the car keys from her hand. I decided to drive myself, and let her chat in the passenger seat. As we sped through the streets I could see her start to relax more in my company and tell me what she'd been up to over the last few weeks.

Keith had found a new apartment and was trying to stick to a regular schedule for visiting the girls. He had no idea that she was taking the break up as bad as she was – even now, pride drove her to make sure she looked perfectly well if she knew he was calling to pick up the kids.

"I think the hardest thing about all this is that I don't even know when he properly checked out? I talk a good game about knowing we were toast but I still find myself trying to figure out when it all fell apart. I still don't know, maybe I never will. I just want to get to a place where I stop hating him, he did give me the girls after all," she continued.

"You will, you both have their best interests at heart so you're just going to have to keep working to get there. It'll take time – give yourself time," I said.

"I have an idea. It's completely irresponsible and petty but it might make you feel better?"

"I think we'd better just get you to therapy," she replied.

"Really?"

"Fuck no, we'll do your plan super quick and you can go after to talk about your terrible life choices."

I took a left off the road we were travelling on and stopped at a corner shop, leaving a confused Elle in the car. I returned to the vehicle a few minutes later with my secret purchases and headed towards our destination.

We pulled up outside Smug Club and I stopped the car. I reached into the carrier bag and took out a card which said 'thank you' on the front with a teddy holding a flower underneath.

"I thought we could write something nice to Mrs Clunting. Thank her for bringing us together and bury the hatchet," I explained.

"Are you kidding me? You know she started a Facebook group about me telling people to boycott my classes because I was a secret swinger who used boogie bounce to pick people up? You want me to be the bigger person? She's lucky I don't walk in there and make a scene claiming she owes me money for heroin."

"Hear me out: firstly, I didn't know she did that and secondly, I'm completely screwing with you – we're here to egg the place."

I took out the box of eggs and handed her one.

"Aren't you afraid that Joseph will disown us for reigniting the gangland war on his doorstep?" said Elle, in mock indignation.

"Nah, we've carved out a reputation for being these utter bitches so we should probably just give the public what they want, besides they have to catch us first."

We both shuffled over to the car park and decided against egging the building – we didn't like the thought of causing more of a clean-up job for the maintenance worker, we just wanted to get a rise out of our nemesis.

We took aim at her car and spent a frantic twenty seconds lobbing eggs at the back windscreen and laughing like hammy Bond villains.

For some reason, I thought a dozen eggs would have lasted longer, but it was probably a good job they didn't or we were running a bigger risk of being seen by someone from inside the building.

We were breathless as we returned to the car and took off in a rush. By the time we got around the corner, I went back to the speed limit – I didn't fancy explaining what led to me getting a speeding ticket to Ben.

I set off towards the therapist's office and thought about why I was doing this, why I was going to confront things I'd spent my adult life avoiding.

This time, I wasn't afraid of what lay in front of me. This time I wanted to get better for my family – and I meant all my family, Elle was included. She needed me too and I wanted to be well enough to get her through the next few tough months.

This big-hearted weirdo saw something in me. Perhaps it was my potential – or my desperation – I didn't care which. We needed each other.

Elle had brought me back to life and now it was my turn to return the favour. Besides, the swear jar in Joseph's could definitely help towards mum's cruise.

"What are you thinking of over there?" she asked.

"Ah, nothing; I was just listening to you prattle on like a boring old, biddy."

We pulled up to Dr Kelly's office, and I felt less brave about going ahead with my appointment.

"Are you waiting? It could be an hour," I said.

"Yeah, I'll go for a walk and see if I can get any inspiration for my new career. What do you think of a website that offers masturbation techniques for your pet? I've always thought there could be something more rewarding for them than just humping a cushion."

"Perhaps," I said as kindly as I could, "Maybe, just maybe, we should maybe keep thinking."

"That's one 'maybe' too many. Fair enough, I'll keep thinking; there's bound to be a millionaire-making idea rattling around in there somewhere. I mean it can't all be useless general knowledge or weird facts about Neil

Diamond. Speaking of which, I decided to update his *Wikipedia* page to include the stuff about hamsters."

I grabbed my bag and took one more big breath before I got out to start the next battle against my brain.

The inner bitch had been quiet as of late but I wasn't foolish enough to think she'd gone.

I stopped at the door and started to lose my nerve.

I looked back at the car and saw Elle, standing outside, waving enthusiastically.

"Go on, bitch! Go show 'em what Amy fucking Cole is made of!"

And so, I did.

Elizabeth McGivern

AMY COLE WILL RETURN IN:

AMY COLE
IS ZEN
AS F*CK

ENJOY AN EXCLUSIVE EXCERPT
NOW

AMY COLE IS ZEN AS F*CK

"Have you ever been sent a dick pic?" asked Elle.

I managed to cover my mouth before coffee came spluttering out.

"What?"

"A dick pic," she repeated, as if saying it again would make the question any less bizarre.

"I bet you've got a whole host of them stashed away somewhere. Ben seems like the type."

"You're saying my husband 'seems like the type' to take pictures of his penis and send them to me?"

"Don't make it sound weird, it's quite fun – here look at this one."

She shoved her phone into my face and there it was; a rather flaccid-looking penis.

"Why are you showing me this?" I said, as I tried to shield my eyes, "That image is now burned into my retinas. I feel like that constitutes some sort of assault."

"Stop being dramatic, Amy, I just wanted your opinion on it. I haven't seen anyone's penis – other than my scumbag ex's – in a very long time. It doesn't look like Keith's. Does it look like Ben's? Should I show it to Michael and Joseph and see if they think it's normal looking?"

I grabbed her hand to stop her from leaving the table and showing the picture to any other unsuspecting bystanders.

"It looks a bit sad," I said.

"Yeah, doesn't it? I know I'm new to this internet dating, malarkey, but surely he could have taken a better picture than that? Or maybe that *was* the good picture, that's a depressing thought."

Going against my better judgement, I picked up the phone and looked at the picture again.

"Do you think he's used a filter, or is it really that purple?"

"I hope it's a filter, or else I should just reply now and tell him to go get it checked out."

She sighed as she put down the phone and flopped back on her seat.

"I'm bored of being single, Amy. I just want to meet a nice guy, who likes me and the girls and possibly has a normal-coloured penis. All I'm getting are these idiot 'lads', in their twenties, who just want to meet up for a quick fumble. I hate that I'm not happy on my own – I really never thought I would need a relationship to feel whole, but here I am. It's pathetic."

I tried not to have a sympathetic look on my face but I was caught out and told to 'stop it'.

"You'll meet someone, the right someone. I doubt you'll get much success on that app you're using by the sounds of it."

"No, I was told this was the one you needed to download if you wanted to find your soul mate. I'm sticking with it. Especially because it cost me £1.99 to download," she added.

"Let me see it then, maybe it's something you're exuding on your profile which is making all these undesirables flock to you. A bit of an edit could make all the difference."

She reluctantly handed over her mobile and I clicked on her profile.

Her username was Elle's Bells and the bio read:

Hi to all you sexy guys out there. My name is Elle and I'm a 29-year-old, fun-loving MILF who knows how to party hard and fuck even harder.

I stared at her incredulously.

"Seriously, Elle? You think that profile is sending out an 'I'm looking for a serious relationship' vibe?"

"Look, I know I said 29 but I figure the picture I'm using is a few years old and if we met at a dimly lit restaurant I could probably get away with it," she replied.

"I'm not talking about the age lie - although I think we should circle back to that – I'm talking about the party-girl persona who sounds like she's here for the ride."

"Do you really think it reads that way? Seriously?"

"How can you not think that? Of course these morons are you sending you dick pics."

"Well, that's really given me some food for thought. I figured if I'm up against real 29-year-olds I should have a catchy bio to reel them in."

"Look, if you want to screw around and have some uncomplicated, casual sex then go right ahead. I support you 100%, but don't complain that you're not being matched with Mr Right when you have 'no gag reflex' listed under the *Special Skills* section."

I could see that she was mulling things over and weighing up the advantages of just having a few one-night stands, compared to getting involved in a new relationship.

"What do you think I should write then?"

"Just be yourself, your awesome, 35-year-old self," I smiled.

"What should I do about purple penis?"

"Delete the photo and maybe never say those words to me ever again,"

"You're no fun, now that you're not mental anymore," she said, sulkily.

Acknowledgements

When I was five-years-old, I invented an imaginary world called: Congo, Bongo Land.

Reading that back now, I realise I sound like a racist MP but when I was five, this place was amazing. I could do anything or be anyone. I eventually told my primary school teacher, Mrs Cunningham, about this place and she encouraged me to write about it. She gave me a jotter and - despite not being able to write yet - I drew pictures and bored my mother with endless stories about what they meant.

Twenty-seven years later I'm still boring my mother with stories I want to write but this time, one has finally made it to print.

I'm beyond grateful to so many people that have helped and inspired me to keep going with this project, despite my daily doubts that I'm a complete fraud and what I've written is utter shite.

I'm very lucky to be surrounded by a huge, encouraging family that is always on hand to help. I could probably fill an entire book listing them here but a special thank you should be made to:

Mum and Rachael, who made it through the first draft, in record time, and didn't say it was awful.

To Hannah-Louise and Natalie, who made it through the second draft and didn't disown me.

To Ciara, who told me to: "Just, fucking write."

To Dad and Martin who said they aren't going to read the book, but will check it out if it ever becomes a film.

To Mandy, Jenny, Carmel, Sarah and Lasairiona for the *many* nagging text messages to ask if it was finished yet. Your guilt sent me back to the laptop.

To Ryan's creativity, design skill and love of the colour lilac...

To the McCarrunningbelliotts group for all the late-night procrastination conversations about Michael Fassbender and pushing me to go ahead with publishing.

To the Carroll, McCamley, McGivern and Toner clan as a whole, thank you for putting up with the incessant pleas to buy this – I won't stop asking, so you might as well just go buy another copy after you're finished with this one.

And finally, to my one true love: Colin Firth. Your framed photo on my desk inspires me to be a better person.

I suppose I should mention something about my husband and kids at this stage? Fine.

My children are the human embodiment of perfection and I'm thanking no one else for that but me, so that just leaves my husband, Conor.

Thank you for believing in me and this book, more than I did. Thank you for helping me deal with the frustrating setbacks and rejections with compassion and irritating optimism; and thank you for not starting divorce proceedings when I turned into a raging bitch during the editing process.

Finally, (no really this time) thank you to every person that reads, comments and gets in touch with me through my blog, *Mayhem and Beyond*.

What started out as a way to journal my early days as a parent turned into a place where I could be honest about being a mum who struggled with mental health issues. Each and every time you reach out and share your support – or tell me you're going through something similar- it helps make a stay-at-home mum feel a little less isolated.

I hope you enjoyed meeting Amy Cole as much as I enjoyed writing her, you have made my five-year-old self very happy.

Elizabeth McGivern is a former journalist turned hostage-in-her-own-home surrounded by three men and a horrible dog named Dougal.

In an effort to keep her sanity she decided to write a parenting blog after the birth of her first son so she can pinpoint the exact moment she failed as a mother.

In an unexpected turn of events, the blog helped her to find a voice and connect with parents in similar situations; namely those who were struggling with mental health issues and parenting. It was because of this encouragement – and wanting to avoid her children as much as possible – her debut novel, *Amy Cole has lost her mind*, was born.

Elizabeth lives in Northern Ireland although wishes she could relocate to Iceland on a daily basis. To witness her regular failings as a parent you can find her on:

www.mayhemandbeyond.com
Twitter: @mayhembeyond
Facebook.com/mayhemandbeyond
Instagram: mayhemandbeyond

Lightning Source UK Ltd.
Milton Keynes UK
UKHW02f1919250718
326291UK00005B/351/P